The Wages of Sin

Books by Dale E. Lehman

Howard County Mysteries

The Fibonaci Murders
True Death
Ice on the Bay
A Day for Bones
The Wages of Sin

Bernard and Melody Capers

Weasel Words
Rooftop Sonata

Science Fiction

Space Operatic
The Belt
Penitence

Short Story Collections

The Realm of Tiny Giants
Found by the Road
Manifest Secrets

THE WAGES OF SIN

A Howard County Mystery

DALE E. LEHMAN

Chase, Maryland

The Wages of Sin
Dale E. Lehman

Copyright © 2026 by Dale E. Lehman

This is a work of fiction. All the characters, organizations, and events portrayed in this book are either products of the author's imagination or are used fictitiously.

Cover art by Proi
https://99designs.com/profiles/proi

Text set in 11-pt. Calluna
Chapter headings set in 18-pt. Imprint MT Shadow

Published by Red Tales, 2025
Baltimore, Maryland
United States of America
https://www.DaleELehman.com

ISBN: 978-1-958906-12-5 (trade paperback)
978-1-958906-13-2 (digital)

For Eve, the family foodie, who would enjoy both Clare Fleming's carrot cake and dinner at the Elkridge Furnace Inn.

"If ye become aware of a sin committed by another, conceal it, that God may conceal your own sin. He, verily, is the Concealer, the Lord of grace abounding."

~ Baha'u'llah, *The Summons of the Lord of Host*

Chapter 1

Tuesday, March twenty-seventh.

She had just opened the letter when a cloud passed over the sun, quenching the light raining through her balcony door. A chill infiltrated the apartment as she read the opening lines.

You don't know me. If you did, I'm sure you'd kill me. I wouldn't blame you. I deserve it. I ruined your life.

The single sheet of paper was lined with ragged edges torn from a notebook. The ink was blue, the writing barely controlled. The writer might have been an untrained four-year-old or a tremor-ridden centenarian. She flung it onto the table as though she'd plucked a handful of poison ivy. It felt like it. A deep urushiol itch crawled along her fingers, across her palms, up her arms, edging toward pain, fed by the noxious mixture of anger, grief, and fear.

I wish I could undo what I've done. I really do. I wish I could change a lot of things. God, how I wish that. I've destroyed us all.

Hers wasn't a luxury apartment. One bedroom, a Walmart loveseat and smoked glass table crammed into the living room, a kitchenette with barely room to pirouette, a dining area overstuffed with this cheap round table and two chairs. Still, she loved it. For three years it had been her paradise. She lived nowhere near the ocean, but some mornings she swore she heard waves rolling up a beach and children splashing in the water, pattering along the sand, building dream castles. She was happy here, happier than she'd been since the day the police brought tragedy to their door and her mother tumbled into depression.

That day dragged them both into hell. Over time, they clawed back out. Pain morphed into dull ache. Days became weeks became years. She was out on her own now, an adult charting her own course, figuring out her life. She wasn't rich, didn't have it all, but in a way she did. She was free, walking along that beach, splashing through the warm waves where the children played, toes sinking into the sand with every step. She didn't quite know where she was going, but each step was hers now, nobody else's, and whatever turn she took, it would be all right.

Now this letter arrived, and her beach froze over. The chicken-scratch handwriting catapulted her back to that horrible day in an instant. She'd been cast out from paradise, flung once more into hell. She nearly collapsed, caught herself at the last moment, pressed palms to tabletop to steady herself. Hovering over the paper, she read without touching, denying the words truth by refusing them contact. This was a joke, a sick joke, a stalker, a blackmailer, a...

I need to explain, but it will only deepen your pain. It sure won't erase mine. Nothing can save me. I know. I went to his brother's church. It seemed the place to go. I went to his brother's church and confessed, but the priest wouldn't absolve me. Not even God will forgive me. I'm already in hell. I've moved five times, used twice as many aliases, do menial work for cash, never sleep through the night. I don't see myself in the mirror. A zombie stares back.

Bile clawed up her throat. She barely forced it back down. Who had written this? Why after all this time would they tell her things she no longer cared to know?

I wasn't always a fallen woman. I thought I was a good person. But I was in a tough spot, and I needed the money. It seemed harmless at first, just a joke, a dirty little joke that became more and more real until I couldn't escape. A lot of men followed me to hell, but not him. He deflected my advances. When he realized what I was after, he confronted me, threatened to turn me over to the FBI. I was terrified. It wasn't premeditated. I swear it wasn't. It was pure terror.

A fresh wave of anger crashed over her. Of course he hadn't fallen! He wasn't like that, wasn't like this demon, whoever she was, whatever she'd done. But beneath her anger, pride stirred. He at least died doing the right thing. He was at least a hero.

I've paid for it every day since. My boss is a monster. He was the one I feared, not the FBI. I still fear him. He's hunted me for years. He almost caught me several times, and now he's closing in again. So once more I'm running. Maybe I'll leave the country this time, if I can. I don't know where I'll land. I only know you deserve to know the truth. Please believe me when I say this: he was a good man. He really was.

I won't ask your forgiveness. If God won't forgive me, how could you? But I am sorry. Truly, I'm sorry.

She groped for the chair, sank into it as tears washed her cheeks.

Why? Why upend her world just when she'd managed to right it? She couldn't allow it, wouldn't allow it. The bitch would pay. She'd see to that. Whoever this was, whatever the cost, she'd make them pay.

†

Early afternoon on Saturday, April twenty-first couldn't have been more perfect. The sun blazed in a cloudless sky. A warm breeze danced with the young leaves in the trees. It was a day of promise and nerves, beginnings and endings, and above all love. Detective Sergeants Corina Montufar and Eric Dumas stood before priest and altar in St. Augustine Catholic Church in Elkridge, Maryland, she in a simple white gown, he in a black tux, as Father Ed Tyler administered their wedding vows.

St. Augustine wasn't Montufar's home church. That was St. John the Evangelist in Columbia's Oakland Mills Interfaith Center. But St. John had never felt quite right. Not the physical space, anyway. She liked the people, liked Father Owen, but the building belonged in a business park. Even the interior lacked inspiration. Comfortable, yes, but its wood-paneled walls, abstract window designs, and plain table for an altar exuded a conference vibe.

St. Augustine, though, radiated divinity. A stone structure perched on a hill above Old Washington Road, its interior glowed with light raining down from lamps on high and splintered sunbeams pouring through stained-glass windows. Far above, stars were sprinkled across deep blue vaulted ceilings. Statuary and flowers clothed the church inside and out. Candles flickered.

A touch of incense perfumed the air. Beyond its walls, a cemetery flowed over the hillside to the northeast, while on the southwest, an L-shaped brick complex housed a convent and school, separating the church from nearby homes. It just felt right. But of course it did. The parish had been established in 1844 and the present church consecrated in 1902, long before the birth of the strange notion that peace might be established between religions by stripping them of their identities.

Montufar opted for a full nuptial mass. She'd dreamed of such a wedding since childhood, but she worried Dumas might balk at it. He wasn't Catholic. Worse, he couldn't share in the eucharist. She didn't want him to feel separated, not even in a single detail. But when she expressed her reservations, he didn't flinch. "Go for it," he said. "It's your dream. I'd do a cliff-dive ceremony to marry you."

Typical Eric.

And now here they were, man and wife, a photographer's dream, Dumas a lean six-foot specimen, Montufar five inches shorter, a slip of a woman who might have blown away on the breeze had he not been holding her. She almost felt she was rising with the wisps of candle smoke, rising into the light as she melted into his embrace. Perched on the cusp of laughing and crying, she wondered how Dumas would survive kissing her in front of so many witnesses.

He did himself proud. It seemed to last an eternity.

When they turned to face the world as one soul, the smiles and tears of friends, colleagues, and family greeted them. Montufar's family, at least. Dumas had no family anymore, no blood family, but hers had adopted him, as had the department. His good friend Officer Kevin Graham stood in the middle of the gathering, applauding so loud nobody dared stop before he did.

At Montufar's side, her younger sister and maid of honor Ella sniffled and cast a glance across the way at her fiancé, local reporter Jack Collins. Collins winked back. Long anticipated, their engagement had been unveiled the day after Montufar and Dumas announced their wedding date. They'd barely begun planning, although Montufar figured the whole gang would return to this church before the year was out, a few roles reversed.

The rest of the party consisted of colleagues, save one. Montufar's other bridesmaids were Detectives Theresa Swan and Holly Ross. Dumas' best man was their boss, Detective Lieutenant Rick Peller, and the final groomsman—the odd man out—was Dumas' neighbor, Ozzie White, who after more than a year of treatment following a psychological trauma remained barely functional. Dragging him up here had been as easy as open-heart surgery, but Dumas and Montufar hoped it might do him some good.

Ozzie survived it. So did the rest. Corina Montufar was now Corina Montufar Dumas, appending her husband's name but in keeping with her family's culture still answering to Montufar.

It had been as perfect a wedding as perfect could be.

And then they stepped outside.

†

Peller noticed it first, just after the gathering showered the newlyweds in red and white rose petals, just before the photographer, a twenty-something woman built like a marathoner, began herding the wedding party back inside.

Rather than follow the flock, Peller stepped away to catch a breath of vernal air. He needed it. He was happy for Montufar and Dumas, but their wedding had transported him back to his own and filled him with longing for Sandra. She'd been killed five years and eleven months ago, and while the pain had long since receded, emptiness often ambushed him. He missed her every day, some days more than others.

The temperature had reached the mid-seventies, but it felt much warmer in the sun. Newborn leaves chattered in the breeze. A herringbone courtyard of gray pavers edged by a low wall connected the church with the parking lot on Peller's right and the rectory, a handsome white house, on the left. The rectory had two entrances, one in front surrounded by a small concrete porch, the other on the side by the church, accessible via ramp.

The courtyard overlooked a portion of the cemetery and the hill descending to the road below. Atop the wall to the left, a statue of Jesus raised its hands in blessing. To the right, a crowned Mary extended her hands palms up, her downcast eyes keeping watch over the mortal world. Domed lights slumbered at the foot of each statue, awaiting twilight to wake.

But something else caught Peller's eye. Something that shouldn't have been there. A smear of bright red atop the wall at Mary's feet. Before he could investigate, the photographer tapped his shoulder. "We need you inside," she said.

"I'll be right there," he promised. After she skittered off, he approached the statue and inspected the smear just as Father Ed came to his side.

"We're taking photos," the priest said. "Let's…" He caught his breath when he saw what had drawn Peller's attention. He strangled a cry of anger and turned away in disgust.

Peller snapped a photo with his cell phone. The smear wasn't a smear. It spelled out a message in red paint.

Romans 6:23

He couldn't chapter-and-verse, but the priest likely could. "What does it mean?" Peller asked.

Father Ed refused a second look. "It means we have a vandal."

"The verse, Father."

"The text?"

"Yes."

"For the wages of sin is death, but the free gift of God is eternal life in Christ Jesus our Lord."

Although a message laden with both hope and menace, the vandal hadn't likely intended the former. The first clause must be the point. A death threat. But against who?

"You'll report this to the police, I hope," Peller said.

Father Ed turned his gaze on the graves below. "We don't want to mar Corina and Eric's big day. Let's get those photos done." He waved toward the church and started for it.

Peller figured that meant no, but that was fine. The cops were already here. He followed Father Ed inside, where the wedding party subjected themselves to flash after flash of the photographer's camera. After, eyes swimming with spots, the party dispersed.

The guests had already driven off to reconvene for the reception at four o'clock at a rented hall in Columbia. The wedding party arrived twenty minutes later, and the festivities went into overdrive. Dinner ensued, followed by music, dancing, and laughter, not to mention cake cutting and various silly—in Peller's view—traditions. He didn't see much of Guatemala in the party. It seemed Montufar had gone full-blown American. Not surprising, really. She'd only been fourteen when her family came to the U.S. Now thirty-seven, she'd spent well over half her life here and had worked hard to fit in.

At seven o'clock on the dot, the happy couple debarked on a week-long honeymoon down the Blue Ridge and into the Great Smokey Mountains, blissfully ignorant of vandalism. Peller told no one. Father Ed had been right on that score, anyway. The culprit shouldn't be allowed to deface Montufar and Dumas' wedding day.

The party lingered on and on. People began to drift away around ten o'clock. Long before then, Peller felt an urge to return to the church with technician Geri Franklin in tow to scour the grounds. Alas, they were both stuck here, Peller because his companion for the evening, Joan Churchill, wanted to stay, and Franklin because Montufar had tasked her with ensuring Ozzie White made it home safely. White himself displayed no interest in moving. None at all.

"I'd dance with him," Franklin confided to Peller, "but I'd have to sling him over my shoulder. I've seen corpses with more life."

Which was almost literally true. Peller whispered back, "So sling him. It might snap him out of it." Although honestly, he wasn't sure Franklin had ever danced in her life. A party girl she was not.

She smiled a pinched smile.

"What's his problem?" Churchill asked, also in a whisper.

On the opposite side of the round table, White stared without interest at the dancers. Or more likely, at nothing at all. His eyes didn't move, almost didn't blink. He probably wouldn't have heard his companions had they been shouting.

"Short version," Peller said, "he fell for a woman who turned out to be a killer. She pretended to be in love with him to get close to Eric. Her accomplice killed two officers right in front of Ozzie while she distracted them."

Franklin eyed White as though scrutinizing a crime scene. "That would do it. What was he like before?"

"I don't know him well, but from what I hear, he was a bubbly character. Outgoing, optimistic, full of schemes that never quite worked out." Peller grinned at Franklin. "Just your type."

She rebuked him with another of those smiles. Physically, she could have been a perpetual teenager. Professionally, she was a machine, focused, efficient, barely ever cracking a joke. Seldom in Peller's experience had she spoken of anything but work. She was the best crime scene tech on the force but weird in most people's eyes. "If I wanted a boyfriend," she said, "I'd look up Albert Einstein."

"He's too old for you," Churchill told her. "And too dead."

"The good thing about dead guys is, they never argue with you."

Churchill laughed in agreement, Peller in amusement.

"You think I'm joking?" Franklin rose, circled the table, sat next to White. He didn't notice. "Tell me something," she said.

He didn't tell her anything, didn't even look at her.

"Does that bitch get to dictate the rest of your life?"

That got his attention. He turned a frown on Franklin. "Huh?"

"You heard me. Dump her in the landfill. Flush her down the sewer. Get on with your life."

Peller leaned back, fascinated and a bit disturbed by Franklin's chutzpah. Churchill put a hand to her mouth to cover a horrified smile.

White's gaze drifted away. "I don't know how," he mumbled.

Franklin stood. She might have been short, but she towered over him. He wasn't tall himself, particularly when seated. She thrust her hand out. "Come on."

He frowned at her fingers. He might have been counting the joints for all the interest he showed. "Where?"

"You'll see." When he didn't move, she snatched his hand and tugged. "Come *on*."

White exhaled and, whether irritated or resigned, permitted her to lead him from the table. Peller's gaze followed as she hauled him onto the dance floor and all but forced him to move to the music. Nobody paid them heed, nobody but Peller and Churchill. Fifteen minutes passed before White loosened up. After that, he seemed almost normal. He even half smiled now and again.

Churchill pointed at Franklin. "You work with that lady?"

"I work with someone who looks like her. I think this is her evil twin."

"I like her."

"Now you're scaring me."

Churchill laughed. "I didn't think you ever got scared, Sherlock."

Peller wished she'd stop calling him that. If any of his colleagues overheard, he'd never hear the end of it. But he had to admit, it had become… endearing. "Well, that message at the church sure made me uneasy." He said it without thinking. He should have kept his mouth shut.

"What message?"

He couldn't obfuscate, not with her. By now she knew how to read him. He related the details, what he believed it meant.

"You think Father Ed's in danger?"

Peller shrugged. The threat could have been for anyone in the St. Augustine community. One of the priests. Someone in the parish office. Any church member. Given that, he found Father Ed's reluctance to report it curious.

"What will you do?" Churchill asked.

"If he doesn't call it in by Monday, I'll report it myself."

"It could be nothing. Somebody's idea of a joke."

Could be. But Peller trusted his instincts, and something told him this was no joke.

†

Father Ed had politely declined the invitation to the reception. The Montufars weren't from his parish, and he had five o'clock mass to celebrate. He could have stopped by after, but he didn't relish the thought of driving to Columbia and back so late in the day.

Besides, this vandalism preyed on his mind. He didn't want his parishioners upset. The graffiti had to be removed or at least hidden before mass, which left very little time. Worse, he was pretty sure it was a threat. Lieutenant Peller thought so, too. Father Ed could tell from the set of Peller's mouth, the tone of his voice. By all rights, the incident *should* be reported.

And yet...

Wasn't this an internal matter, a Church matter? Best not have it splashed all over newspapers, TV, and the web. They didn't need that kind of publicity. The Church had received enough negative press as it was. And could they be sure it was a threat? Maybe some anti-Catholic fool found it amusing to deface Church property. There were idiots like that out there.

No, he'd take care of this himself.

The church was silent now, wedding party gone, volunteers for the upcoming mass not yet present, church office closed. Father Ed was momentarily alone. He stepped outside and stood before the Mary statue. Paint on stone. Could he scrub it off? He set a finger to the red. Nope. Dry to the touch. He'd only make a bigger mess if he tried to remove it. He needed a professional, and fortunately, he had one.

He dug his cell phone from his trouser pocket and called his parish secretary Lilith Forbes at home. "Sorry to bother you," he said when she answered, "but I need Carl Weber's number."

"At this hour on a Saturday?" Hearing her on the phone, anyone would swear Forbes couldn't be more than forty, but her eightieth birthday was only a month off. Age hadn't dulled her, maybe never would. She was sharp as a master chef's knife, knew all the regular churchgoers and half the Christmas-and-Easter parishioners. The Weber clan was among the regulars. They'd attended St. Augustine for three generations. Carl owned a hardscape business and had done a few small jobs for the church over the past decade, usually at cost.

"It's an emergency," Father Ed said.

Forbes gave him the number. "What's the problem? A safety hazard? Better take care of that before mass, I suppose. But on such short notice, I don't know."

Father Ed let her assume what she would. "Thank you, Lilith."

He next called Carl Weber. Weber's wife Gina answered. "Oh, hello, Father! This is a surprise."

"An unwelcome one, I'm sure. I need to speak with Carl. We have a problem."

"Of course, let me get him."

A moment later, Carl Forbes greeted Father Ed. "What's up?"

"A bit of a mess. Red paint on the top of the wall, right in front of the Mary statue. I was wondering if you could get rid of it, or at least hide it, before five o'clock mass. It might upset people."

"Paint?" It was hard to tell if Weber was dumbfounded, amused, or both. "How did that happen?"

"Vandalism."

"Oh, damn. How fresh?"

"I think it was done during a wedding this afternoon. We found it afterwards."

"Then it hasn't cured, but it's soaking in. Yeah, I should be able to remove it, except the stone will likely be stained. What was it, splashed on? A big pool?"

Father Ed hesitated, but there was no point in hedging. Carl would see when he arrived. "A message. Written rather neatly."

Weber didn't reply at once. Father Ed expected him to ask what it said, but he didn't. "That could be worse. The words might be legible in the stains when I'm done."

"Can't you clean the stains off?"

"Sure, but I might damage the stone. Your best option is to replace the affected slabs. But you'll want a good match. If I don't have the right material in stock, I'll have to order it. Maybe we should cover it up for now, throw a tarp over it and set up a barricade. If anybody asks, just say the wall was damaged and is awaiting repairs."

That would work. The main thing was to keep the message out of view. "I'll trust your judgement," Father Ed said. "How soon can you get here?"

"Call it twenty minutes. Hiding the evidence will be quick work."

Father Ed wasn't sure he liked the way Weber put that, but at least he had one less thing to worry about. He pushed all other cares aside and focused on the upcoming mass.

Weber arrived in his black Ram pickup right on time. Father Ed directed him to the problem and watched from the church door. The contractor read the message, hands on his hips, before setting to work. He draped a cloth tarp about Mary's feet, concealing the problem, then weighed down the edges with cream-colored pavers that almost matched the wall. Finally, he set a pair of orange sawhorses on either side and hung a strip of yellow caution tape between them. The effect wasn't elegant, but it got the point across: keep out.

Saturday evening mass was lightly attended, as usual. Father Ed could remember a time when the church was half full on Saturdays and packed on Sundays. Attendance had fallen in the past couple of decades. Some days he worried about that, but today it was a relief. He felt guilty in his relief, even though he carried this extra burden. Maybe it was encroaching age. Too many years shouldering too many burdens. He could use a break. He hadn't pondered retirement, but he was sixty-two, a reasonable time to give it some thought. Though he had a solid decade of service left in him, God willing, reduced activity might be good for him. Sooner or later, he would hand over the pastor's reins to someone else. After all, age caught everyone eventually. Age or death.

After mass, he returned to the rectory living room and sat in silent contemplation while his housekeeper and cook Clare Fleming rattled about the kitchen. Flemming was an energetic black woman, thirty-four years old, divorced, probably too curvy for her own good. At least, her confessions mostly involved sexual indiscretions. She always seemed contrite when unburdening her soul, but she'd made zero progress toward rectifying her conduct. Father Ed liked her, though. She was kind and witty and too smart to spend the rest of her life as a housekeeper. He encouraged her to go back to school, always remembered her in his prayers, always held out hope she'd find some self-control. And yet, she was still here, still staking claim to the same sins.

"You look like a man with a problem, Ed."

The willowy voice startled Father Ed from his reverie. Father Walter Simmons had materialized before him, leaning on his walker, a wisp of a smile on his face. Father Walter was a retired priest-in-residence who had lived at St. Augustine for three years. Now seventy-nine, he'd come from a parish outside Boston after fracturing his hip in a bad fall down a set of icy steps. Several surgeries later, he could get around with the aid of that walker or, on good days, with a cane. He'd moved here because his sister Janice and her family lived nearby in eastern Columbia, just across I-95.

They visited him regularly, took him on outings and to family gatherings. He still had the energy and certainly the intellect to assist Father Ed with the burdens of their office, but watching him move could be painful.

"Feeling a bit old, I guess," Father Ed told him.

Father Walter grinned. "Men feel old five times in their lives. When they turn thirty, forty, fifty, sixty, and seventy. After that, it's smooth sailing."

"What's it like, being retired?"

"Same as not being retired. Only the pace is different. Clare's got dinner on the table. Come on."

Father Ed rose and followed Father Walter as he made his way into the kitchen. The table was set for three. A carved roasted chicken awaited, with mashed potatoes and gravy and corn and green beans. The priests and the housekeeper took their seats. Father Ed said grace, then the food was passed around.

Though it wasn't unusual for them to eat in silence, tonight the quiet hung heavy over them. Father Ed felt Flemming's eyes on him, felt Father Walter avoiding his companions. They knew something was amiss, knew he was withholding news.

Fleming had already guessed at it. "What's with the wall?"

Father Ed couldn't face her. "What do you mean?"

"The tarp and caution tape. You'd think someone drove a truck into it."

"It would have been better if they had," Father Ed mumbled, then wished he hadn't.

Father Walter glanced at him but didn't press the matter.

Fleming was another matter. "Why? What happened?"

Setting his fork down, Father Ed sighed. "I don't want to alarm anyone, so keep this to yourselves. Someone painted words on the top of the wall. It's being taken care of."

"What does it say?"

"Clare, please."

"Come on, Father. Hiding things never makes it better." She raised an eyebrow.

Father Ed knew what she meant, but this wasn't confession. He was trying to protect his flock.

"I think the three of us can keep a secret," Father Walter said. "If it has to be kept."

Three people already knew: himself, Lieutenant Peller, and Carl Weber. How much could it hurt if he told these two? Maybe none, maybe a lot. He didn't worry about Father Walter, but could he trust Fleming to keep her mouth shut?

She pleaded with her eyes and a smile. She was good at that. Too good.

Father Ed gave in. "It says, 'Romans 6:23.'"

Fleming pouted. Of the three, she was the only one who didn't know it by the numbers. "Which is?"

"'For the wages of sin is death, but the free gift of God is eternal life in Christ Jesus our Lord.'"

Silence.

Father Ed shrugged.

"Is that a threat?" Fleming asked.

Probably. Maybe not. What could he say? "I don't know, Clare. I hope not."

Father Walter seemed to age another fifteen years in two seconds. His face ashen, he pushed back from the table, fumbled for his walker, struggled to stand. "Please excuse me," he whispered. "My hip is hurting something awful this evening. I'd better go take my horse pill."

They watched him go.

Fleming leaned on the table. She looked frightened "You don't think..." She swallowed and bit her lip.

No, he didn't. Father Ed couldn't see any reason anyone would target Father Walter. Father Walter was the kindest, most harmless man in the universe.

"You don't think..." Fleming began again. "...they're after *me*?"

Chapter 2

Wednesday, March twenty-eighth, seven fifteen A.M.

Nearly seventeen hours had passed since the letter. She hadn't eaten. She hadn't slept. Her father's killer had placed a confession in her hands, and she didn't know what to do, only that she must do something to find and punish the nameless woman.

She went for a walk. Maybe that would shake the confusion and fear from her soul. Dad had always said walking was good for clearing the head, for meditating, for working things out. She hadn't done it much since his death, but now, running on fumes, she heard his whisper in her brain.

Get out there. Walk. Don't think, just move.

With March drawing to a close, the air was cool, the sky half overcast. She left her apartment and shuffled down the sidewalk alongside the complex, beyond the complex, beyond the townhouses to the south. Squirrels romped through the grass and up the trees. Songbirds twittered. Robins hunted worms. She turned west along Frederick Road, passed by more shaded townhomes.

And then footsteps sounded behind, soft, matching her pace. Her blood turned to ice. Which was stupid, because, come on, who would be following her? Someone else was out walking, that was all, someone getting their morning exercise, maybe someone who, like her, had been crushed and tossed aside by life. They must be nobody, no danger, but she couldn't help it. She had to be sure. She stopped abruptly and turned.

The young man had been closer than she realized. He nearly ran into her.

"Whoa!" he yelped. His hands caught her shoulders, and the duo executed a clumsy dance to avoid falling. He hadn't meant to grab her. It had just been reflex, but once balance was restored, she pushed him off and backed away as though he'd assaulted her.

He put up his hands. "I'm sorry! I'm really sorry! It *was* your fault, though. I mean...no, never mind. I'm sorry."

Her heart hammered while she laughed in relief. "Yeah, my fault. Sorry."

He squinted at her. "Are you okay?"

Of course she wasn't okay. Her father's murderer had sent her a letter. Not that this guy could know about that. "Not really," she said. "Sorry." Stupid thing to be doing, walking the streets in her mental state. She started back the way she'd come.

He eyed her as she passed by. "Hey, do you... Do you need help? I mean... Food? Money?"

She stopped and gaped at him. "Really?" She wanted to slug him, but then she saw his face, his confused, awkward, geeky face, and she couldn't. It was almost comical, him offering help when he couldn't be in much better shape than she. Financially, anyway. He hadn't likely received a note from a killer.

"You look like, you know..." He waved vaguely.

She looked down at herself. Okay, her jeans had tears in the legs, her long-sleeve t-shirt had seen better days, but she'd thrown them on to go for a walk, not out clubbing.

"I mean," he sputtered, "You look...great. Really, um, great. I mean..."

She laughed at him stumbling all over himself. "Hot?"

He blushed. "No! I mean... Well, yeah, but... Oh, hell. I just thought you might, you know, need something to eat."

He got that right, anyway. Suddenly she was starving. "Probably do. I had a long night."

"Are you homeless? Damn it, I shouldn't... Never mind. I'm sorry."

She didn't know why she did it. Later, thinking back, she couldn't fathom it. Maybe she just wanted this jumble of a conversation to end, or maybe she already liked him, or maybe she needed another human being—if that's what he was—to talk to. Whatever the reason, she shrugged in mock misery, turned away, took one halting step. Then she paused and waited for the inevitable.

He came to her side and tentatively touched her shoulder with his fingers. It was light, tremulous. Nerves? Desire? Both? "I haven't had breakfast. Want to join me?"

She pretended to hesitate. She looked down, faking embarrassment.

"What's happened to you?" he whispered.

"Something awful."

"I won't hurt you. I promise. I just want to help."

"Well," she said. "Okay. Thank you."

†

The good weather continued through Sunday into Monday. Peller thought it a shame he had to work, which for him was an odd thought, but there was plenty to do around the house and in the yard on such a day, and not just maintenance. He hadn't changed a thing since Sandra's death nearly six years before. Maybe the time had come for some upgrades.

The anniversary of that tragedy was almost upon Peller, less than a month off. As he climbed into his F150 that morning, emptiness blindsided him once more. Sandra was gone, long gone. There was but one way he'd be with her again, and barring some unforeseen event, he wouldn't pass that way for decades. He couldn't mark time forever. He had a strange urge to repaint the whole house, brighten it, make it new, maybe expand the rose bed he and Sandra had planted together, maybe remake Jason's old bedroom into a study. His life had been on hold for almost six years. Wasn't that enough?

Of course.

Maybe not.

How could he know?

You weren't always this indecisive, he heard Sandra tease.

Only where you were concerned, he told her. But that wasn't quite right. He'd always been sure of her. Himself, that was another matter. Even after all this time, he couldn't be certain her voice was real, that it was her speaking from the beyond and not just the memory of her. But he did have a preference.

He drove to work. Arriving at Northern District Headquarters, he settled into his cubicle on the second floor and whisked through his emails and voice mails, mostly bureaucratic business, a few related to ongoing investigations. Late last week, he'd off-loaded Dumas' and Montufar's work to Holly Ross and Theresa Swan, respectively. Nothing major. A few minor assaults, some idiot shooting off rounds in the woods of Centennial Park, probably at birds or squirrels. Their most serious active case involved a strange series of parking lot collisions, thankfully without injuries, in which witnesses said the perpetrator was an irritable elderly Latina in a powder blue Escalade. Peller rather wanted to take on that one himself if only for its weirdness, but it was right up Ross' alley. Last year, she'd revealed a surprising aptitude for handling unstable suspects when she was taken hostage by an armed killer.

Done with email, he checked for reports of vandalism at St. Augustine. Nothing. He entered one himself, just to have it in the system. No resources would be wasted on it right now. A splash of paint hardly qualified as a priority. But should another incident occur—and Peller bet it would—the link would at least be on file. Out of curiosity, he queried for other recent incidents at Catholic churches in the county, then at churches generally. Synagogues, too. Nothing came up.

†

Detective Theresa Swan almost let the nice weather seduce her. Almost. While she loved being outdoors, it was best to stay alert. When you were hunting an armed suspect—even a dopey teenager taking potshots at wildlife in the woods—you couldn't let your guard down.

Yeah, yeah, that was stereotyping. She didn't *know* she was looking for a teenager. Witnesses, such as they were, had described a teen/twenty-something/thirty-something tall/short skinny/chunky white/black/Asian/Hispanic man/woman. Incredibly helpful. Those Swan regarded as reliable, a mere three who could describe the perp's clothing in at least minor detail, tended toward a younger male, on the lanky side, possibly of darker complexion. But he'd mostly been seen in shadow, so who knew his skin tone? He kept to the trees save once when spotted speed walking over open ground, face turned away from the witness. He was nondescript. Faded blue jeans. Black t-shirt. Black hoodie, sometimes with the hood up, sometimes down.

The upside was, Swan got to walk in the park on a nice day. It was good to be doing something, anything, in the sunshine. She'd spent a fair portion of the previous ten months healing from a gunshot wound to her left shoulder. Her physical therapy had gone well. By now, she could almost believe nothing had ever happened. She relished the sun warming her dark skin, the breeze fluttering her black hair, while she strolled along the path into the woods along the lakeshore. Observers would think she hadn't a care in the world. She almost convinced herself she didn't.

But she did. Another incident had been reported not an hour ago. A young mother pushing her baby in a stroller along the paved pathways heard gunshots in the woods bordering the southern shore of Centennial Lake west of pavilion G. She'd seen nothing, just heard the crack of a gun. Swan called in a trio of patrol officers to canvas the area. No luck. Few people had been there and none but the mother had seen or heard anything. Of course not.

Still, the woman was scared. She hadn't imagined the gunshots. While it was unlikely the perp remained in the area, this stand of woods offered plenty of hiding places. The path cut through the trees along the lakeshore and emerged at a boathouse where paddle boats could be rented. Swan searched for footprints or trampled undergrowth, but the tangled vegetation revealed nothing. Foliage hadn't fully emerged on the deciduous plants, allowing greater visibility into the woods. Anyone hiding there must be well back.

The crack of a branch and a rustling of dead leaves snagged Swan's attention. She paused, peered into the darkened woods. Nothing caught her eye at first, then she heard it again and spotted a gray squirrel scampering from the forest floor up a tree trunk. It perched on a low branch, something clutched in its front paws, its tail curled into a question mark behind it.

"You got a license for that tail?" Swan asked.

The squirrel chattered a warning: *predator alert!*

Swan didn't have a taste for squirrel soufflé. She walked on, spotting the lake now and again through gaps in the trees. No criminal activity there. She almost ignored the next rustling until movement caught her eye. She stopped, barely breathing. Alongside an old tree trunk, all but merged with it, a shadow undulated, as tall as a person but with an odd shape, like something from a horror film.

At least I'm dressed for this, Swan told herself, as though that trumped all other considerations. She wore jeans and work boots and a long-sleeved shirt. Her pocket-holstered handgun pressed reassuringly against her right thigh as she crept from the path into the trees, trying to keep silent. It wasn't at all easy. Deadfall and foliage shed over the winter crackled beneath her feet as she worked her way toward the shadow. And yet, whoever or what-ever it was didn't notice her approach. She drew close enough to hear sounds, human sounds. Giggling. Muffled words. She paused and listened.

Two voices, one male, one female.

"Figures," Swan grumbled.

Still, best not to take chances where firearms might exist. She continued her measured approach and soon was close enough to make out half the words the couple exchanged. The talk was nothing she needed to hear. Keeping partially behind an oak trunk just in case, she called, "Howard County Police. Zip up and step out where I can see you."

The woman yelped. The man grumbled, "You gotta be kidding." They tugged their clothing into place and stepped away from the tree. They were a young couple, probably early twenties, he of average height and a bit on the heavy side, she only an inch shorter, both blonde. The man was trying to smirk. It made him look ill, not cool. The woman struggled to hide her fear.

Swan approached and gave them both a once-over before circling the tree they'd been using for support. No guns in evidence, but just to be sure, she asked. "Either of you carrying weapons?"

The man's smirk turned sarcastic. "You wanna see my weapon?"

"You want me to book you for indecent exposure and disorderly conduct?"

He looked down and shook his head.

"We received a report of gunshots fired in the area," Swan said. "Are either of you responsible for that?"

"No," they muttered in unison.

"Did either of you hear anything?"

They shook their heads.

She supposed not. They probably hadn't been here at the time, and even if they were, they'd have been too focused on each other to notice a cannon going off. She stepped aside and waved them toward the path. "Get out of here," she said. "And keep it in the bedroom."

They hurried on their way, crashing through the leaves, eyes downcast as they passed her by.

"Mondays," Swan grumbled.

Since she was here, she tramped through the woods for a time, but nothing of interest turned up. Just more squirrels.

†

This was the fifth time in thirteen days. Different places around North Laurel, different victims, all the same story. A car parked a bit too close to the line or over the line or just in an inconvenient location for an angry old lady in her big blue Escalade. And then a dent or scratch or broken mirror or cracked bumper, and an irate plaintiff. This one was a chunky 19-year-old male in a *Call of Duty* t-shirt. He all but accused Detective Holly Ross of being the culprit. Over and over.

Ross had tried to maintain eye contact with him while he ranted, but she was getting sick of it. She let her gaze wander the strip mall parking lot and the façades of stores lined up like a brood of baby ducklings. Ugly ducklings. Strip malls sure could show their age, once they came of age. The storefronts faced All Saints Road, surrounded by brick apartments and town homes shaded by old trees. Not an inspiring site, but yeah, the sort of place you'd expect an accident. Not an accident involving an Escalade, but an accident.

"Are you even *listening?*" the guy complained. Roark Caldwell, his driver's license had said. It hadn't been a great photo, even for a driver's license. Stringy blond hair covering his ears, his face puffed up like he'd had the mumps that day.

The pair of responding officers, who had arrived a good ten minutes before Ross, were leaning on their squad car by the curb of the strip mall, trying not to smirk. They'd had their turn with Mr. Caldwell and were now enjoying the show. Probably they wanted to see how far Ross would let him push her. She'd gotten a bad rep the previous year when, in a fit of zeal, she leaned too hard into several witnesses. One particularly, who responded by slicing Ross' left cheek with a garden trowel. Thank God Theresa Swan had been there to cover her. Ross learned her lesson. It wouldn't happen again. Not today, anyway.

She returned her gaze to the plaintiff. "I heard every word, Mr. Caldwell." *Several times,* she didn't add out loud. "We're looking for the vehicle."

She gave his car another once-over. It was a piece of junk anyway, a 1997 Dodge Neon, silver except where it was rusted or blackened, in serious need of a bath, and with more dings, dents, and scratches than you could count in a month. The front bumper was now split wide open, its driver's side dragging on the ground. Caldwell had parked badly, a good two feet too far forward, no doubt the reason the culprit had decided to teach him a lesson. But seriously, the damage couldn't have lowered the car's value by more than a hundred bucks.

"Meanwhile," she added, "contact your insurance company and be thankful you weren't injured."

"Of course I wasn't injured! I wasn't in the car! I was in the deli!" He jabbed a finger at the Sally's Subs storefront. "How stupid can you get?"

Ross gave him a pinched smile and left him standing there. Waving to the officers, she got into her car and pulled away. In her rearview mirror, they laughed and waved back. Caldwell gave her a goodbye gesture, too, neither friendly nor amused. She wondered if he'd have dared do that to Eric Dumas. Probably not. Dumas was a man. She was just a woman, an oval-faced Cherokee woman, without even a uniform to bolster her position. Detective or no, many men didn't take her seriously. You'd think by now people would have gotten beyond their prejudices, but they ran deep, sometimes cutting their way to the surface, eroding pretensions to civility.

Too bad Dumas was off having fun with his bride. Not that Ross begrudged her boss the time off. She was happy for him, for them both, but she sure could have used his advice, or at least his sympathetic ear. She shouldn't have been on this case in the first place. Auto accidents weren't the province of detectives. That's what patrol officers were for. Except this time, it wasn't an accident, not even an isolated incident. This was someone with anger management issues intentionally ramming half the vehicles in the county. If the perp's SUV lasted that long, she might injure or kill someone.

Pro bono publico, Ross reminded herself. *For public good.*

In this case, the public good demanded quick apprehension of the suspect. Unfortunately, only a few things were known. A light blue Escalade, license number unnoticed. The driver was consistently described as Latina or Hispanic or a few times as "an immigrant," with or without "illegal" prepended, depending on who did the talking. Most called her old or elderly, with two witnesses explicitly stating she had gray hair.

Five incidents in a baker's dozen days. Ross had mapped them. Her initial hypothesis: they were close to the perp's domicile. For a time, that seemed likely. The first three incidents, two of which occurred before the case was tossed to Violent Crimes, had indeed been in the southeast part of North Laurel. But the next pair bled north along the I-95 corridor into Elkridge. And then this incident, back in North Laurel. Ross still bet her little old lady came from somewhere around here. Too bad she'd been wily enough to avoid getting caught in the act.

The lack of suspect or license left one route: vehicle registrations. Ross had already put in a request with the MVA. Escalades were expensive, roughly in the fifty-five K range. Total U.S. and Canada sales last year had been under forty thousand, so there weren't likely more than a thousand of them on the road in the entire state of Maryland. Most of those would be in the D.C. area and a few other locales where the bulk of the money lived. With luck, Ross could narrow it down to a handful of candidates in the target area. Then she could pay a visit to their owners and see if any owned a Cadillac tank that had been used as a battering ram.

It was a plan, anyway. Not a fun plan, but dogged research and a little logic was how most cases got solved.

At least the county paid her to do it.

Chapter 3

Still Wednesday, March twenty-eighth.

Her first day as a faux homeless person was her last. She couldn't keep up the pretense. Lying wasn't her forte.

He figured it out over breakfast, strawberry toaster pastries and coffee served in the kitchen of his apartment. "Where have you been sleeping?" he asked, and when she couldn't think of an answer, she saw the realization in his eyes. But he didn't press her. He fell silent, allowed her space, and after the meal told her he had to get to work.

"I guess I should go," she said. Not that she wanted to. She felt drawn to him, to his kindness, to his concern. She'd never met anyone quite like him, which was ridiculous because she hardly knew the guy. He hadn't exactly been open about himself thus far. Yet the thought of leaving him filled her with sorrow. She deserved to be kicked out, of course. She wished she hadn't lied to him.

But he surprised her. "I telecommute. I have an office in one of my spare bedrooms. You can stay out here or in the other bedroom, if you want. Just don't bother me while I'm working."

"This is a three-bedroom?"

He grinned. "Sure is. I have a good job."

"Wow." That sounded stupid, but what else could she say? He must have the biggest unit in the complex. She had the smallest.

She spent the whole day in his apartment. The spare bedroom was spare indeed, just a dumping ground for things he didn't much need. A pair of lamps sat unplugged on the floor. A disused nightstand. A broken desk chair. A box of castoff clothing, its top open, its contents tossed in haphazardly. She chose the living room instead and daydreamed about how her furniture would look in that bedroom.

Wait, why would she fantasize about that?

Oh, of course. How obvious. Her paradise had burned to the ground. She needed a new home, and she could do a lot worse than this. She returned to the spare room for a bit and stood at the window. Behind the building, a thick stand of trees obscured the view, its tangled branches covered in young leaves freshly burst from their buds. A wilderness view, not a beach, but she could live here.

They had lunch together. Bologna sandwiches and chips and sodas. They had dinner together. Chinese carry-out, which he fetched while she watched the six o'clock news with zero interest. Only after dinner did he ask where she lived.

"Down the street," she admitted. "I have a small apartment on the south end of the complex. Lease is up this year. I was going to renew, but…"

"Can't you afford it?"

"Not anymore." Which was true, but not the sort of affordability he meant. "Something's happened. Something…oh, I can't explain it."

He leaned across the table and took her hands in his, his touch as gentle as before. "Sure, you can."

She pulled away.

"I mean…" He curled his fingers into fists and stared at them as though they had offended him. "I just mean I'll listen. You can tell me. I won't judge you. I promise."

"I can't," she said. "Please don't ask."

Crestfallen, he rose, cleared the table, tossed the trash in the waste-basket under the sink, washed the utensils and dropped them in the dish drainer. Then he leaned his backside against the counter, arms crossed over his chest, and gazed at her with a determination she hadn't seen in anyone's eyes since her father had died. "Don't pretend you haven't been hurt. Let me help you, damn it."

Of course she had been. That's why she couldn't talk. But that look, it hurt, too. Or the memory of it did. Still, she found comfort in it, in the thought that her father might be watching over her, might have sent her out for that walk so she could run into this nerd. And then the incongruity of the situation overwhelmed her. She laughed.

"What's so funny?" he demanded.

"You don't know a damned thing about me, yet you're ready to rescue me from the dragon."

"There is a dragon, then."

What could she say?

"What is it? Or who?"

"I don't know. That's the problem. How do you slay a dragon you can't find?"

"Tell me. Tell me everything. Don't leave anything out."

She was afraid, but the fire in his eyes gave her comfort. Maybe she'd found a protector, a champion even, after all. She swallowed her fear and made a start. "I got a letter," she said. And once that leaked out, the dam broke and a deluge ensued.

†

Aside from the frustration of not making any progress on their cases, the first half of that week bored Holly Ross and Theresa Swan.

Ross didn't receive her list of Escalades of interest until Thursday, whereupon she spent a day at her desk, whittling it down. Sort of. She arrived at seventeen candidates, assuming she was right about southeast North Laurel being the target area. Owner's names didn't help much. While witnesses identified the driver as an elderly Latina, three-quarters of the vehicles were registered to men. That meant nothing. The perp could have been a wife, a girlfriend, even a mother or sister or cousin. Whoever she was, she might be driving a vehicle registered to John Smith.

Swan, meanwhile, acquired two new leads in the Squirrel Shooter case, as she began calling it. Alas, neither helped. Panicked reports of gunshots in Centennial Park flowed in on Tuesday and Thursday. Responders found nothing. Witnesses provided nothing but sound vectors. Swan didn't bother visiting either site or talking with the witnesses. They had nothing to tell. She added their location data to a map of the park. Her map captured eight incidents now, all on the south side of the lake where most of the park facilities were arrayed. Woods shrouded the northern shore. Over seven miles of paved paths traversed the park, paths used by walkers and runners and bikers, yet the shooter had kept to the area near the pavilions.

"I think Squirrel Shooter's lazy," Swan told Ross late Thursday afternoon. They had retreated to the break room to bemoan their lack of progress while drinking what passed for coffee. Misery loved caffeinated company. Dingy walls, maybe tan, maybe a bit on the gold side, surrounded them. A few of the ceiling tiles bore brown water stains. No expense had been lavished on the place.

"Lazy?" Ross asked.

"Yeah. He/she/it is keeping near their car."

"At least you have a clear target area. I only have an educated guess."

They faced each other over a round table, fiddling with their mugs, taking occasional sips. Swan's mug featured a pink breast cancer ribbon. On Ross', Susie Derkins from *Calvin and Hobbes* glowered at the world.

Swan figured Ross was ahead. Her colleague at least had a list of vehicles. She only had so-called witnesses waving at the woods. "I considered increased patrols in the area," she said, "but Whitney would click her pen at me."

Ross laughed. Every detective on the force had been on the receiving end of those irritated pen clicks at one time or another, sometimes directed at them, sometimes performed absently while Captain Whitney Morris pondered the annoying, the frustrating, or the merely puzzling. "You need Kevin Graham. With him wandering the park, nobody would dare shoot off as much as a bang snap."

"You don't shoot those off. You throw them on the ground."

"You know what I mean."

Swan did. Graham was an imposing officer, a big Jamaican well-practiced in the art of intimidation. Eric Dumas liked to partner with him in psychological games of good cop/bad cop. They made a formidable team. Outside such encounters, Graham was all good guy. He had his sweet side, although Swan would never suggest that to his face. "If we ever catch Squirrel Shooter, I'll get Kevin to give him a nasty look. That would set them on the straight path."

Ross sipped her coffee. "You know, I could use him, too. When I find a banged-up powder blue tank, I'll be facing down an angry granny. Not a situation I want to be in. Not again."

Swan cracked a lopsided smile. "It wasn't a granny last time."

Ross touched a finger to the scar the trowel had left on her face. "Damn angry, though. Hmm. I think I'll start calling her that. Angry Granny."

"Oh, fine, you get dibs on Kevin."

Rick Peller strolled into the break room. "Ladies," he said, and got himself some coffee. "Not too bored, I hope?"

"No, sir," Swan said. "More frustrated than bored."

"Detectives? Frustrated?" Peller grinned, but then his expression turned serious. "There's something I'd like the two of you to see."

The women finished their coffee and rose in unison. "What's up?" Ross asked.

"Vandalism," Peller said. "At a church. I'll drive."

†

A short ride, less than a mile and a half, brought them to St. Paul Catholic Church in Ellicott City, a towering stone structure perched atop a hill. An arc of buildings surrounded it, mostly old, a couple newer, one contemporary. The church looked down on the road from above a retaining wall. Unlike St. Augustine, no statuary adorned the grounds, possibly because there wasn't much ground to spare. The buildings and the parking lot behind took up the bulk of the land. Signage said the church had been established in 1838.

GPS brought them down Main Street in Ellicott City. The church was only a block to the south of the intersection of Main and Maryland Avenue. Making the turn, Peller flinched as he passed a traffic light mounted on an old green pole. He only half realized he'd done it.

"What's wrong?" Swan asked.

"That signal," he said. "It saved me from drowning last year."

Neither Swan nor Ross commented. The whole department knew the story. Peller had been assisting in the rescue of a woman and her children trapped in their car as a flash flood swept down Main Street. He and a group of good Samaritans had gotten the family out, but a chunk of debris in the water had bowled Peller over. They'd nearly lost him that day.

Peller rounded the front of the church. They craned their necks to gaze up the retaining wall, up the gray and brown face of the church, up the stained-glass windows and bell tower to the tip of the spire and Celtic cross piercing the sky. Heaven felt a long, long way off. That probably wasn't the intention.

The road ascended the hill and forked. The entrance to the church parking lot was to the left. Signage identified the buildings, including the parish office this side of the church and the rectory at the far end. The latter was a tree-shrouded house flanked by a white garage. The garage caught their attention as soon as they turned in. Even from a distance, the red lettering painted across the bay door was unmistakable.

Ecclesiastes 8:11

The message was writ large, large enough to span the width of the door.

"Anyone know that verse?" Peller asked. He parked in front of the parish office.

Ross looked it up on her cell phone. "It says, 'Because the sentence against evil-doers is not promptly executed, therefore the hearts of men are filled with the desire to commit evil, because the sinner does evil a hundred times and survives.' The last bit is part of verse twelve. I'm reading from the New American Bible, the one Catholics use."

"Are you Catholic?" Peller asked.

"Free agent." Ross tucked her phone away. "My Cherokee ancestors worshiped Unetlanvhi, the Great Spirit. Most of our people are Christian today, primarily Baptist and Methodist. My family's been largely noncommittal for the past few generations."

"But when in Rome," Swan quipped.

They climbed out of the car and entered the parish office, where a fortyish woman sat at a desk, staring at a computer screen. Her eyes had a faraway look, not focused on what it displayed. Her hair, a silvery blonde, was styled with side bangs and long strands in back. She looked like she hadn't slept in a week. That might have been from the stress of the day.

"Are you Ms. Beck?" Peller asked. The vandalism had been reported by one Shelly Beck.

The woman rose. "Yes, are you the police?"

Peller showed her his ID. "Detective Lieutenant Rick Peller. These are Detectives Theresa Swan and Holly Ross. We've seen the graffiti."

"It would be hard to miss," Beck said. She tried to laugh it off, but she might have been choking.

"Are you aware of any other vandalism, or is that it?"

"I didn't think to look. When I saw it, I called Father Dan. He said to call you."

At least one priest was thinking clearly. "When did you notice it?"

"When I arrived at one o'clock this afternoon."

"Nobody else was around this morning?" Swan asked.

Beck rubbed her forehead as though thinking was too much for her. "Daily mass is at eight, but nobody reported seeing it, as far as I know. Father Dan sounded surprised when I told him."

Which put the window of opportunity between nine fifteen or nine thirty A.M. to one P.M. Anyone could have sprayed the message without drawing attention. Between the hilly terrain and the trees, the garage was invisible from the road, save right by the parking lot entrance. Only someone driving south on College Avenue would glimpse it, and then only for a second as they rounded the uphill curve bending away from the church. No drivers' eyes would be on the parking lot just then, not if they wanted to stay on the road.

"I'd like to talk to Father Dan, if he's available," Peller said. He turned to Ross and Swan. "Get photos and check the grounds for any other signs of vandalism. Let me know if we need a tech on site."

Swan and Ross nodded and got to work. Shelly Beck called Father Dan. "The police are here," she said. "They'd like to speak with you. Okay, I'll send him over." She cradled the receiver. "You can go to the rectory, by the garage. Father Dan will be expecting you."

Peller thanked her. His eyes played over the buildings and grounds and parking lot as he approached the rectory, but nothing seemed amiss. No other obvious signs of vandalism, nothing one wouldn't expect. It was quiet save the swish of traffic in the distance. When he reached the rectory door, the black-garbed priest already had opened it. His form filled the frame. Peller put his age at about fifty. Nearly six foot himself, the Lieutenant had to look up to meet Father Dan's eyes.

Father Dan extended his hand and introduced himself. Peller accepted the handshake and was escorted inside, where a comfortable living room furnished in ornate early twentieth-century décor greeted him. A pair of steaming teacups sat on coasters on a dark wood coffee table.

"You've been expecting me." Peller nodded at the cups as he sat opposite Father Dan.

"Of course. I had Shelly report the incident, after all." There was a twinkle in Father Dan's eye, as though he was playing a satisfying game of chess with Peller.

"You didn't make the tea several hours ago. You saw us drive in."

"I saw an unmarked car, Lieutenant. How could I have known it was the police?"

Peller raised an eyebrow and took a sip.

Father Dan laughed. "You're right. It's a dead time of day. I wasn't expecting anyone else."

"Your last name isn't Brown, is it?" Peller asked, referencing the fictional British priest-sleuth.

"Adkins. You know your Chesterton. I'm impressed."

"Occupational hazard. I mostly read westerns. When did you notice the vandalism, Father?"

The priest picked up his cup and took a sip, then frowned at it. "I forgot the sugar. Oh well, that would make my doctor happy." He set the cup down again. "I wasn't the one who noticed it. Shelly did. She reported it to me. I only looked after telling her to call you."

"What time was that?"

"Early afternoon. I didn't check the clock, but I guess shortly after one. That's when she arrived."

"What do you think it means?" Peller sampled the tea again. Father Dan was right. No sugar. But it was Earl Gray, which Peller had always thought perfect without enhancements.

Father Dan leaned back and studied the textured ceiling. "It's a curious verse."

When he didn't continue, Peller prompted, "Curious how?"

"I just mean it's not one you often hear cited. It's curious to find it sprayed on a wall. I don't suppose you're interested in a theological analysis. Basically, it says when punishment for wrongdoing is delayed, people are emboldened to continue in their wickedness. And yet, God doesn't deliver swift retribution. He's patient. He desires we obey him out of love, not merely to avoid punishment. But His patience encourages the wayward. It makes them think there will be no retribution, which is tragically wrong-headed."

"Why spray it on your garage?"

"It's either a prank or a warning, I suppose. If the latter, it's likely directed against the Church herself, but it could mean nothing at all."

It meant something. At least, Peller sensed it did, though he didn't yet know why. True, it could be a vendetta against the religion. Two Catholic churches had been targeted in the same manner. Yet there was another possibility. Someone might have a close connection to both parishes. Only nine miles separated St. Paul and St. Augustine, a fifteen to twenty-minute drive. They weren't neighbors, but they weren't that far apart.

Father Dan reached for his cup again, frowned at the sugarless liquid, and downed another gulp. His face contorted, possibly from lack of sweetener, certainly from the thoughts swirling through his brain. "I do hope it's nothing, but let's be brutally honest. You know what's been in the news."

Peller did. The clergy sex abuse scandal refused to die down, including allegations that church officials had sought to cover it up.

"It will only get worse," the priest predicted. "These malefactors are tarnishing the good name of all priests and the Church herself." His hands shaking, he returned the cup to its saucer, spilling a bit as he put it down. "It's not Christian, and I'm ashamed to admit it, but if I had my way, every one of them..." Jaw locked, he frowned at the spilled tea.

"Most people would agree," Peller told him.

Father Dan's disgust was all but written on his face. He loathed the scandal, loathed the abusers, maybe loathed himself for loathing them. A priest of all people should be able to forgive.

Peller let him simmer a moment before asking, "You didn't put that message there yourself, did you?"

"What?" Father Dan gaped at Peller. Then his tension melted into a small laugh. "No, Lieutenant, no. It wasn't me. I don't blame you for thinking it, though."

"I wasn't seriously thinking it, but I had to ask. Was any other vandalism noticed around the property?"

"Not that I'm aware of. I didn't look." He leaned forward, suddenly concerned. "Do you think there might be?"

"Probably not. My team's scouting the grounds, just in case. We'll let you know if we find anything." Peller passed Father Dan his business card. "If anything occurs to you, or if anything else happens, contact me directly."

After taking his leave, Peller returned to the car just as Theresa Swan and Holly Ross emerged from opposite ends of the complex and joined him. They reported nothing else amiss.

"Did Father Dan say anything helpful?" Swan asked.

"No," Peller replied. "I didn't expect him to."

Ross squinted at the graffiti as though it blinded her. "Why did you bring us here?"

"This is the second incident." Peller told them about the message at St. Augustine and Father Ed Tyler's strange reaction. "I wondered if Father Ed wasn't telling me everything, but this puts a new spin on it. Father Dan suggested it could be a reaction to the sex abuse scandal."

"If so," Swan ventured, "it could be harmless vandalism. Just somebody blowing off steam."

"Could be."

Ross opened the rear passenger-side door. "But you don't think so."

Peller wasn't sure what to think. Maybe this was nothing. Maybe he just wanted it to be something because nothing near as interesting was going on. He didn't like to think he would think that way, but nothing aside from work gave life much meaning anymore, not since Sandra's death.

You're hopeless, she chided in the recesses of his brain.

I know, he admitted. *But I don't know how to change it.*

The detectives stood by their open car doors and didn't get in. They stared down the red letters as though demanding they explain themselves.

"What would Corina say?" Swan asked.

Absently, Peller replied, "That we need more data. Which we do."

Ross smirked. "Yeah, but Eric would have some wild idea anyway."

That might have been the right thing to say. Peller suddenly realized what he was looking at, maybe part of what had been niggling at him. "That writing," he said.

The women frowned at it, unable to see what he had seen. But of course they couldn't. They hadn't seen the message at St. Augustine.

"What about it?" Swan asked.

"It's in a different hand. The messages were painted by different people." The only common letters were *a* and *s*, but something was off. The spacing of the letters, the slant of the strokes, something. It wasn't the same writer.

"Does it work like that?" Ross asked. "Handwriting, sure, but spray painting?"

Another unknown. Fortunately, Peller knew an expert who could tell them. "Let's find out," he said.

†

"I was about to go home," handwriting analyst Jacey Alexandre complained, spinning her aggrievement to ridiculous heights. She sounded as though the world would end if she had to do five seconds more work.

Peller cracked a smile, which is what she wanted, at a minimum. She liked to put on a show. Although they'd only ever talked on the phone—Jacey worked at the Maryland State Police forensics lab in Pikesville—he'd been on the receiving end of her theatrics a few times over the past ten years. "Oh, come on," he said. "How often do you get a fun request like this?"

"More often than you'd think. And yes, people do write in largely consistent form, whether in pen, crayon, chalk, dry erase marker, or spray paint. Graffiti artists show consistencies from one work to the next, too, like any other artist."

"This isn't an artist, just someone spraying messages onto available surfaces."

Jacey uttered a heavy sigh.

"What?"

"As you may recall, I was about to leave."

"You know you're interested."

"At least tell me the messages are clever. I've had my fill of crude."

Peller let her hang for a moment.

"So?" she asked.

"Bible verses. Book, chapter number, and verse number. We had to look up the text ourselves."

"That's clever?"

"Possibly."

"Come on, Rick. Don't hold out."

"Would I do that?"

"Obviously. Cut to the chase, and it better be proselytizing with extreme prejudice."

Peller might have laughed in other circumstances, but she'd hit closer to the mark than she knew. "They may be death threats."

The whole world fell silent.

"Jacey? You didn't go home, I hope."

"Biblical death threats," she said with a little too much glee. "Sick. Send me the photos. You'll have my report by noon tomorrow, graphology included, no extra charge."

"I'm less interested in profiling than finding out if my hunch is right. I suspect two people were involved."

"No, no, no, Rick. You can't stop me, not once you charge my battery and press start. You know that."

"My mistake. Photos are on the way." He texted her the materials. She confirmed their arrival, and he let her get to it. He doubted she'd stay too late. She had a husband and a pair of teenage girls waiting at home. But he figured she'd know before she took to the road whether his suspicions were true. If Peller could pick out the differences in the lettering, Jacey would instantly see them.

Assuming he wasn't imagining things.

Chapter 4

Thursday, March twenty-ninth.

He made his couch into a bed for her. A bit awkward, really. She didn't mean to sleep in his apartment, and he didn't ask her to. Not verbally. He just brought out spare sheets and a blanket and gave her one of the pillows from his own bed. It smelled like him and a bit like his cologne. She had the odd feeling as she bedded down for the night that she was putting her head on his shoulder. Strange, but part of her liked the sensation.

She slept in her clothes, of course. She hadn't gone back to her apartment to get anything, and she wasn't about to undress in his living room. When morning came, she felt a bit stiff, quite rumpled, and longed for her toothbrush. He emerged from his room dressed for another day of telecommuting in jeans and a faded Green Day t-shirt. He served up more coffee and toaster pastries. Chocolate this time.

"Is this all you eat for breakfast?" she asked. It probably came out more plaintive than she meant.

If so, he didn't notice. "Pretty much. I'll get us something different for tomorrow, if you want. Frozen waffles, maybe?"

Tomorrow? Would she still be here tomorrow? No, she couldn't move into a near-stranger's apartment. Or could she? She had no other place to go. Her apartment had been defiled, and she couldn't go back to her mother. Mom would know something was wrong, would insist on hearing everything. She didn't dare inflict that letter on Mom. It would plunge her back into depression.

He smiled as he lifted his mug to his lips. It was a friendly smile but timid. Hopeful but afraid. He wanted her to stay, yet he couldn't make himself ask.

"Looking for a roommate?" she teased.

He almost choked on his coffee. "Uh, no, not really. I mean...I'm not kicking you out. You can stay a bit. You're...you're..."

When he couldn't find the continuation, she supplied one from their first conversation. "Hot?"

"Oh my God," he muttered.

She laughed. "It's okay. You're not bad yourself, in a nerdy sort of way."

He blushed. "I was thinking," he said a bit too quickly. "Can I see that letter?"

That cold penetrated her skin again. She stared at him, horrified.

"I'm not afraid of it. Maybe I can help you figure out who sent it."

She didn't ever want to touch that letter again, didn't ever want to see it. But damn his logic, it made sense. She couldn't do this alone. Whatever "this" was. If she was ever to make that demon pay, she would need someone steady. Someone like him.

She nodded.

A short time later, they walked to her apartment. He held her hand. She didn't know when he had taken it, but his touch steadied her. Strength seemed to flow from his body into hers. She led him to the dresser drawer where she had hidden the thing. She refused to handle it, but he picked it up without hesitation and read, eyes narrowed almost to slits. He read it once, twice, thrice. When he was done, he placed it back, closed the drawer, and stared out the window at the trees and their swelling buds. Then he asked just one question.

"Which church?"

†

Seventeen Escalades of interest. What fun.

Holly Ross set out to track them down on Friday, which wouldn't be as easy as it sounded. She knew where the vehicles lived. She had no idea if they'd be home when she got there. Probably not. Their drivers would be at work or shopping or halfway across the continent on vacation. At best, she might cross a few off her list. But she had to be cautious, had to avoid tipping off the owners. She needed a look at the vehicles, not a confrontation. Her target Escalade had been used as a battering ram, so it ought to bear damage on the front and sides. With five incidents in thirteen days, there'd been zero time for repairs, unless maybe the owner operated a body shop.

When Ross checked the map, she discovered that nine of the addresses on her list were in a gated community off Gorman Road, an expanse of single-family homes and townhouses wrapped around a lake. That neighborhood was cut off from surrounding areas by woods. The other eight addresses were more scattered. She would chase those down first, while she was fresh.

The day had turned cooler, cool enough she nudged up the heat as she cruised south on U.S. 29 toward North Laurel and took the State Route 216 exit. From there, she navigated residential roads to her first target, a comfortable home of light brick and pale siding that reposed in the shade of middle-aged trees. False shutters flanked the windows. The professionally designed landscaping had grown weedy. A few cars sat in nearby driveways and along the curbs, but at this place?

Nah. Of course not.

She rang the doorbell while robins hopped about the front yard and a crow cawed on high. The door didn't open. She rang again, then a third time with no response. She made a quick note on her cell phone and moved on. The next house waited a few blocks away in the same neighborhood. With a bigger tree but less landscaping, in style it was a sibling of the previous. The garage door was raised a crack. Not much, just a few inches, too little for even a toddler to squeeze under, but it suggested carelessness.

Ross rang the bell and waited, rang and waited. She pondered the blue security company sign stabbed into the ground near the front door. Unlike the garage door, that bespoke caution. People could be so inconsistent. After a third ring with no response, she made a note and proceeded to her third target, a Georgean home with a brick façade near a United Methodist Church on Scaggsville Road. A faded wooden privacy fence held the back yard in its wide embrace. A black sedan rested in the driveway. No Escalade, but maybe someone was home. Ross went to the front door. No doorbell button. She knocked. A dog barked inside.

Do you own a blue Escalade? she thought at the dog. *Bark! Thank you, sir. Can you tell me if it's been in an accident recently? Bark bark bark! I'm sorry, sir, could you repeat that? Bark bark bark! Yes, I suppose I am barking mad.*

The door opened. The dog was there, a mid-sized mutt that could have been a cross between a boxer and a poodle. A forty-something woman accompanied the critter. She squinted at Ross as though her visitor was radiating an excess of light. Being not old and not at all Latina, she probably wasn't the culprit.

"Hello?" she said while the dog continued its racket. Ross could barely hear her.

"I'm Detective Holly Ross, Howard County Police." Ross displayed her ID. "I'm investigating a minor incident. Could I ask you a couple questions?"

The woman's squint didn't change, but after inspecting Ross's credentials, she raised her index finger, then led the dog away. It didn't want to go. While she tugged at its collar, it strained for the door, bared its teeth, and snarled. Somehow, she corralled the beast, returned, and stepped outside. "How can I help you?"

"Does anyone living here own a blue Cadillac Escalade?"

"Yes, it's my husband's, but he's at work right now. In D.C."

Out of your jurisdiction, Ross finished for her. *Have a nice day.* "Does anyone other than your husband drive it?"

The woman shrugged. "I do sometimes. Not often."

"Nobody else?"

"No. Why do you want to know?"

"Nothing serious. Just trying to narrow down possibilities regarding small traffic incident."

"It's never been in an accident, if that's what you mean."

So the woman claimed, but that just made Ross itchier to get a look at that vehicle. *Down, girl, down,* she told herself as though addressing the dog. *No confrontations.* "Thank you, ma'am, that will be all." She stopped herself from adding an ominous *for now.*

That was Ross' whole morning, visiting houses where nobody was home or, if they were, where the vehicle wasn't. She hit up that gated community with the same results, just at more expensive homes. Seventeen visits, eleven no-shows, six interviews with people who couldn't have been Angry Granny, probably weren't even related to her, and who insisted that their vehicles, all taken to work by family members, had never been in accidents. She had no reason to doubt any of them, but she rather wished she did. She wanted a quick win.

Yeah, but you don't want to wind up back with that therapist.

She resigned herself to making phone calls.

†

Squirrel Shooter must have taken a day off from hunting. Without any phantom gunshot reports to liven up her day, Theresa Swan wrapped up some paperwork, made routine phone calls on a few boring cases, and tried not to think about the church graffiti. It wasn't her case. Peller had just asked for a bit of help. Maybe. He never explained why he took Ross and herself to the church. Maybe he wanted their observations and insights. Maybe he wanted them working it.

No, forget it. It wasn't her case.

Then again...

Swan accessed Peller's report on the St. Augustine incident and compared the writing to the photos they'd taken at St. Paul. The boss had a point. The letters slanted to the right in the first case, stood mostly vertical in the second. But did that mean anything? Maybe, maybe not. The *modus operandi* was identical, at any rate. If there were two writers, they must be working together for a common purpose. Except they didn't seem to be on the same page. One message a death threat, the other, not so much.

As she pondered the conundrum, her cell phone rang. She nearly jumped out of her chair. Recovering, she checked the caller. Ken Bauer, her boyfriend. She answered with, "Hey, handsome."

"Hey, beautiful. What's wrong?"

"Why would anything be wrong?"

"Your voice is shaking."

"I was deep in thought when the phone rang. You scared me out of my wits."

Bauer laughed. "You need some time off."

"I'm hardly on at the moment."

"Great. Then you can spare a day for me."

If only. They didn't pay her for spending time with him.

He didn't give her a chance to object. "There's this new Greek place we gotta try. Say yes."

"Yes, when I'm off duty."

"You will be," Bauer said. "Saturday."

"Deal. Where?"

"D.C."

Swan about choked. She hated going down there, hated battling traffic and crowds. "Just for a restaurant?" she complained.

"Nah, we'll make a day of it. Do the museums, see the cherry blossoms."

"We missed peak bloom time."

"Too bad. You already said yes. I'll let you get back to hardly working, but we'll talk details tonight. Love ya."

"Love ya," she parroted with a smile.

D.C. Okay, sure, for him, she could deal with it. At least there wouldn't be anyone taking potshots at wildlife or spraying menacing messages on walls.

Probably.

Then again, it *was* D.C.

†

Jacey Alexandre's report arrived via email at 10:43 AM. Peller had spent most of the morning forcing his thoughts elsewhere. Best not to speculate on what she would say. When it showed up, he dove in and took three laps through it to ensure he didn't miss anything.

The primary conclusion: different people had almost certainly written the two messages. The spacings and slants of the letters differed, and the common letters, *a* and *s*, had been formed differently.

The graphology report got into minutiae Peller didn't fully understand. He wasn't sure he subscribed to the idea that handwriting revealed personality, although the notion had some traction in the law enforcement community. Be that as it may, Jacey made a good go of it, but with a few caveats, the main being that the writing samples were too small to permit more than a few basic conclusions. That was offset by the consistency of the lettering. Great care had been taken in the application of the paint.

So...

The writer of *Romans 6:23* was emotional, passionate, a creative personality. They were independent and self-centered. They would take charge of their own destiny and act according to what they believed was right. *Great*, Peller thought. *A crusader.*

The writer of *Ecclesiastes 8:11*, on the other hand, was even-tempered, controlled, a balanced individual but rather private, possibly with something to hide.

Conclusions: The first writer had planned the vandalism and recruited the second to assist. Both were meticulous. If the second writer had any doubts about what they were doing, the first had convinced them it was right.

Great in theory, except Peller had no suspects. This pair could be anybody in the county who matched the profiles, any two people working in concert to achieve an end they believed justified the means. But what end? Nothing had been seriously damaged. No stained-glass windows smashed, no statuary chipped or shattered, no altars defiled. Warnings had been issued, but warnings of what? Against what? A reaction to scandal, as

Father Dan Adkins speculated? Maybe. But Father Ed Tyler obfuscated and suggested nothing, which was odd. Was he the one with something to hide?

Another word with Father Ed was in order. Peller didn't seriously think he was involved, but maybe he knew more than he was admitting. Was he aware of the St. Paul incident? Did he know of any connection between the two churches? Might he open up now that another incident had occurred?

On the way out, Peller stopped by Captain Whitney Morris' corner office. Morris was busy banging out emails when he arrived. The windows behind her revealed another pleasant day, mostly sunny, new leaves quivering in the spring breeze. A bank of bookcases filled with tomes on law and police procedure covered most of the walls. As always, her desk was clear save her computer, a notepad and pen, and photos of her husband the doctor and their three children.

"You look like a man on a mission," she commented without shifting her gaze from her monitor.

"Everyone needs a hobby. Yours seems to be battling the bureaucracy of which you're a part."

"A cynical man on a mission." She pushed back and grimaced at the screen. "Let's just say a few of our local politicians have achieved such proficiency in lying via statistics that they're beginning to believe even themselves."

Peller laughed.

Morris didn't. "I suppose you're here to tell me you're not here."

"I need to pay a visit to a priest. That business at St. Augustine."

"Rotten thing to find at a wedding. Did something else happen?"

"Yes, but not there. A similar message appeared at St. Paul the other day. I'm curious what Father Ed has to say about it."

"Want to swap jobs?" Morris gave him a hopeful look, only half in jest. She'd been a good detective before promotion robbed her of the opportunity to get out in the field.

"Nope. I'll take an intractable priest over politicians any day."

"And I thought you liked your boss."

Peller grinned as she returned to her emails.

An uneventful drive later, he pulled into the St. Augustine parking lot, dismounted his F150, and took a long look about. The otherwise quiet neighborhood was awash in the rush of nearby traffic. U.S. 1 ran by a mere thousand feet to the northwest. Beyond it to the north, a trio of highways—I-95, I-895, and the airport expressway I-195—intersected in a roughly equilateral triangle a mile long on each side. Together, the thoroughfares kept nearby neighborhoods alive with sound. Peller barely noticed background noise most of the time, but standing before the church this morning, he could understand why some people would rather live in the middle of nowhere.

He was alone save one other person, a contractor repairing the defaced stone at Mary's feet. The contractor's white van, parked by the wall, bore the name Weber Hardscapers on the driver's door. Peller decided to talk with the fellow before seeking out Father Ed, but he stopped short when he noticed something strange.

Statuary dotted the grounds, some about the church, some about the convent and school, and some on the drive up from the road. St. Augustine himself greeted visitors just beyond the entrance, looking serene in his mitre, with his crosier in his right hand and a book in his left. Peller knew Catholics imbued imagery with symbols but wasn't versed in their meanings. It occurred to him that the vandal—vandals, rather—might also be revealing themselves through symbols. Attributes of handwriting that revealed their personality traits. Biblical references as warnings or threats. And here, possibly, was another: alongside the church beside the parking lot, the head of the statue of St. Francis of Assisi, who had birds at his feet, in his hand, and on his shoulder, was covered with a wooden bushel basket such as watermen used in crabbing. Peller almost laughed at the incongruous sight. Why would anyone do *that*?

But he knew. Nobody would, not even for a joke. Nobody save the vandals. He snapped a photo with his cell phone, then called for a crime scene technician. If they were lucky, maybe the basket would offer up fingerprints.

He walked to the front of the church and said good morning to the contractor. A stocky man not nearly as tall as Peller, he acknowledged the greeting without pausing in his work. He had removed the two damaged stones from the top of the wall and was setting replacements in place. The work was complicated by the footlight below the statue. The new stone required a hole to accommodate it.

"I'm Detective Lieutenant Rick Peller," Peller told him. "Howard County Police. Could I ask you a few questions?"

The contractor straightened and turned in slow motion. "I guess so," he said, though his tone said otherwise.

"Don't worry, sir. I already know about the vandalism. I was the one who discovered it. What's your name?

After a puzzled silence, the other replied, "Carl Weber."

"Weber Hardscaping is your company, then."

"Yes, sir, it is."

"You're a member of this parish?"

"My grandparents attended St. Augustine. We've been in the community a long time."

Peller nodded at the removed stones, which Weber had set graffiti-side down. "Must've been a shock, seeing that."

"Yeah." Weber eyed the stones as though accusing them of blasphemy. Maybe he was. "Unbelievable what some people will do."

"I don't suppose anyone has any ideas about who did it."

"Not that I know of."

"What about the paint, Mr. Weber? Any thoughts on that?"

Weber shrugged. "The application was smooth. Steady hand. Not much scatter. I'd guess it was spray paint, available at any home center or hardware store, applied at close range." He shrugged again. "That doesn't tell you much, I'm sure."

Maybe, maybe not. Plenty of people had steady hands. Artists. Craftsmen. Contractors.

"What do you think it meant?" Peller asked.

There was that shrug again. "Christianity's always had enemies."

"So has every other religion. I don't suppose anyone came by while you were here?"

"Not that I noticed, but I've been busy."

"Did you notice the basket?"

Weber stared at him.

Peller pointed. "Around the side of the church. There's a basket on St Francis' head."

Balling his fists, Weber strode to the parking lot. Peller followed. Upon seeing the offending object, the contractor growled, "Damn it, what is this?" and started for it, intent on removing it.

Peller stepped in front of him. "I'll have to ask you to leave it, Mr. Weber. I have an evidence technician on the way. We'll deal with it."

Weber made a face. "Yeah, all right. Just get it out of here."

"We will. I'll let you get back to your work. Thank you for your time."

Peller escorted Weber back to the wall to make sure he didn't change his mind about leaving the basket to the cops, then moved on to the rectory. He wondered which entrance to use, the side door with the ramp or the front door? Probably Father Ed used the side door most of the time. More convenient. But who knew where that door led. Maybe the kitchen. Peller went to the front and rang the doorbell. It was only a moment before a curvy young black woman answered. She had a white dish towel draped over her shoulder. She smiled up at Peller and asked, "Can I help you?"

Peller displayed his ID. "Detective Lieutenant Rick Peller, Howard County Police. Is Father Ed available?"

She put a hand to her chest and morphed from happy to aghast. "Um, well, yes, he's here. Is something wrong?"

"Nothing terrible." She might not have known about the vandalism, since Father Ed had been so keen to keep it quiet, so Peller didn't mention it. "Could I ask your name?"

She spluttered a bit before finding her words. "Clare. Clare Fleming. I'm the rectory housekeeper."

"Well, don't worry, Ms. Fleming. I just need a quick word with the Father, then I'll be out of your hair. He already knows what it's about."

She leaned forward and whispered, "That message?"

That answered that question. "That message. Did you see it?"

"No. Father Ed told me about it. Do you know who did it?"

"We're investigating. It's probably nothing to worry about."

She grabbed the end of the dish towel and squeezed it. Then she whipped it off and scrunched it into a ball. "'Tween you and me, Lieutenant, I think it's a death threat. I think someone needs protecting."

Peller watched her ball up and stretch out and ball up the towel. "May I come in?"

"Oh, yes, sorry, this way." She led him into the living room, a small space, comfortable if not fancy. A plain white sofa and matching loveseat, a pair of white bergère chairs, a couple of walnut end tables. Religious art on the walls, of course.

Fleming settled Peller in one of the chairs and asked if he wanted coffee or tea or anything, which he declined. Then she perched on the edge of the sofa and rambled on, still kneading the towel. "It's about sin and death, that verse. Somebody knows something about somebody. They're threatening to kill them because of it."

A straightforward interpretation, but she wouldn't be that upset if she didn't think she knew the target. Peller didn't ask who she feared the intended victim might be. He didn't need to.

She leaned forward, once more speaking in a whisper. "I'm not a very good person. I've done things I shouldn't. Maybe they're after me. Could that be?"

It could be anything. Peller found it hard to believe a rectory housekeeper could be in *that* much trouble. Still, stranger things happened. All the time. "Nobody's perfect," he assured her. "But most of us don't have targets on our backs."

Before she could offer a reason why she would, Father Ed poked his head into the room. "Lieutenant? What brings you here?"

Fleming flipped the towel over her shoulder and sprang to her feet. "I gotta finish up the dishes," she said and fled.

Father Ed watched her zip by. "What was that about?"

"The vandalism has her upset."

"Yes. I didn't want to tell her about it, but she knew something was amiss. She twisted my arm." Father Ed sat where Fleming had been and settled back, completely relaxed, or at least doing a good job of faking it. He crossed one leg over the other and stretched out an arm along the back cushions. "What can I do for you?"

"There was another graffiti incident," Peller informed him. "At St. Paul in Ellicott City. I don't suppose you heard about it?"

Father Ed gaped, just for a moment. "Not until just now. Same verse?"

"Rather different. Ecclesiastes 8:11."

Brow furrowed, Father Ed thought about that. "That has to do with people persisting in waywardness when punishment is not swift."

"Basically. I spoke with Father Dan Adkins about it. He had his parish secretary call us." Peller let that hang for a moment, intending it less an accusation as a prompt.

Father Ed uncrossed his legs and straightened. "It was an internal matter, Lieutenant. I felt it better to handle it myself than allow it to upset and frighten my parishioners."

"I respect that," Peller said, although he didn't. "But it's gotten bigger. Two parishes are now involved, and my instinct tells me it won't end there. In fact…" He allowed a bit of dead air until Father Ed shifted uncomfortably. "When I arrived, I noticed something new. Your St. Francis statue has a crab basket on its head."

"A what?"

"A bushel basket of the sort used for transporting crabs."

Rising, Father Ed glowered at nothing. "I'll have it removed at once."

"No, Father. I'll take care of it. It may be nothing, but that basket might be evidence. We're going to check it for fingerprints and anything else we can lift from it, or around it. I have a technician *en route* as we speak."

"But…" Father Ed sank back onto the sofa. "Lieutenant, please. I don't want this turning into a media circus."

"You'd rather these incidents multiply? You can't hide them forever. Eventually it will come out, and believe me, it could be far worse then. Maybe that first message wasn't a death threat, but suppose it was. Suppose someone is murdered. Do you want that on your conscience? If you don't let me handle this, it very well could come to that."

The priest grimaced. "What if you can't stop it, either?"

"Then that's on me. But at least we can say we tried." Peller pulled up the photo of St. Francis on his phone and showed it to Father Ed. "All I want for now is the basket. Unless there's something you're not telling me."

Father Ed refused to look, then looked, then sighed. "All right," he said. "Take the basket. Just get it out of here."

Peller tucked away his phone and rose. "One last thing. You might want to talk to Father Dan. He seems pretty sharp. Maybe between the two of you, you can ferret out the reason for these incidents."

The priest didn't respond. Peller left him sitting there, lost in whatever he was contemplating.

†

"You called me to pick up a basket," Geri Franklin said.

Peller waggled his hand. "To remove a basket from a saint's head."

"A stone saint."

They both stared at the basket.

Franklin sighed and pulled on her gloves. "I'll be a laughing stock. You owe me, Rick."

"I'll take you to dinner tonight," Peller offered knowing she wouldn't accept. Social activities weren't Franklin's forte.

But she surprised him. "I'll take a rain check. I'm going out with Ozzie tonight."

"Ozzie?"

"Ozzie White."

"I know who he is," Peller said. "How is it you're going out with him?"

"He asked me. Before you did."

"I guess that dance did him some good, huh?"

Franklin gave Peller a dull look. "Don't make more of it than it is. He's just expressing his gratitude that somebody bothered to help him."

Peller didn't know about that. Dumas and Montufar had been trying to help him for most of a year and gotten nowhere. It was a minor miracle they'd pulled him into the wedding party. And according to Dumas, Ozzie had a reputation with the ladies before tragedy struck. "If you say so. Enjoy yourselves."

Franklin lifted the basket, revealing St. Francis' head. "I always do," she said, as stone-faced as the statue.

Chapter 5

Friday, March thirtieth and onward.

The days blew by like leaves in a squall. They had one conversation half a dozen times. The words varied, but the gist never changed.

"It's just a letter. Shred it. Burn it. Forget about it."

"But what about the church? *You* said that's the connection. The priest knows who she is. He must know!"

"Don't be stupid. Anyone can walk in and confess. Maybe she came from a different parish. Maybe she wanted to be anonymous. Hell, maybe she wasn't even Catholic."

"Catholics can't get absolution."

"Which is exactly what she said happened!"

"Why would she ask for confession if she *wasn't* Catholic?"

"How should I know?"

"She had to be."

"Fine, suppose she is. Suppose the priest knows her. Why wouldn't he absolve her?"

"Because she wasn't penitent! She murdered him and she didn't regret it!"

"That's not what the letter said."

"So she's a liar *and* a murderer!"

"You're driving yourself crazy. Nothing will bring him back. Let it go. For God's sake, even if you're right, the priest is bound to silence. He can't ID her or tell you anything she said."

"It's murder! How can the Church conceal it? How can they say it's all right?"

"It's not like that. You know it's not.

"It sure feels like it. I'm talking to him."

"He won't tell you anything."

"I'll make him tell me."

"How? By holding a gun to his head?"

"If I have to."

"You can't and you won't. It wouldn't change a thing, except you'd go to prison. For the love of God, just let it go!"

"I can't!"

"Not even for me? I only just found you. I don't want to lose you!"

It always ended the same way. He pulled her into his arms. She soaked their faces with her tears. He whispered that he was there for her, he'd always be there, he just wanted her to be safe and happy and *please* let it go because what was done was done.

But she found no comfort in his words, in his embrace, not even when he kissed her hair and told her he loved her. Because the killer had told one truth, at least. She had indeed ruined both their lives, and damn it, she had to pay for that!

Somewhere in that blur of days, the idea formed. She wouldn't press a literal gun to the priest's head. She would use a metaphorical one. She would scare him, scare the hell out of him until something shook loose, until he let something slip. Priests were human, too. They could make mistakes. And when he did, the path to justice would open. That's all that mattered. Justice.

He tried to logic her out of that, too, warned against the sin of revenge, but she didn't care. It wasn't revenge she wanted. It was justice. And hell, even if it *was* revenge, what was one more sin? She'd already lied about being homeless, and now, as the days ran their course, she traded the couch for his bed, not by request or invitation but by unspoken agreement. He said he cared for her, and she had to admit, she cared for him. Despite his protestations, it might not have been love. Not quite. But they were bound to each other, if only by her rage.

Besides, he wasn't so innocent, himself. She found that out when she violated his cardinal rule one day. He was shut in his office, working, while at the kitchen table she relived the day her father died. Once more, she felt her life bleeding away. She couldn't face it alone, not again, so she went to him for comfort. She went quietly, to avoid startling him. She didn't want to bother him, just to be in the same room, just to see him sitting there. He didn't realize she had cracked the door and slipped through, didn't notice her ease it not quite shut behind her.

He was on a call channeled through his computer, on speaker, no headphones. The voice on the other end was scratchy, accented, almost undecipherable to her ears, though he seemed to have no trouble understanding. He was negotiating. Hourly rates. Timeframes. Technical gibberish she couldn't fathom. When the call ended, he leaned back, caught a glimpse of her, and turned, half horrified, half enraged.

"What the *hell* are you doing?"

She backed against the door. It snicked shut. "I'm sorry. I didn't mean to bother you. I just—"

"I told you not to disturb me when I'm working!"

"I just needed—"

He looked pale. He clasped his quivering hands and pressed them into his lap.

"I just...I just need to be with you. Please don't be mad."

"What did you hear?"

"Nothing. Just...I guess you were...buying something?"

He covered his face in his hands, turned away, muttered words she couldn't hear. When he turned back, he had regained control. "Don't tell anyone. Promise you won't tell anyone."

"Tell what? I don't know what it was."

He eyed her the way her father sometimes did when he wasn't sure she was telling the truth.

She couldn't take that look, not from him. "Do you love me?"

He slumped. "Yes."

"Then trust me. I'll keep all your secrets. I promise. Just don't keep secrets from *me*. I haven't kept any from you." She went to him, sat in his lap, put her arms around him.

He pulled her tight against his body and stroked her hair. "You won't like it."

"I won't care," she whispered. "Unless you're a drug dealer or trafficking women."

"Of course not!"

"What are you, then?"

"Broke." He buried his face in her hair. "I went to Vegas last year and went a bit wild. I spent like crazy, lost a ton of money gambling, maxed out two credit cards."

"More than a bit wild. But you can afford it, right? You make a lot, don't you?"

"Yes and no. It's a good salary for someone my age, but not as much as you might think. I needed more, so I launched some side gigs. Short-term government contracts. But there aren't enough hours in a day. I can't do all these jobs and have time to sleep, so I..." He shrugged. "I outsource them."

"Outsource?"

"I hire developers in India. I charge the government U.S. rates for the work and pay my guys India rates. The difference between the two is... substantial. I make a good profit."

It sounded brilliant. "Is it legal?"

"Not exactly. Nothing I handle is classified. If it was, I wouldn't be working from home. But some of the information my guys need to complete the work isn't supposed to be released to unauthorized parties. I could get in huge trouble."

She kissed him, then she made a zipping motion across her lips. They never spoke of it again.

From that day on, he ceased pressuring her to alter course. Instead, he charted it with her. He knew he couldn't extinguish the fire that burned in her soul, but he could bank the flames, direct the heat, keep her as safe as possible.

It did make a difference. Ejected from paradise, she now saw a glimmer of hope. She informed the leasing office she was leaving her tainted apartment. She moved in with him. She took over the spare bedroom, loaded it with her living room furniture, stashed her clothing in the closet, moved the rest into storage.

It wasn't paradise regained, but it was a start. Maybe she'd find her beach again someday, once her quest was fulfilled. If she did—when she did—she wanted to share it with him.

†

Since Geri Franklin threw Peller over for Ozzie White—Peller laughed more than once at that—he had nothing on for Friday night. Situation normal. He rarely did since Sandra's death. He usually spent evenings reading; sometimes called Jason, Belinda, and his grandkids Susie and Andrew; sometimes did odd jobs about the house. Joan Churchill might stop by, although Saturdays had become their usual nights out together.

Tonight, he would call the family, especially Susie. Her eleventh birthday was tomorrow. After, he would just relax and read. But first, dinner.

As he broiled himself a burger and set out the fixings, he found himself thinking about Joan. Not in any way that made sense, not as he'd thought about Sandra when they first met, but in an oddly detached, analytic fashion. Detective fashion.

What were Joan's motives? How truthful was she? What might she be hiding? She'd been burned twice by men who cheated on her. Why risk further heartbreak? She knew the strength of the bond between Peller and Sandra. Wasn't she afraid it would get in the way, that she'd be little more than a replacement, an understudy?

That's your fear, Sandra whispered in the back of his mind, *not hers.*

It should be hers, he replied.

Sandra didn't answer, but she might have given him an indulgent smile. He could almost see it. And she might have a point. He'd invested so much in Sandra. He liked Joan, but she wasn't Sandra, could never be her. If he let Joan in, let her see him as fully as he'd let Sandra see him, would she like the view? Could she ride out his occasional storms, give him room to sulk, feed him her insights when he needed them, withhold them when he didn't? Could she be the partner Sandra was?

Does she have to be? Sandra asked.

He didn't know. Logically, no. Joan only had to be herself. But relationships weren't based in logic, were they? All he had was a balance sheet. On the assets side: companionship, someone who cared about him, someone he could care for. On the liabilities side: question marks, question marks, question marks. The possibilities impelled him to jump. The uncertainties bound his ankles.

He grabbed one of his recent acquisitions, *Blood Meridian* by Cormac McCarthy, and buried himself in it while he ate. By the time dinner was consumed and cleanup done, he'd detached completely from relationship anxiety. Then, of course, another relationship imposed.

When his cell phone rang, he barely had to glance at the name. Shania North. He took the call.

"Hi Shania. Is everything okay?"

He sounded a bit frantic, even to himself. Shania didn't much call unless she was in trouble. Over two years ago, he found her at death's door, ravaged by opioids and on the verge of suicide when she couldn't wake her dead boyfriend. He convinced her to enter a treatment program, but it was a damned difficult addiction to beat. She rose to the surface only to be dragged back down several times over. Last he heard, she was at least treading water.

"Yeah," she said. "Everything's great. Win helped me get a new job."

She was fond of one-syllable names. Win was Winston Marley, another of Peller's contacts from a prior case. Peller roped him into helping Shania because he had a connection with another of her boyfriends, one who had also met a tragic end. Plus, Marley was stable, and he was a Bahá'í. Peller figured the woman could use some spiritual guidance. All of which had been presumptuous, but somehow it worked out. Marley befriended Shania, and Peller quietly stepped into the background, although they still had occasional contact. Shania thought of him as a kindly uncle.

"That's wonderful," he said. "Where are you working?"

"Maryland Food Bank. Win thought I should do something to help others. I guess so I don't think of my own problems all the time."

"Sure. That can help."

"I started today. I really like it. It's kind of physical, but I guess I can build back my muscles. About time." She giggled a little. She didn't often do that. Whenever she did, it gave Peller hope.

"You'll be competing in weightlifting contests in no time."

She giggled again.

"I'm happy for you," Peller said. "Keep me posted. I'd like to know how it works out."

"Kay, I will."

"And tell Winston I said hi."

"Yep. And hi from me to Joan."

That was another positive. Joan hadn't been too keen on Peller's involvement with Shania at first, but the women eventually warmed to each other.

They said their goodbyes, and Peller sank into his recliner with his book. Once the dinner hour had passed in Denver, he called Jason. Or rather, Susie. Jason guessed Peller's intention and let her pick up.

"Hi, Grandpa!" she chirped.

"Hi there, birthday girl. All set for your cake and ice cream?"

"I sure am! Did you send my present yet?" Her tone turned sly as she asked.

Peller laughed. She'd grown so much in the past few years. He wondered where the time had gone. If he blinked, she'd be graduating from high school. "There's something in the mail for you," he promised.

"Like what?"

"Now, that's cheating."

It was her turn to laugh.

"Whatever it is," he promised, "you'll like it. It can't fail."

"Oh, money! That works."

"Keep that up, and you'll take my job from me."

"I don't think so. I want to be a geologist. You should see my rock collection!"

Peller hadn't heard of that interest before. "I guess I'll have to come visit, then. Maybe around Thanksgiving." He hadn't made holiday plans yet, but it would be good to see the family again, and Susie could take him rock hunting in the mountains, at least at lower altitudes. By then, the higher roads would be well and truly snowed under.

After Susie, Andrew came on the line. He was antsy for the end of the school year. His ninth birthday waited in the wings—end of July—so he had a long wish list for his grandfather. Then Jason and Belinda hopped on the call together for a quick catch-up. Not that there was any earth-shattering news. All was well in the suburbs of the mile-high city.

After, Peller resumed reading and eventually fell asleep in the recliner, where he remained until sometime after midnight.

†

Sometime after midnight. That's all Father Walter Simmons knew. Sometime after midnight, something struck his window hard enough to wake him. Shaken, he half sat, supported by his elbows, and stared into the darkness. Although the window was covered by a blackout curtain, a smidgeon of light leaked in around the edges. He listened, heard no further sound, no breaking of glass, no rustling to suggest someone had gained entry. Just that bang, then nothing.

He half sat in bed in the dark, first quivering and listening, then whispering a prayer to St. Michael for protection, then listening further. Nothing happened. Nothing at all. Maybe a bird had struck the window. Or a bat. No, bats used echo location. They wouldn't run into a window, would they? A fallen branch, maybe? Father Walter heard no wind, but an old, decaying tree limb might have broken under its own weight.

Nothing. Nothing else happened.

He laid back on his bed and closed his eyes.

He recited the Act of Contrition. Over and over, he recited it.

He didn't sleep again for an hour or more.

Come morning, he hobbled to the window without his walker, without his cane, and opened the curtains, expecting to find cracked glass or a branch or a dead bird on the ground. He found none of those. Instead, he found words, black words on the glass.

James 5:16

Father Walter stumbled back, groping for the bed. It was too far away. He lost his balance, pitched over backwards, and struck the back of his head on something. A terrible pain flared in his right knee. He thought he cried out, but his voice was so thin, so feeble, he feared no one would hear.

The last thing he remembered was uttering something, something in Latin. Probably it had been *mea culpa*.

†

On Saturday night, Peller picked up Joan Churchill from her apartment and took her to see *Zodiac*, a new film about the Zodiac Killer who had terrorized northern California in the late 1960's and early 1970's. She had requested the film. "You should like it," she told him. "It's right up your alley."

Peller didn't know about that. Most crime films and TV shows, even when based on fact, made sharp left turns away from reality. But then, reality was often less entertaining. In the end, he did enjoy the film, particularly Robert Downey, Jr.'s portrayal of reporter Paul Avery. Only one thing marred the experience. His cell went off not once but three times in succession, silenced but vibrating in his pocket, refusing to be ignored. He ignored it anyway and only discovered, as they left the theater with Joan hanging on his right arm, that the call was from dispatch. He should have checked earlier.

After tucking Joan into his car, he got behind the wheel and said, "I have to call in. Something must be up."

"You're off duty," she reminded him.

He called anyway.

The dispatcher gave him the rundown. "We received a frantic call about two hours ago from a woman at St. Augustine Catholic Church. She insisted on talking to you. We couldn't get much info, but one of the priests is in the hospital. It sounded like they had an intruder. I have her number if you want to call back."

"Were officers dispatched?"

"No. She said she wanted to talk to you and nobody else."

That was a great way to get ignored. Whoever took the call must have been in a good enough mood to humor her. "Hold on, let me get something to write with." Peller reached in front of Churchill and rummaged in the glove compartment, where he kept a notebook and pen, just in case. "What's the woman's name?"

"Clare something. She was babbling half the time."

"I know her. I met her the other day. Go on."

The dispatcher relayed Fleming's cell number.

"What's Father Ed's condition?" Peller asked.

"Is that the priest? I didn't catch his name. It sounds like he's alive, but like I said, she was babbling half the time."

"Okay, I've got it from here. Thanks." Peller disconnected and flashed Churchill an apologetic smile.

"Call," she said. "This is what I get for dating a detective, isn't it?"

"Definitely a bad move on your part." He punched in Clare Fleming's number and when she answered said, "It's Lieutenant Peller. What happened?"

"Oh, Lieutenant. Thank God. Father Walter's been attacked!" The words rushed by like a hurricane gust. "He's in the hospital now, and there's another message. It's all so horrible and all my fault. I just don't—"

"Clare," Peller said. "Calm down. One thing at a time."

She sucked in a breath. "I'm sorry, I'm just..." She choked down a sob.

"I know, I understand. Who's Father Walter?"

"A retired priest who lives here. He broke a hip or something a couple years ago and can't walk too good. He lives at our rectory 'cause he has family in the area."

"You said he was attacked," Peller said. "What happened?"

"I don't know. He didn't come out for breakfast this morning. I found him on the floor, all banged up. There was one of those messages on his window."

"Were the police called?"

"Father Ed called 911 and got an ambulance." Fleming pronounced it Baltimore-style, *AM-blance*. "I told him to ask for the cops, too, but he didn't wanna."

That priest was starting to get on Peller's nerves, but likely there had been no need for police, at least where Father Walter was concerned. Paramedics would have called them in if they suspected violence rather than an accident. In her agitated state, Fleming had probably misread the situation. Except... "What did the message say?"

"James 5:16. Written on the outside of the window, backwards, so you can read it from the inside."

Which meant it had been intended for someone on the inside, possibly Father Walter, if the vandal had known it was his room. "Was the glass broken?" Peller asked.

Fleming hesitated before saying, "No."

"Was the window open?"

"No."

"Was it unlocked?"

"I—I don't think so."

"It doesn't sound like Father Walter was attacked," Peller said. "It sounds like he took a fall. I'll check up on him at the hospital tomorrow."

Churchill tapped Peller on the shoulder and whispered, "Tomorrow's Sunday."

He nodded in acknowledgement but didn't change his mind. He'd been known to work Sundays before, on the clock or not. It could be important, and what else did he have to do with his time? "I doubt there's any danger," he told Fleming. "Everything will be fine. Try to calm down and get some rest. I'll be in touch when I have news."

After they'd said their goodbyes, he pocketed his cell phone and started the car. "At least your time with me isn't boring," he told Churchill.

"Far from it. Want to grab some dessert?"

He glanced at the car's clock. "All the restaurants are closed."

"I bought a half chocolate cake at the store today, and I have ice cream."

He backed out and headed for her apartment. "I don't know. It's getting late."

"Nonsense, Rick. The night's still young."

"I'm not."

Churchill sighed dramatically.

Peller felt tension seep through his body as part of his brain said yes, part said absolutely not.

"I have a feeling you never said that to Sandra." Her tone was light, teasing, but she'd struck a nerve and probably knew it.

She's right, Sandra said.

"I wasn't so old back then."

"Come on, you know you want to." She stroked his neck. "I have chocolate syrup, too."

"Well..."

"And caramel."

He laughed.

"And peanuts. You can't say no to peanuts."

"I could if I was allergic to them."

"Are you?"

He flashed her a grin before admitting, "No."

Churchill didn't say another word. Peller figured she knew she had him. The funny thing was, once he admitted it, that naysayer in his brain backed off. Maybe a much younger Rick Peller had replaced him. He wondered if she had any of those colored sprinkles, too.

†

Churchill lived on the third of four floors at Orchard Meadows, a handsome if average apartment building off route 29. Small trees dotted the parking lot and grounds, some blossoming in the spring warmth. Her place was comfortable and on the feminine side, done in muted colors, soft furnishings, and lots of pillows. Her preference in art was flowers and forests, all sunny and bright. Peller wondered if the décor reflected her natural personality or if she'd surrounded herself with light to chase off the darkness of her past. They had both suffered losses, but of divergent sorts. He coped with Sandra's death by preserving his home as it had been. Joan burned all her photos in a vain effort to purge the pain.

This evening wasn't overshadowed by either past. They ate cake and ice cream with more toppings than were good for a person while they talked about family and work. Churchill found Peller's accounts of Angry Granny and Squirrel Shooter amusing, the church incidents not so much. By comparison, her office experiences were mundane, or so she claimed. She handled customer service for a local medical billing company. Even so, Peller found her tales of confused and irate customers entertaining. People were people, no matter where you encountered them.

By the time Peller noticed the time, it was well past midnight, and he was exhausted. "I guess I'd better go," he said.

She put a hand on his shoulder. "You can sleep on the couch."

"I shouldn't."

"You say that every time I offer."

He did. The idea of spending the night, even in separate rooms, made him uncomfortable. He always made some excuse.

"You're too tired to drive, Sherlock. And isn't driving under the influence of chocolate syrup illegal?" She winked.

She had a point, at least where exhaustion was concerned. Peller could barely keep his eyes open. It sure would be illegal for him to drive in that state, but he tried to rise anyway.

She pushed him down with surprising ease. "My geriatric neighbors won't notice. I know you worry about that, but really, they won't."

"I sure hope not."

"I'll get you a blanket."

He didn't object further. Maybe he was too tired. Maybe part of him wanted to stay. Whatever the case, she brought the blanket, and after the lights were out and she retreated to her room, Peller sank into a sleep from which he didn't wake until the morning sun seeped in around the curtains and the clank of cookware rang in the kitchen. Momentarily disoriented, he sat. Every muscle in his body ached, as though he'd been tied in a knot half the night. He stood and stretched and examined his crumpled clothing. That was another argument against sleeping over. Now he'd have to go home and change before interviewing Father Walter. Or trying to interview him. The priest might not be in any shape to talk.

Peller shuffled into the kitchen. Churchill was busy cooking pancakes and sausage. She was wrapped in a light green bathrobe. A pale yellow nightgown peaked out below the robe's hem mid-calf. She was still barefoot.

"You didn't have to go to all that trouble," he said.

She glanced over her shoulder and smiled. "And you don't have to work on Sunday. But you're going to anyway."

"Only because it's important," he objected, although that wasn't entirely true. He suspected Fleming's report of a break-in was overblown. It was just another piece of graffiti.

"So's this. Anyway, I like doing nice things for you. Don't complain. Enjoy it."

"Is that an order?"

"You bet it is."

Peller sat at the kitchen table and watched her work. He hadn't realized before, but she moved a lot like Sandra. From behind, he could almost mistake one woman for the other. He even had a momentary urge to take Churchill into his arms, as he would have had she been Sandra. The impulse was as disorienting as waking up on her couch.

Churchill plated the food and brought it to the table along with butter and a bottle of maple syrup. "I was thinking," she said, then she didn't say what she was thinking.

Peller applied the butter and syrup and passed it to her. "That sounds dangerous."

"Probably is."

"Better tell me, then, so I can perform an intervention."

"Oh, I forgot the coffee. Hold on." She got them each a mug, then settled into her chair and took a bite.

"Are you being mysterious," Peller asked, "or dramatic?"

"Nervous."

He couldn't imagine why. Well, he could, but he didn't think she would be so bold as to suggest combining households. It might be in the back of her mind, but they weren't within a hundred miles of that yet.

"I'm afraid you'll say no," she added.

If she *was* that bold, he might. "You won't know until you say it."

"I'd like to go with you."

In mid-bite, Peller set down his fork and stared at her.

"To the hospital," she clarified, although she didn't have to. Where else would he be going?

"Why?"

Churchill didn't answer. Peller couldn't imagine an answer. They stared at each other in befuddlement.

"I've done it before," she finally said.

Yes, once, but only because she'd wanted to see him just when he had a quick errand to run, and he hadn't had the heart to say no. "This is different," he said. "For one thing, I'm interviewing an injured man in a hospital. You're neither a relative nor a cop. I doubt they'll let you in the room. For another, there are confidentiality constraints."

"I'll stay in the lobby while you do your work. I just...I just want to spend time with you."

"We spent all of yesterday evening together," Peller pointed out. "And breakfast this morning."

Churchill stared at her plate. "Is that enough?"

Ouch. *How do I answer that?* he asked himself, as though he might have an answer.

Don't ask me, Sandra's voice teased in the depths of his mind.

He could think of only one reply, and it wasn't the reply he wanted to give. Or maybe it was. Truth be told, he did enjoy her company, once he stopped fighting himself. "I didn't mean it that way. Sure, you can tag along. But it might be a longer and more boring ride than you expect."

Moisture dotted her eyes as she smiled. "Thank you. And no, I won't be bored for a minute."

†

Once he was up and moving, the wrinkles fell out of his clothes, so he skipped the detour home. They said little on the drive to Howard County General. The Sunday morning traffic was light, the sky half obscured by mid-level clouds. Churchill was content to look at the passing trees and homes and businesses. Upon arrival, she took a seat by the lobby windows where she could see the potted plants and trees along the front of the building. Peller showed his ID at the desk and received a visitor badge and directions to Father Walter's room. When he arrived, the priest was watching a televised Sunday morning mass. A half-consumed breakfast cooled on the tray beside him. Peller took a seat and waited in silence as the old man went through the motions from the confines of his bed.

Twenty-five minutes passed before Father Walter turned off the TV and smiled at Peller. It was a tired, gentle smile, a bit befuddled, too, since he had no idea who his visitor was. "I used to be up there," he said, gesturing at the TV. "At the altar, I mean, not on camera. Seems a lifetime ago."

"I know," Peller told him. He showed his ID. "I'm Detective Lieutenant Rick Peller, Howard County Police. How are you feeling?"

"Police? Whatever for?"

Peller waited.

"I'm fine. It's my own fault. I should know better than to walk about without aid. I fell. Hit my head, twisted my knee. I think they said nothing was broken, but I've been a bit fuzzy. The pain meds have that effect on me."

"I'm sure you're in good hands," Peller said. "You're certain it was an accidental fall?"

"I'm not *that* fuzzy." Father Walter winked.

"Nobody tried to harm you?"

"Ah, I see. You suspect elder abuse."

"I don't suspect anything, Father. I'm just asking a routine question."

He nodded and closed his eyes, maybe hoping that would make Peller go away.

"What's James 5:16?"

The smile vanished.

"I'm told it was written on your window."

The priest didn't respond, didn't open his eyes, didn't move. Peller guessed it was a fear response. Some people froze when confronted with facts that implicated them. But what could Father Walter possibly have to fear?

"It's not the first time such a message has been left at St. Augustine," Peller said.

"I know." Father Walter opened his eyes and gazed at the ceiling. "James 5:16. 'Therefore, confess your sins to one another and pray for one another, that you may be healed. The fervent prayer of a righteous person is very powerful.'"

"The message was written so as to be read from inside the room."

Father Walter nodded absently. He looked out the window at nothing, really, except maybe his own past.

"Did it frighten you? Is that why you fell?"

"I'm very tired, Lieutenant. I should sleep."

"I'm concerned for your safety," Peller said. "If someone is threatening you, help me find them so we can put a stop to it."

"We all live under a threat. And we have but one Savior."

"Father—"

Father Walter slid down and pulled up the sheet. "The seal of the confessional is absolute. I couldn't tell you if I wanted to."

Peller waited a few minutes more, but Father Walter said nothing. He might have fallen asleep. He might have been pretending. Either way, they were done. Peller rejoined Joan Churchill in the lobby. He wished Montufar and Dumas were with him. He could use their insights just now. Especially Montufar's insights as a Catholic. But that would have to wait for their return tomorrow.

✝

Since he was out and about, Peller decided to visit St. Augustine. Churchill had no objections. She might have been happy to ride shotgun with him to the landfill. She didn't even need conversation, just his presence, although when they were a mile from the hospital she did venture a question: "How's the Father?"

"He says he's okay."

"You have doubts?"

"You know how people are. Some insist their coronary was no big deal, others are dying from a hangnail."

Churchill laughed. "My dad was both. Did you learn anything?"

"Not really." Which wasn't entirely true. Father Walter's comment about the seal of the confessional suggested he knew what the verses were about. Someone must have told him something that led to this. Peller couldn't imagine what. Given that priests were duty-bound to protect what they were told in confession, nobody would have cause—no rational cause, anyway—to fear exposure. Not that threats always had rational bases, but these messages seemed intentional and targeted. Well, likely targeted. The St. Paul incident threw doubt on that.

When they arrived at St. Augustine, Peller left Churchill in the car while he visited the rectory. Clare Fleming answered the door and breathed a huge sigh of relief when she saw him. She led him into the living room and fussed over him for a bit, offering coffee or tea or cookies or anything he might want from the kitchen. He politely declined and asked her to have a seat.

"When we spoke, you said Father Walter had been attacked."

Fleming nodded so vigorously, her head might have been half detached. "Yeah, he didn't come out for breakfast. I went to check on him and found him on the floor with a cut on his head and that message on the window like it was pointing a finger at him."

"But no signs of forced entry? The window was closed and locked and not even cracked, right?"

She folded her hands in her lap and frowned at them. "Yeah, I guess."

Peller gave her a break. She'd been frightened and panicky. "He's doing fine. No serious injuries as far as I know."

"Thank God for that."

"Is the message still there?"

"No, I scraped it off."

Peller cocked his head.

Fleming shrugged. "I couldn't bear the thought of him coming back to that."

"I don't suppose you thought to get a photo?"

No, she hadn't. But she wasn't going to say so.

"Was it red paint, like before?"

"Black."

Maybe the vandals had run out of red. Or maybe the color change had been to make it more visible on the window. In any case, Peller doubted that had significance. "Did it look like the same person had written it?"

"I didn't see the other one, only heard about it."

It was a longshot, but Peller pulled up the photo of the first message on his phone and showed it to Fleming.

She studied it, shivered, shook her head. "Maybe, maybe not."

So much for that. "Can I have a look at Father Walter's room?"

Fleming led him down a short hall to a bedroom near the back of the house. It was modest, comfortably furnished with a plain twin bed, an old blue recliner, some bookcases, and a small wooden table along one side that served as an altar. Icons hung on the walls. The lone window looked out on a small stand of pines beside the rectory and a line of trees bisecting the cemetery. The weathered headstones and obelisks arrayed along the hillside lent an October feel to the place. The bogeyman might be hiding behind one of them.

"This used to be Father Ed's office," Fleming told him. "The bedrooms were upstairs. But Father Walter can't handle the stairs, so Father Ed put him here and moved his office up." She pointed at the ceiling.

"How long has Father Walter lived here?"

Fleming quickly counted on her fingers. "Three years."

Did the attacker know this wasn't Father Ed's office anymore? Peller approached and studied the window. No sign of vandalism remained. Fleming had cleaned it well. Her devotion to the priest was commendable, unless that hadn't been her motive. Recalling his earlier conversation with her, how she wasn't a very good person, how she'd worried that she was the target, Peller gave her a once-over. She was a good-looking woman, some men would say voluptuous, but to Peller she just looked scared. "Are you afraid for Father Walter?" he asked. "Or for yourself?"

"Um." She went to the window and ran a finger over it. "Both, I guess."

"I don't know what these messages are about, but something tells me we'll see more of them. If you know who's behind them, or what's behind them, even if it's just a wild guess, now would be a great time to tell me."

"Who would want to harm a sweet old man like him?"

"Who do you think?"

"Nobody. Nobody!" She slapped the wall then winced at the sting.

But that only answered half the question. "Who would want to harm you?" Peller asked.

"I dunno." Her voice had dropped to a near-whisper. She gazed out over the tombstones. "I don't always remember names. Or even get them."

Peller assumed that meant sexual indiscretions. One-night stands, sometimes with men who had wives or girlfriends about whom Fleming neither knew nor cared. Betrayal could lead its victims to dark places. But then why paint a threat on a hobbled priest's window? Or even on Father Ed's, if the vandal thought this was his office? More likely, guilt had led Fleming to rash conclusions about the danger to herself.

Unless the culprit, targeting the housekeeper, had picked a window at random.

But then, that St. Paul incident...

Nothing made sense yet. Peller gave Fleming his card. "Call me directly if anything occurs to you. Or if it happens again. Unless it's an emergency, then call 911 first."

She took the card but didn't look at it. She looked like she wanted to cry.

Chapter 6

Very early Monday morning, someone—nobody would say who, but it had the hallmarks of Detective Lieutenant Bill Trengove's schemes—decorated Eric Dumas' cubicle as a dungeon, replete with black plastic chains, fake barred windows, and printouts of torture devices, while Corina Montufar's was done up in fairy tale princess décor, all light and pastel and awash in cute forest animals. When the happy couple arrived for their first day of work as husband and wife, there were confetti and pastries and lots of laughter and joking around. Not much work got done that first hour, but then most of the cases were of that annoying and not incredibly serious variety that nobody much wanted to work anyway. They could wait one hour.

When Dumas and Montufar got back to business, they began by catching up. Reviewing the statuses of cases with their underlings, deleting nonessential emails, flagging or responding to those of importance. Exciting detective stuff. Dumas didn't care. In his mind, he was still hiking the forested mountains with his beloved, passing in and out of wisps of cloud, far from all this. He couldn't even find much to fret over in the Angry Granny case Holly Ross was now detailing for him. Nobody had been hurt, and Dumas' instinct whispered that the property damage was collateral. Whatever had set off Angry Granny, it wasn't other drivers. Besides, Ross had made a good start. She wasn't satisfied with her progress, but she seldom was.

He invited her to his dungeon—cubicle, whatever—to review what she'd learned so far. She summed it up in one word, muttered with equal parts embarrassment and anger: "Nothing."

"You have a list," Dumas said as though that would help. Or cheer her up. Or at least get her to look at him.

"Seventeen, of which only six are eliminated, unless they aren't."

"Come on, Holly, you know how it works."

That earned him a look, although a pinched one. "Give me a little credit. I haven't goaded anyone into attacking me. Not yet. And believe me, I really wanted to once or twice."

"There you go, then." Dumas gave her an encouraging smile. Not that it would have much effect.

"I haven't seen any of these vehicles. One's got to be banged up. If I could just *see* them..." She shook her head. "But all I can do is make phone calls and try to set up appointments, which will tip off whoever's responsible."

Dumas supposed so, but given the frequency with which Angry Granny was smashing things up, he doubted it would be possible to hide the evidence. He told Ross so.

"I thought of that. If only I could find out which are in the shop. And where. There can't be more than two or three."

Dumas leaned back and waited for the rest. Ross wanted to prove herself, so he gave her space to do it. Her pinched lips and laser gaze at nothing told him she was working it out.

"Insurance claims," she said. "MVA can provide insurance info for the vehicles. The insurers should be willing to check on recent claims, given the circumstances."

"Good idea," Dumas told her. "And while you're waiting for that, make the phone calls. You can cross a few names off, anyway."

She perked up now that she had a plan and Dumas' approval. "By the way, did you see the reports on the church graffiti?"

"No, what's that about?"

"Someone's been painting Bible verses on Catholic church property. Rick's looking into it."

Dumas wondered why that had landed on Peller's desk. It seemed too small a thing for his attention. "What church?"

"Two, so far. St. Augustine—yeah, that one—and St. Paul in Ellicott City. The messages sound like threats."

Dumas pulled up the case on his computer and skimmed the reports. "The first incident occurred during our wedding? How did we miss that?"

"We were inside at the time," Ross said. "Rick noticed it when we went out, but only he and Father Ed saw it."

That would be Peller. If anything was even a little out of place, he'd catch it. "Why didn't he tell us?"

"And mess up your wedding day?"

Fair enough. "A strange time to pick," Dumas mused. "Vandalizing a church while it's full of cops."

Ross leaned back and frowned. "I hadn't thought of that," she said. "I wonder if the perp knew."

†

Montufar's protégé faced a different challenge. Swan's map showed everywhere Squirrel Shooter had struck, along with dates and times, but it offered no more than a vague idea how to catch him.

"I wouldn't mind spending all day in the park for the next few weeks," Swan said, "but I don't think I'd get approval."

Montufar laughed. "I'd approve it if I could tag along. But Rick, no, and Captain Morris, definitely not."

"Do we have to tell them? The descriptions from the few likely reliable witnesses suggest a young guy, possibly of dark complexion, but maybe that was just because he was in shadow. He was wearing jeans and a black hoodie, sometimes with the hood up, sometimes not. The times of day are all over the place. Some morning, some afternoon, once just before sunset. He must have time on his hands. Unemployed or doing work on a rotating schedule? A college student with different class schedules on different days?"

Montufar nodded. Good guesses all, but the evidence was way paltry.

"He's not hurting anyone, just scaring people, probably unintentionally. But a shot fired in the wrong direction…"

Exactly. They needed uniformed patrols at random intervals. That might convince Squirrel Shooter to put away his gun, but would he come back once they vanished? Better to nab him if they could, which meant stealth. Lots of stealth, more than Morris would authorize. The Captain had enough trouble fending off calls for reorganizations and staff cuts and God knew what else.

"What can we do?" Swan asked. The question was as much for herself as for Montufar. "We're stuck in react mode. He fires off a few shots, someone complains, we investigate and find nothing. Holly and I were fantasizing about siccing Kevin Graham on him. If only we could."

Montufar liked the image of Graham lifting the shooter by his hood and carting him off to jail. If nothing else, it was amusing. In fact, now she thought about it, enlisting Graham wasn't a bad idea, but they'd have to pull strings and convince him to trade his uniform for plain clothes. That would be a tough sell. He liked his uniform. "Maybe Eric can wrangle him for a special assignment," she said. "He and Kevin have a long history of working together. Let me talk to him."

Swan relaxed, as though the whole problem was solved. "Has Rick told you about the graffiti yet?"

Montufar couldn't imagine what that would be about. Graffiti wasn't a detective's province, not unless it connected with something bigger. "What graffiti?"

Swan bit her lip.

"You're making me nervous, Theresa."

"I probably should let him explain."

"Is there a short version?"

"Ah…" Swan glanced over her shoulder as though Peller might be stalking them. "It might upset you."

"I'm a big girl. I can handle it."

"It started at St. Augustine. During your wedding. Rick was the only one who noticed it that day."

Of course he did. But how did the rest of them miss it? "Where did they write it?"

"On the wall under the statue of Mary. Then it happened two more times, once at St. Paul in Ellicott City and once on a window of the St. Augustine rectory."

Montufar pulled up the active case list, filtering for those opened in the last week. It came to the top. She scanned the reports while Swan folded her hands together and almost squeezed the life out of them. "Two church targets," Montufar mused, "all three messages dealing with sin. And...huh. St. Francis' head covered with a basket?"

Swan leaned forward. "I missed that one." She read Peller's report and the attached lab findings. "A lot of fingerprints on the basket, probably from at least three individuals, none matching anything." She sat back and made a face at the monitor. "Why would anyone do that?"

"That's the right question," Montufar said. "The Catholic Church is heavy on symbolism. Covering St. Francis' head could be covering his eyes so he can't see, or his ears so he can't hear. See or hear what, though? He's known for humility and compassion, charity, service to the poor, simplicity, care for all living beings. He's patron saint of environmentalists. I don't see where that intersects with the messages, do you?"

"Rick's done all the interviews," Swan said. "Holly and I just helped him scout around St. Paul. We found nothing beyond the message itself."

"Well then," Montufar said as she closed the file. "Only my first morning back, and already a second meeting in my future."

†

The newlyweds ambushed Peller once they caught up on every-thing. By then it was just shy of noon, and he wanted to treat them to lunch. When he offered, they looked at each other, laughed, and as one said, "Our Chinese place."

Peller inwardly groaned. He'd been thinking crab house, but it was their choice, so he allowed it.

"Their" Chinese place was a small establishment in Columbia tucked away in an almost hidden strip mall. Dumas and Montufar had frequented it for a couple of years, sometimes to hide, sometimes to celebrate, sometimes to talk business. Peller had never been there, although he'd heard them mention it. After due deliberation, he ordered sesame shrimp. It was, at least, seafood. Montufar chose kung pao chicken, over which she expertly wielded a pair of chopsticks, and Dumas stuck with his traditional General Tso's chicken and a fork. Peller wondered where Montufar had acquired her skill with wooden tweezers. And why.

As the meal commenced, Dumas glanced at Montufar while asking Peller, "What's with this church vandalism?"

Peller had been nervous about this conversation. It was inevitable, but it might disturb them. Montufar particularly. But at least he didn't have to break the news. "Holly and Theresa filled you in, then?"

"They mentioned it. And we read the reports."

"I expect it was coincidence it started the day of your wedding. That was just a window of opportunity for the vandal. There's nothing to suggest otherwise."

Montufar put down her chopsticks and patted her mouth with her napkin. "Especially since the other incidents happened while we were away and involved a second church."

"Exactly," Peller acknowledged.

"Then again, let's keep an open mind." She folded her hands on the table and met Peller's eyes. Her own were like steel. If this was bothering her, she wasn't letting on. "What do you think it's about?"

"I don't know yet. Initially, Father Ed Tyler didn't want police involvement. I thought that odd. Father Dan Adkins had his parish secretary call in their incident. He suggested it was directed against the Catholic Church generally, not against a specific parish or individual. Clare Fleming,

Father Ed's housekeeper, thought it might be directed against her, but that's hard to credit. She pretty much admitted to sexual impropriety, but I can't imagine an irate wife or girlfriend going this route. If anyone seems to be a specific target, it would be Father Walter Simmons, the retired priest at St. Augustine, since the last message appeared on his window. But maybe the vandal didn't know it was his window. That room used to be Father Ed's office."

Peller paused and shook his head. Too many conflicting circumstances, and he hadn't mentioned the handwriting yet.

Dumas did. "With two graffitists—is that a word? Graffitists?"

Montufar nudged him. "Was it in your word-a-day calendar?"

"Not in this year's. With two of them, the question would be, are they working to a common purpose, or do they have different agendas? Maybe the second got the idea from the first."

"They must be associated," Peller said. "Father Ed tried to cover up the first incident. He had a contractor on it almost immediately. I quietly reported it, but we didn't start investigating until the second occurred."

"Okay, associated, but not necessarily the same agenda."

Montufar picked up her chopsticks and toyed with her food.

"I know that look," Dumas said.

"Everyone in the department knows it." Peller winked at Dumas.

"It's one agenda," Montufar said. "The cited Scriptures all deal with sin. One speaks of death, one of delayed punishment encouraging sin, and one calling for confession. Different angles, but a common theme. And that basket could be along the same lines. The covering of St. Francis's head suggests preventing him from seeing something. Or preventing his qualities—compassion, charity, maybe—from being expressed. Is the vandal accusing someone of that? Or are they admitting their own sin?"

Dumas watched her for a moment, then raised an eyebrow at Peller. Peller had nothing to say, so Dumas filled the void. "That's...deep."

"It's just symbolism." Montufar popped a piece of chicken into her mouth.

"Which could suggest the perp is Catholic," Peller suggested. "Or at least understands how Catholics think."

Montufar nodded.

"Oh good," Dumas said. "That narrows it down to, what, a million Marylanders? Unless we're dealing with an import."

She gave him a long-suffering wife look.

†

When they returned to Northern District Headquarters, Peller found a sticky note on his computer monitor instructing him to call Shelly Beck, parish secretary at St. Paul. "URGENT" was scrawled across the bottom. He called immediately.

Given the gravity of the note and what she had to say, Beck sounded curiously calm. "Thank you for getting back so quickly, Lieutenant. We've had another incident."

"What happened, ma'am?"

"We cleaned off that paint after you left the other day, but today a new message appeared. I'm afraid it's rather ugly."

"What does it say?"

"Psalms 50:22."

In the pause that followed, Peller wondered if she expected him to have the whole of the Bible memorized. "Which is?"

"Like I said, it's ugly."

"How ugly, ma'am?"

"Taken out of context, I mean. I don't mean the Bible itself is ugly."

Peller rubbed his eyes. "I know."

"It says…" Paper rustled in the background. "It says, 'Now consider this, you who forget God, or I will tear you in pieces, and there will be no one to save you.'"

Ugly for sure. "We'll be right out," he said. "Don't let anyone touch anything. Keep the parking lot and grounds clear until I get there."

She acknowledged. Peller put in a call for Geri Franklin and photographer Scott Sahin to meet him at the church, then summoned Dumas, Montufar, Swan, and Ross to his cubicle and related the news. "All brains on deck," he said. "It feels like an escalation. The next incident could involve more than just words."

Dumas had the most passenger space, so Peller and Montufar rode with him, although Montufar ribbed him, saying, "My Firebird would get us there faster."

"We'd have to fold Rick in half to fit him in," Dumas replied. "Anyway, Holly wouldn't be able to keep up." Ross and Swan were following in Ross' white Ford Fiesta. Since it was just the two of them, nobody in that vehicle required folding.

Montufar turned to Peller, who was sitting behind Dumas. "He refuses to drive more than eight over the speed limit. And I thought he was a Maryland cop."

"It takes all kinds," Peller said.

Upon arrival, they found the new message, *Psalms 50:22*, painted in the same red on the same garage door. Sahin was already there, photographing the message in full and close-up detail, while Franklin, gloved and intense, prowled the periphery, scouring the scene for anything that might offer a clue as to who had done the deed. The detectives parked by the church office and walked to the vicinity of the rectory. They stared down the message as though it might start talking and reveal the vandal's purpose and identity.

"What do you think?" Montufar asked Peller. "First writer or second?"

"Second," Peller said without hesitation. He snapped a photo of his own with his cell phone, then compared it to those he'd previously taken. He showed them to the group. "Look at the spacing, the slant of the letters, the differences between the a's and s's. Jacey's report noted all of those. Romans and Psalms both contain an m. That looks different to me, too."

Dumas pondered the message. "Definitely personal," he said.

"How do you know?" Ross asked.

"I don't know. I feel it. Someone's out for revenge."

"Or justice," Peller suggested.

"True," Montufar said. "The first message coincided with our wedding. That could have been an attempt to bring the matter to our attention."

Dumas shook his head. "It's the tone of the verses. They sound... angry. Whoever did this wants their target to suffer."

Peller's gaze strayed to Geri Franklin who was now bent over, staring into the grass on the side of the garage opposite the rectory. Sahin had retreated to his car and was leaning against it, waiting for Franklin to find something worth photographing. Peller suspected she already had.

Swan picked up on the thought. "Holly and I will see what Geri's got, then we'll have a look around." Peller nodded. The younger women joined Franklin, and a subdued conversation ensued as all three studied whatever the tech had found.

Peller turned his thoughts back to Dumas' hunch. He agreed. There was malice here. They were missing some link between events at the two churches.

"Corina," he said, "talk to Shelly Beck. She probably can't tell us much, but she may be able to provide the time frame for this incident. And see if she knows of any connections between St. Paul and St. Augustine. Shared activities, people moving between the parishes for any reason. Whatever. Eric and I will talk with Father Dan."

Montufar nodded and made for the church office.

"Let's see what vibe you get from this priest," Peller told Dumas. "He's an interesting fellow."

†

Father Dan shook Dumas' hand, his grip strong, a twisted smile on his lips. "Sergeant," he said. "A bit unusual, isn't it, being married to your colleague?"

Dumas's eyes widened. He tried not to give away his position during interviews, but the priest caught him way off guard.

Father Dan winked at Peller.

"If he hadn't been a priest," Peller told Dumas, "Father Dan would have been a detective, too."

"That's either intriguing or scary," Dumas said to deflect his disquiet.

"Your ring," Father Dan said. "It matches hers." He waved toward the office, where Montufar had gone. "I admit I cheated a little." He went to a table by the window, picked up a pair of binoculars, and held them out for inspection. "I'm a backyard birder, so I keep these handy. Sometimes my curiosity is piqued by subjects other than birds."

"Like beautiful young detectives?" Dumas cracked a smile to show he was ribbing.

Father Dan returned the binoculars to their place and motioned Peller and Dumas to be seated. He settled himself facing them. "I should probably plead the fifth on that."

"Tell me about today's reading," Peller said.

The priest leaned back and folded his hands in his lap. "For starters, Psalms 50:22 is a threat, but not pure threat. You must understand the context. Chapter fifty contains twenty-three verses. It opens by praising God, recounting that He created the world, and summoning His people—Israel—to judgement. It commands the people to make their sacrifices and pay their vows to God and to call upon Him in times of trouble. In turn, God promises to rescue them. Over half the chapter is dedicated to that theme."

He paused a bit too long. Peller prompted, "And the rest of it?"

"The rest is a warning to the wicked among the people of Israel, those who talk of God's laws and covenant, but who are undisciplined, who take criminals and adulterers for friends, and so forth. It's mostly a recitation of the evil such people do."

Pausing again, Father Dan picked up a Bible from the end table and opened it to a bookmarked page. "The last three verses read as follows:

'These things you have done and I kept silent; You thought that I was just like you; I will rebuke you and present the case before your eyes. Now consider this, you who forget God, Or I will tear you in pieces, and there will be no one to save you. He who offers a sacrifice of thanksgiving honors Me; And to him who sets his way properly I will show the salvation of God.'" He closed the book, set it down, raised an eyebrow as though challenging the detectives to work out the meaning.

Peller glanced at Dumas. Dumas knew what he was thinking. "Similar to the previous verse you were gifted. A warning that God's patience doesn't mean there will be no judgement."

"In part," Father Dan acknowledged. "It's also a promise that those who turn away from their wicked ways will be saved. The threat 'I will tear you in pieces' shouldn't be taken literally. It follows a promise of rebuke, of making plain to the evil-doer what they have done. I read it as a threat of spiritual torment, not physical, brought about by clear knowledge of one's own doings."

That made sense to Dumas, but he wasn't so sure the vandal understood or meant it that way. "What do you make of these incidents?" he asked.

"Like I told Lieutenant Peller before, the Church has always had enemies, and it is undeniably composed of imperfect people. I would guess it's a statement of outrage over..." His jaw worked for a moment, but he didn't continue.

Peller leaned forward. "Father, your church isn't the only one receiving these messages. It started at St. Augustine in Elkridge. Two messages were left for them, as well."

"That settles it, then, doesn't it?"

"I'm not so sure."

"What were the verses?"

"Romans 6:23 and James 5:16."

"That's interesting." Father Dan didn't need to pick up the Bible this time. "Sin and confession. Very interesting."

When he didn't elaborate, Dumas asked, "What's interesting?" But then he realized what it was, why he'd sensed a personal vendetta behind the messages. "The verses at St. Augustine are both New Testament, calling for confession. Those here are Old Testament, warning against persisting in waywardness. Together, they form a warning. Come clean, or else." He turned to Peller. "Corina was right. Someone is sending a message to someone. By why at two different churches?"

"Speculations, Father?" Peller asked.

Father Dan shook his head. "Nothing comes to mind, but it is curious that the messages are divided the way they are."

"We're proceeding on the assumption that these incidents are personal, connected, and possibly death threats." When Father Dan shot him a surprised look, Peller added, "We have to, at least until we're sure no one's in danger. Do you know of anyone with a connection to both churches?"

"That's a tall order, Lieutenant. Catholics are encouraged to primarily attend and participate in the community life of the parish in which they live, but they aren't required to do so. People sometimes continue to attend a church in a parish they've left. And anyone could, for a variety of reasons, attend a different church now and again. Membership records wouldn't cover most of the bases. I want to help, but I don't see how we can."

Dumas wondered about that. Father Dan was likely sincere. Then again, he was observant and smart. He'd make quite the adversary if he chose to mislead them.

Peller didn't comment. He gave Dumas a look to ask if there were any other questions. Dumas shook his head. "All right, Father. If anything does come to mind, or if any other incidents occur, you know where to find me."

Father Dan escorted them to the door and bid them a somber farewell.

Chapter 7

Shelly Beck brushed a hand through her silvery bangs and donned a look of extreme concentration as though mentally scanning the entire parish membership list. "I don't think so," she said. "But honestly? It would be hard to know."

"No problem," Montufar replied. "I was just curious." She had mentioned, without giving details, the incidents at St. Augustine and asked about possible connections. Parishioners moving from one locale to the other, frequent visits between the two churches, joint activities.

"Father Dan and Father Ed know each other, of course. But they don't communicate often, as far as I know. A few times a year at most. That retired priest over there—what was his name? I think he visited us once last year. I don't recall why."

"Father Walter?"

"Yes, him."

"When was this?"

"In the summer, I think. Oh, and their housekeeper filled in for ours a few times."

"Clare Fleming," Montufar said.

"Maybe," Beck said. "I didn't catch her name."

Why would Fleming come here? Wouldn't that leave a vacancy in her own parish? "Is that a common practice?" Montufar asked. "Swapping housekeepers?"

Beck's gaze strayed to her computer monitor while her fingers fluttered over the keyboard. "She needs extra money sometimes. She doesn't mind filling in for us on her days off when our regular housekeeper is away. Father Dan says she's nice and works hard."

Montufar wasn't sure how significant these visits were, but they did at least establish a link between the two churches. That Father Walter might be the target unsettled her. She'd rather it be a housekeeper than a priest, but she couldn't let emotions get in the way. Priests were as human as anyone. There had always been wolves among the flock. Besides, the trigger for the graffiti might not be so sinister. An unthinking word, a misunderstanding, an accident—any careless act might trigger an attack, even a homicide.

"Thank you, ma'am," Montufar said. "I'll let you get back to your work."

"Let me know if I can be of further help," Beck offered. But her lack of eye contact suggested she'd had her fill and just wanted things back to normal.

†

The three women stared at the object in the grass. A yellow plastic flag stuck in the ground next to it bore the words *EVIDENCE—Do not touch*. They stared far longer than necessary. Theresa Swan bit her lip. Holly Ross' face wrinkled in revulsion. Geri Franklin gazed on her find with scientific curiosity. "This is a first for me," she said.

"From a distance," Swan said, "I thought it was a dead bird. I couldn't figure why you were so interested."

Ross turned away, part distressed, part angry that she hadn't been stronger. After everything she'd been through in recent months, she ought to be able to handle this.

"You okay?" Franklin asked.

"Yeah, just...I've never seen...one of those...without the rest of the dog."

"Me, either. I'm guessing it's symbolic. Like that basket on St. Francis' head."

Swan came to Ross's side and wrapped an arm around her shoulders. "At least nothing was cut up that time," she said.

Ross was grateful for Swan's friendship and support, and for Franklin's detachment. She'd drawn strength from both colleagues more than once, and now again. Regaining control, she turned back just as Franklin, motioning Scott Sahin over, said, "Many crabs were carried to their doom in that basket."

Sahin, camera in hand, stopped short when he saw his subject. "Is that…"

"Yep," Franklin said. "Male dog genitalia. I doubt it found its way here by accident."

Having documented homicides a few times, Sahin wasn't too affected, save one thing. "I hope the animal was dead when this was done."

So did Ross. Frightening people with graffiti was one thing. Animal abuse was quite another.

†

Upon return to HQ, the team assembled in the conference room. Clouds thickened outside, a portent of the rain predicted for that night.

The mood in the room mirrored the weather as Peller settled into a chair opposite the windows. Montufar and Swan flanked him. Dumas and Ross faced him across the table. He sensed their thoughts were aligned. The messages had grown more sinister. Whatever lay behind them, it was personal. Specific. Potentially deadly.

"Let's consider the pattern," Peller said. "What are we seeing?"

Montufar spoke first. "Two churches, three messages left at each. In both cases, two scriptural, one symbolic. New Testament verses at St. Augustine, Old Testament at St. Paul. The former speak of sin and confession, the latter of changing one's ways. In both cases, one message implies a death threat."

"What we saw today," Dumas said, "combines the 'tearing in pieces' message with a literal illustration. One suggesting sexual impropriety, maybe."

Peller agreed. "Clare Fleming implied someone might be targeting her for that very reason."

"Except…" Swan shook her head.

"Go ahead," Montufar prompted.

"Isn't that sort of threat usually leveled at men?"

Peller knew of no statistics on the subject, but he supposed so.

"We should talk to Fleming, ASAP," Ross suggested. "Get details. Names, if she has them. Theresa and I could take that on. She might be more open with us."

Fleming had almost talked to Peller, might have if Father Ed hadn't intruded, but Ross had a point. "All right. Get her away from the rectory. Take her someplace private. Make her comfortable."

Swan and Ross nodded in unison.

"If messages aren't about Fleming," Peller continued, "they're likely aimed at one of the priests. The rectories seem to be particular targets."

"Let me talk to Father Ed," Montufar suggested. "I know him a little. I'll find out about his and Father Walter's connections with St. Paul. Eric can see what Father Dan has to say. Let's see if they tell the same story."

Peller felt a twinge of annoyance. His team was cutting him out of the action. But no, that wasn't their intent. Getting different eyes and minds on each piece of the puzzle could help resolve it before anyone got hurt. That was why he pulled everyone in to start with. Besides, the only one with whom Peller had established any rapport at all was Father Dan. That one moment with Fleming aside, everyone else was keeping him at arm's length. "All right," he said. "Let's make some headway before it gets worse."

Just as they were rising, Ross' and Swan's cell phones went off simultaneously. They turned away to take their calls, then turned back annoyed. It was almost comical, except the news couldn't be good.

"Now what?" Peller asked.

"Squirrel Shooter shot someone in the leg," Swan grumbled.

Ross pressed her hand to her forehead. "Angry Granny injured a pedestrian."

Dumas cracked a lopsided smile. "It never rains but it pours."

Outside, it began to rain. Hard. Hours earlier than predicted. Montufar came to his side. "Look what you did," she said as she gave his shoulder a light punch.

†

The potential for violence might have been greater in the Church case, but the actual trumped the probable. Swan and Ross had to deal with their calls pronto.

Swan's windshield wipers slapped away the rain as she made for the tennis and basketball courts situated at the east end of Centennial Park. The complex huddled in a stand of trees, where a parking lot served it as well as Pavilion H. The woodland and lake paths connected there.

The rain tapered off just as Swan parked. The flashing lights of a drenched ambulance and two squad cars scintillated in the droplets on her vehicle. Getting out, she surveyed the woods wrapping the northern fringe of the parking lot and the field. The wet grass drew her eye to the lake's edge on the northwest. Trees and undergrowth were thick there. Everything was dripping.

Two things occurred to Swan. First, Squirrel Shooter hadn't expected the rain. She hoped they got a good soaking. A little karma was better than none. Second, she wondered at the odds of a stray shot fired within the woods finding a clear path to an innocent bystander. Bullets did funny things sometimes. Their high momentum had that effect. But still...

Swan approached the squads. Two of the officers were talking with a willowy young man seated on the back of the ambulance while one of the paramedics dressed a wound on his ankle and the other spoke into her cell phone. The remaining officer, a big black man in a dripping raincoat, leaned on his squad car, arms crossed, expression world-weary. He gave Swan a half-smile. "Always something, eh lady?"

"Kevin," Swan said, returning the smile. "They didn't say you were on the scene."

Kevin Graham shrugged. "They must figure you detectives already know the important stuff."

She leaned on the car next to him. They watched the paramedics work. "We aren't psychic, you know. Unless Eric is."

Graham raised an eyebrow.

Swan laughed. "I begged Corina to ask him for your help out here."

"Bad enough I got one boss. Don't give me four."

"It's just a request." She nodded at the victim, who was waving off the paramedics. They kept working on him anyway. "Not quite an emergency situation, I guess."

"That's a matter of perspective. Usually is an emergency, if you're the one who got shot, but not this guy. It only nicked him. He doesn't want the hospital experience today."

"Can't say I blame him. What do we know for sure?"

"That he got shot."

"All that, huh?"

"All that." Graham pushed himself off the car and pointed at the woods. "He says it came from that way, right before the rain hit. We got three other witnesses who say the same. One was over there—" He pointed to the far end of the parking lot. "—and two on the court. Mr. Seth Weisselberg—" Graham indicated the victim. "—was on the lake path. I figure you smart folks can triangulate, for all the good it'll do. Once the sirens screamed in, I doubt your guy stuck around."

"I take it nobody saw him."

"Not a one."

"Oh, well. Thanks, Kevin."

"Sure thing. Tell my buddy Eric I said welcome home. And that I'll help, if my real boss lets me."

"I will."

Swan walked to the ambulance and introduced herself to Seth Weisselberg. Aside from being soaked to the skin, he seemed okay. "I know you've already told the story," she said, "but humor me."

He winced as the paramedic finished up the dressing. "I was walking by the lake. Just before the rain started, I heard a crack. Next thing I knew, I was on the ground with my leg screaming at me. A woman ran up and asked if I was all right. We both saw I was bleeding. That's when the deluge started. I told her someone shot me, and she called 911. That's it. I didn't see anything."

"How bad's the injury?" Swan asked the paramedic.

"Almost superficial. A bit of a gouge. It looks like the bullet winged him mid-calf." To Weisselberg, he said, "You really should see a doctor."

Weisselberg waved that off.

Swan stepped aside to scan the field, path, and lake. "I wonder where the bullet is now."

She was asking herself, but Weisselberg answered. "Probably in the lake."

"Which way were you walking, and where exactly?"

He motioned. "West, maybe a hundred feet prior to the bend."

"Where's the wound?" With the dressing already in place, Swan couldn't tell.

The paramedic indicated the outside of his left leg, slightly to the back. "About here."

No, the bullet wasn't in the lake. It winged him on the landward side. A tree and bench reposed left of the path where it bent a bit north to follow the shoreline. Otherwise, there was only empty field. The proverbial needle in the haystack, but that bullet was out there. It had to be.

"All right, sir, thank you. I won't bother you further. The officers got your contact information, right?"

He nodded.

Swan returned to Graham's side and mulled over the information.

"Whatcha thinking?" Graham asked.

"I need a metal detector."

He glanced at her. He scowled at the field. "Seriously?"

"From what Weisselberg said, the bullet should be out there. If we find it, maybe we can figure out roughly where the shooter was standing and locate a casing, too."

Graham gave the grass a long once-over. "Huh," he said. "Okay."

†

Confusion wasn't quite the word. When Ross arrived at the scene, the parking lot of a Mexican restaurant on U.S. 1 sandwiched between a Super 8 and an apartment building with first-floor storefronts, she found three HCPD squads, an ambulance, and a gang of restaurant employees and customers huddled near the entrance. The latter were chattering, pointing, and videoing the circus with their cell phones.

The focus of attention was an elderly black man with an eighty-year-old face and a teenage temperament. Snapping and snarling, he gestured right, left, forward, backwards, heavenward, and hellward. The paramedics were packing up and grumbling. Ross figured the old man had vetoed treatment. He hardly looked injured, anyway. Two of the officers, a more seasoned pair with long-suffering expressions, were listening to the plaintiff. The other, younger patrolmen stood well to the side, doing their best not to notice the goings on.

Ross drew a breath and waded in. The presumed victim stopped mid-sentence as she planted herself before him and flashed her ID. "Sir, I'm Detective Holly Ross."

"Detective, huh?" He eyed her as though she'd claimed to be a space alien. "That mean you's smarter'n these morons?"

The officers—Porter and Coleridge, their nameplates said—didn't react. Much. Ross waved them off. "I'll take it from here," she told them. "Ask the paramedics to see me before they leave."

"I owe you a donut," Officer Coleridge whispered.

Ross turned back to the victim. "What's your name, sir?"

"Clayton Parker. Folks call me Clay."

"And what happened, Mr. Parker?"

"I says, folks call me Clay." He raised an eyebrow.

"Sorry. What happened, Clay?"

"Lady in a big blue SUV about runned me down. Called me blind, too. Rolled down her window and called me blind, then peeled out. About got in a accident. She must'a been the blind one!"

"Were you injured?"

Parker smacked his left bicep. "Mirror winged me." He pointed at his foot. "Just about runned over my shoe. Brushed my little toe. And the damn witch calls *me* blind! But I seed well enough. Got her license number, I did. Gave it to that dumb cop over there." He pointed at the older officers, who had joined their younger brethren and were now having a bit of a laugh over something, probably at Ross taking on the beast.

Ah, but a license number! Ross felt like whooping. Except…not in front of all these people. The crowd remained at the restaurant door. The paramedics were eyeing her with something approaching malice, probably because she'd stopped them from leaving. And the officers—she didn't want them telling tales. "Can you describe the driver?"

"Little ol' Mexican lady, frizzy gray hair, expression like a snarling wolf."

"Was she a restaurant customer?"

"Nope. Pulled in, parked, and backed out just as I come by." He pointed southbound. "Went back the way she come. Probably lost. Probably so senile, she don't know where she going."

Which meant there wasn't much point in interviewing the crowd by the door, but Ross would run it by them. "Okay, thank you Mr., ah, thank you, Clay. The officers got your contact information, right?"

"If they knowed how to spell. Wouldn't count on it."

Ross humored him. "Better give it to me, then." She recorded his address and phone number on her notepad app, then thanked him and withdrew to the ambulance, where she confirmed with the paramedics that Parker hadn't sustained any significant injuries. Not that they'd been allowed to examine him, but he insisted he was fine and hadn't shown any obvious signs of trauma.

The ambulance and Parker and two of the squads departed. The older officers remained while they ran the plate number Parker had given them. Ross checked with the crowd in the meantime. Nobody knew anything except there'd been a great deal of yelling, after which Parker demanded someone call 911.

The carnival atmosphere notwithstanding, Ross was elated. This was the most information she'd gotten, and that plate number would narrow the field of vehicles to one. Except when she checked back with the officers, it hadn't. There was no registered vehicle with the number Parker had given them.

Maybe the old bat was right. Ross grumbled to herself. *Maybe Parker is blind.* It looked like she'd be digging through insurance records after all.

†

The air had cooled into the low sixties by the time Peller returned home. Surprisingly—or perhaps not—his neighbor Jerry Souter was settled in a rocker on his front porch. Souter waved Peller over. Peller obliged and lowered himself into the rocker to Souter's left. The two men surveyed their neighborhood. An array of moderately old two-story homes lined the street.

"The newlyweds back home?" Souter asked.

Peller nodded. "They showed up today to much fanfare and chaos."

"Sounds about right. You people have a crazy job."

"Not crazier than war."

Souter, an African American World War II veteran who even at ninety-six looked ready to march off to battle, grunted. "Crime's just another form of war."

"I won't argue with that."

They rocked in silence for a few minutes. Peller didn't normally discuss his cases with anyone outside the department, but sometimes

Souter showed an interest, and sometimes Peller let him in on publicly available details. Today, though, the old man didn't seem to care.

"Anything new with the family?" Peller asked.

"One of my great-granddaughters graduates high school end of May. She wants me to come for the ceremony."

"That's great. Is she local?"

Souter turned a jaundiced look on him. "If you call Sacramento local. Closer'n Tokyo, I guess."

Peller laughed, but it would be a long haul for a man Souter's age, even if he was in good shape.

"I suppose I'll go," Souter continued. "Haven't seen her in ten years. She's the only one ever writes regular. The rest of 'em drop me birthday and Christmas cards, but people don't seem to write much no more."

"Texting's the thing now," Peller agreed. "No stamps, no waiting." Souter had a cell phone, but Peller didn't know if he used it for much aside from actual phone calls.

"How 'bout you?" Souter asked.

"I called Jason, Belinda, and the grandkids Friday night. Everything's going well with them."

The older man nodded, cracked a lopsided smile, said nothing.

"What?"

"You didn't mention Joan."

And he didn't care to.

Souter did. "You weren't home most of the weekend."

"You're spying on me?"

"I just keep an eye on things. A one-man neighborhood watch. World's a crazy place. Can't let your guard down."

Yeah, that would be Jerry. Peller let it slide. "We spent some time together."

"I won't pry," Souter promised. "But maybe it's time you got your head on straight."

"Meaning?"

"Don't leave the lady hanging. You got a choice to make. Make it, or she'll make it for you."

Sometimes Peller felt Joan already was making it for him. He wished he *could* make up his own mind. Too many things complicated the decision. He feared he would always compare Joan to Sandra and Sandra to Joan. He feared what that would do to the relationship. Most of all, he felt tethered to the past, not in the sense of constraint but of longing. He feared losing something that had been—still was—a vital part of his being.

You can't ever lose that, Sandra whispered.

How can I be sure? he asked.

"Thing is," Souter continued, "not making a choice is a choice, too. Better to pick your path than let it be picked for you."

Peller stopped rocking. "I'm working on it." It might have come out too sharp. "Aren't you getting cold?"

Souter shrugged.

"I am. And hungry. I'd better get something to eat." He rose and took one last look around the neighborhood. Everything looked so normal, felt so quiet in the cool evening, like nothing was churning in his head, like nobody was out there planning mayhem. What a deceptive place the world was.

Souter gave him a wave. "Catch you later, son."

Peller returned the wave and went home.

Chapter 8

Tuesday. May Day. The midpoint between the vernal equinox and summer solstice, International Workers' Day, Lei Day in Hawaii. Of those, only the second even remotely concerned the detectives, and that only because they received a union email on the subject. Otherwise, they were preoccupied.

Holly Ross sent the MVA a request for insurance information on her list of Escalades. Then she made a note to check the license plate number Clayton Parker had given against the plates on her list. He'd gotten it wrong, but maybe not entirely wrong. He might have substituted a character or two, reversed a couple of characters, left one out.

Having done that, she visited Theresa Swan's cubicle to discuss their approach to Clare Fleming. Swan was finishing a call when Ross settled into the guest chair in her cubicle. "Thanks, Kevin," she was saying. "I'll be out and about at least part of the day. Call my cell if anything turns up."

Once Swan hung up, Ross said, "You got him."

"I got him. Or Eric did. I gather neither his sergeant nor his lieutenant have a high opinion of us anymore, but Captain Morris has an understanding with someone in Kevin's chain of command, so they can't refuse without extenuating circumstances. It didn't hurt he was present when we found the bullet."

"Why don't we make him one of ours? It would be simpler."

Swan cracked a smile. "Eric says he's tried, but Kevin refuses to give up patrol life."

"No accounting for taste. What's the word on the weapon?"

"Twenty-two. I think we found where Squirrel Shooter was stomping around, but no casings turned up. Maybe he recovered them before he left."

"At least you have something for forensics." She'd meant it as encouragement, but she couldn't keep a bit of lament from her voice. She still had nothing but a questionable license plate number. "So, how do we handle Clare Fleming?"

Swan called up the case notes, and they skimmed them together. "She's worried she might be the target of the messages. Let's use that. Fear can be a great motivator."

"Great," Ross joked. "Another chance to develop my sympathetic side."

Swan glanced at her, uneasy.

"Don't worry. I've been to therapy and everything. Being taken hostage might have been my best career move so far."

That got a laugh from her colleague.

Ross looked through the notes again. "Nothing here about her schedule. We want the interview someplace other than the rectory, but she's probably already there for the day."

"Let's find out. Maybe she can step out for a break. To a coffee shop or something." Swan picked up the phone, dialed the St. Augustine office, asked for Fleming. A moment later, she said "Ms. Fleming? I'm Detective Theresa Swan, HCPD. Lieutenant Peller asked me to gather some background information. Would it be possible to meet today away from the church? No, nothing serious, just routine, but we want to protect your privacy. Yes, that'll be fine. We'll see you shortly."

"That was easy," Ross commented.

"There's a burger place on U.S. 1 south of the church. She'll meet us there at 10:00."

"That's too early for burgers."

"They do breakfast, too, I'm sure. Everyone does these days."

Ross checked the time on her cell phone. "There's no rush, but I'm ready whenever you are."

Swan drove, taking her time and arriving fifteen minutes early. It was cooler than last week, with skies half obscured by mid-level clouds and rain in the overnight forecast. One of those days that couldn't seem to make up its mind whether to spring into spring or fall into fall.

To pass the time, Ross asked Swan about her weekend D.C. trip.

"We had fun," Swan said. "Wore ourselves out doing the museums, and Ken found this new Greek place for dinner. I'm glad he was driving, though. I hate that traffic. I fell asleep on the way home."

Ross pointedly looked at Swan's fingers. "No ring yet, huh?"

"I'm in no rush. He definitely isn't."

"I am. I had so much fun in Corina's wedding party, I want to do it again."

"I'll tell Ken that. I'm sure it will motivate him."

They both laughed.

"Anyway," Swan added, "you should talk. You don't even have a boyfriend."

"I've had several, I'll have you know."

"What happened to them?"

"I buried them in the cellar."

"Uh-oh, sounds like I need a search warrant."

Ross smirked. "You'll have to find the place first. I don't own a cellar." She pointed at a car pulling into the parking lot. "I think that's her."

As the newcomer eased into a parking space, the detectives exited their vehicle. Clare Fleming's dark face rose into view. Swan motioned her over. "What really happened to them?"

"I intimidated them," Ross said. "They couldn't handle being attached to a lady cop."

"Good morning, Ms. Fleming," Swan said as their subject approached.

Fleming's eyes flitted nervously between the detectives' faces, as though she expected to be cuffed and stuffed into the back of their car. She stopped just out of arm's reach, fidgeting with a small white clutch.

"I'm Detective Theresa Swan, and this is Detective Holly Ross."

Fleming didn't even nod. She had that deer-in-the-headlights look. "Can I buy you a cup of coffee?"

A few minutes later, seated inside at a corner table with nobody near, paper cups of dark liquid steaming before them, Swan asked, "How long have you worked at St. Augustine?" A simple, unthreatening question that with any luck would put Fleming at ease.

Fleming sipped her coffee but didn't look up. "Almost five years."

"I suppose it's a pretty peaceful job, most of the time."

"Yeah. Just cooking and cleaning. The Fathers don't make too much of a mess."

Ross, looking over the top of her cup, asked, "What did you do before that?"

"Nothing."

"Nothing?"

"My ex-husband Carl made the money. I stayed home and did what I do now, except I did it for him. He was no holy man, I'll tell you that." She picked up her cup, stared into it, set it back down. "The rectory's way better."

"Did Carl hurt you?" Ross asked.

A restaurant employee swept by, cleaning tables. The women stopped talking until he was gone. Ross eyed him, which seemed to make him nervous. He worked a bit faster.

Fleming stared at the worker's retreating back. "He didn't hit me, if that's what you mean."

"Cheated on you?" Swan asked.

"Yeah. Then I cheated on him to get even, and it all went to hell. We agreed to split. Father Ed gave me the job at the rectory. Their last housekeeper moved to Phoenix about that time, to be near her grandkids. For a while it was me and him and a deacon there, then the deacon left and Father Walter moved in."

"When was that?" Ross asked.

"Three years back."

"And that's when Father Ed moved his office upstairs."

Fleming nodded and took a drink. "That's not what you're after, is it? Not just that, anyway."

Ross folded her arms on the table and leaned toward Fleming and spoke softly. "You told Lieutenant Peller you thought those messages were meant for you."

Swan approved of the delivery. This was their pressure point, but it had to be finessed.

"I don't know who they're meant for," Fleming said.

"But you're afraid."

Fleming looked out the window for a moment. "When I saw Father Walter hurt and that writing on his window, I panicked, okay? I thought someone attacked him. But..." She shook her head.

"We know you're scared, but you can trust us," Swan said. "We're here to protect you and the fathers. Please us tell who you suspect."

Fleming set her cup aside, leaned forward with her arms crossed on the table, and spoke in a whisper. "First time you do what you shouldn't, it's hard. Second time is easier. After that, it's like walking. You don't even think about it. I did what I did 'cause I was furious with Carl. Wasn't long before I was doing it for fun. The worst part is, I didn't even think about their wives and girlfriends. Didn't even ask if they had 'em. But sometimes guys would tell me, and it turned me on. I mean, I was doing to other women what Carl's women did to me, and I *liked* it. I know it's wrong, but I can't stop myself. It's an addiction."

"We aren't here to judge you, Clare. If you need counseling, we can suggest resources, but that's more Father Ed's line of work."

Fleming half laughed, half cried. "Poor Father Ed. He's heard this a million times. But he hasn't given up on me, bless him."

"You think one your lovers' wives is doing this," Ross said. But as soon as she said it, she realized it was wrong. Betrayed women didn't leave threatening messages, certainly not messages painted on walls and windows. When they wanted revenge, they went for the jugular. Fleming would be in the hospital if not the morgue. She must know that. Ergo, it was something else.

As Fleming acknowledged. "No. It's...look, I like working at the rectory, but it doesn't pay that good, okay?"

"Sure," Ross prompted.

"So...sometimes..." Fleming snatched up her cup, drained it, stared into the dregs. "Guys, I need help."

Swan leaned forward and spoke in a near-whisper. "That's what we're here for, Clare. Just tell us who you're afraid of, and we'll make sure you're safe."

"It's worse than that. A lot worse. I need protection, yeah, but I also need...what's it called? Immunity?"

Swan and Ross exchanged a glance. "Immunity?" Ross asked. "From what?"

"From prosecution," Fleming said. "I need to make a deal."

†

Dumas gazed into the trees overhanging the St. Paul rectory. He was seated on the porch alongside Father Dan. The porch faced away from the parking lot. From here he could almost believe he was at a cabin in the middle of a forest. The land dropped away to an unseen road below, Mulligans Hill Lane, and the railroad on the other side. The morning was quiet, the air still and cool.

"There's a tattoo parlor down there," Father Dan said. "It's tucked into an alcove in the retaining wall. I always thought it an odd place for one of those. Or maybe not, when you think about it."

"Is the Church against tattoos?" Dumas asked.

"No. Some Protestants are. There's a prohibition against them in the Old Testament, but the Church views that as a ceremonial matter not binding on us today. We just urge people to be thoughtful if they choose to get one, so as not to be offensive." The priest gave Dumas a knowing smile. "I doubt that has anything to do with the case. Or your visit."

"Just curious. My new bride is Catholic. Or had you already deduced that?"

"I didn't have a chance to observe her *that* closely, Sergeant."

Dumas put his hands to his eyes in imitation of a pair of binoculars. "Didn't see her crucifix?"

"Does she wear one?"

"She does."

"You plan to join her?"

Dumas wasn't sure he wanted to go down that path. He respected all religions, Montufar's especially now that she was his wife, but for himself, he was no more than half immersed in any one spiritual practice.

"Just curious," Father Dan parroted.

"I do have a couple of relevant questions."

"Else you wouldn't be here."

"I understand you know Father Ed Tyler."

Father Dan nodded. "He's a good man. Simple, straightforward, cares deeply for his flock."

"How often do you see him?"

"Rarely. We trade emails every month or two, mostly to keep in touch, share news, that sort of thing. I think the last time we were in the same place at the same time was three years ago."

"So it's not a close relationship."

"Not really, no."

Dumas hadn't expected any shocking revelations, based on what Montufar had learned from parish secretary Shelly Beck. If anything useful were to turn up, it would be in relation to Father Walter. He asked about that.

"Father Walter," the priest mused. "Yes, I think he did visit last summer. June or July, maybe?"

"For what purpose?" Dumas asked.

Father Dan shook his head. "Nothing official. Oh, wait. It was a family event. He has a sister in Columbia. I think they were doing a get-together—family picnic or some such—and they all came here for mass that weekend."

"Is this his sister's church?"

"Her son's, I think. I don't recall his name. Maybe Shelly knows. You could ask her."

Dumas made a mental note to check on that before leaving. "We're concerned someone may have it in for either Father Ed or Father Walter," he said. "Can you think of any reason why?"

Father Dan turned a shocked expression on Dumas. "Why do you say that?"

The reaction seemed genuine. Few people could fake it that well. Still, Dumas reserved judgement. "I can't say specifically. But there are indications."

"You must be mistaken, Sergeant. As I said, Father Ed's a good man. And Father Walter? I don't know him myself, but Father Ed speaks highly of him, and he seems to have a good family."

"How do you know that? If he's only been here once and you couldn't immediately recall why, I assume you don't know his family any better than him."

"I don't, but Father Ed once said they visit him and take him on outings. And I have an image of them sitting in church together that day. Just one day, but it's a peaceful, happy image."

It would be, though, wouldn't it? Dumas thought. Not many would present anything less in church. "There's a connection between the events here and at St. Augustine, Father. We're looking for that connection. Aside from Father Ed, Father Walter, and Clare Fleming we haven't discovered any. Do us a favor. If you think of others, let us know."

"Clare? What's she got to do with anything?"

"She works here sometimes, yes?"

Father Dan nodded.

"Then she's a connection."

Father Dan frowned at the trees beyond the porch. "Honestly, I think you folks are trying to herd rabbits. You're talking about some of the most harmless people I know. It's got to be about the Church herself, not about them. The connection you're looking for may not exist."

Dumas thanked him and proceeded to the office, but it was closed. Shelly Beck, he recalled now, didn't get in until one o'clock. That was fine. He'd enlist her help with a phone call this afternoon.

†

Montufar timed her visit to Father Ed to coincide with his housekeeper's absence. When she arrived, she was surprised to find Father Walter before the statue of Mary, lost in contemplation.

She approached cautiously, not wanting to disturb him but with questions swirling through her head. Peller had met Father Walter in the hospital and gotten nothing but a refusal to talk, justified by the seal of the confessional. What had that meant? Had someone revealed something to him? Or was he referring to his own confession? Either way, he wouldn't break his silence, and Montufar wouldn't dream of asking him to. But he knew something. They needed to find a way to enable him to reveal it without betraying his vows.

Father Walter heard or felt her approach. He turned, leaning on his cane, and smiled. "Good morning."

"Good morning, Father. I don't think we've met before. I'm Detective Sergeant Corina Montufar."

"I recognize you. You're the police bride." He laughed lightly. "I've seen a lot of the police lately."

"You're feeling better, I hope?"

"Oh yes, I'm fine. They released me this morning. I'm not supposed to walk around without supervision for a few days, but old men don't like to be babied. Or take orders from doctors."

Montufar came to his side. They both looked up at Mary. A slight breeze stirred the leaves overhead. "Not quite how you envisioned retirement, is it?"

Father Walter smiled at nothing.

"Strange messages," Montufar added. "Police inquiries. Landing in the hospital. Hardly peace and quiet."

"I can take it. Church politics can be worse."

She supposed that was true. Not that she had direct experience of it, but she'd heard a story or two. She was thankful Captain Morris shielded her team as much as possible from the police and county versions. Coming up through the ranks, Montufar hadn't always been so fortunate. Some elements within the force had made it clear a woman from an immigrant family had no business in their world. She'd grown a tough shell to prove them wrong, a shell she was now trying to shed. She'd found enough internal strength that she no longer needed it, but ingrained habits could be hard to break.

"What do you make of all this?" she asked.

Father Walter's smile morphed into the glazed look of someone avoiding engagement. He shrugged.

"I'd tell you what I think, but maybe you don't care to know."

"If you want to talk, I'll listen. That's what priests do."

"That message on your window was written to be read from the inside. I think it was meant for either you or Father Ed."

Father Walter pinched his lips. His eyes remained fixed on Mary. "Father Ed?"

"Your room was his office before you moved in."

"You think the vandal knew that?"

"It's possible."

The priest faced Montufar, shifting his cane to keep balance. "It was probably just a window of opportunity." He chuckled at his own pun.

Montufar looked him in the eyes. He had hazel eyes underscored by dark circles, as though he hadn't slept in a month, maybe the effect of his fall and hospitalization. "No," she said. "That window faces the hillside and the cemetery. Even if the message had been outward facing—which it wasn't—who would have seen it? Only someone in the room. Who would be in that room? You, since it's yours now, or Father Ed, since it used to be his office."

"Hmm." He shifted his cane, turned to face the church, looked up at the stone and stained glass and the bell tower, its tall dome topped with a gold cross. "Why would anyone target us of all people?"

"I came to see Father Ed," Montufar said. "I'll ask him while I'm here. But if you have any thoughts..."

He didn't, or at least none he cared to share.

"If you want to talk," she parroted, "I'll listen. You know where to find me."

She proceeded to the rectory without waiting for a reply, knowing she'd get none, not right now. But that, too, was a reply of sorts. Right or wrong, Father Walter thought he was the target. As did Clare Fleming. But the second message hadn't been meant for her. Or had it? As the house-keeper, she could be expected to come into that room, too, so maybe it had been. But then, why not a window in a common area? Why Father Walter's window?

When Montufar knocked on the door, Father Ed opened before the last rap. He must have been waiting for her. He looked over her shoulder at Father Walter, who had resumed his contemplation of Mary. "Is he okay?"

"So far as I know."

"He's not supposed to wander around for a few days."

"But try and stop him."

Father Ed laughed, stepped aside, and motioned her in. "I've heard he was a dynamo in his youth, almost unstoppable. He seems to be aging gracefully despite his physical limitations. Clare is out, but if you want some coffee or tea, I can manage it."

"I'm fine."

Father Ed directed Montufar to the sofa and sat facing her on the loveseat. He folded his hands in his lap. In his black clothing on the white sofa, he might have been a photo taken a century before. Even his flesh seemed pale. Montufar sensed his tension, too. People often were nervous during police interviews, but this seemed more than that. To put him at ease, she started small, simple, conversational.

"How long have you been at St. Augustine, Father?"

"It seems a lifetime. Longer than average, anyway. The D.C. archdiocese likes to move us around every six years. I've been here eight, nearly nine."

"They must like you here."

"I like it here. And I can be persuasive." Father Ed winked.

Montufar laughed.

He turned pensive, looked over her shoulder at nothing.

"But these incidents have changed things," she guessed.

He began to shake his head, then sat a bit straighter and looked her in the eyes. She got the funny feeling he was trying to comfort her, although he must know she didn't need it. She was here on business, not seeking spiritual guidance. "Yes, of course."

For the moment, she let it slide. "And Father Walter? He's been here three years, right?"

Father Ed relaxed a bit. "That's right."

"What about before that? You weren't on your own, I assume."

"When I arrived, the pastor was Father Henry Blackwood. Everyone called him Father Hank. He was a bit of a stand-up comedian. He always had some joke to wrap around the Liturgy of the Word and Gospel readings. People liked him. Unfortunately, he was diagnosed with pancreatic cancer and passed during my second year. I was appointed pastor after that. I had a deacon serving with me for a while, but he moved on shortly before Father Walter arrived."

"Father," Montufar said, switching gears, "have you heard about the incidents at St. Paul?"

He nodded.

"I understand you and Father Walter sometimes visit that church."

"Infrequently. Father Walter went with his sister's family last year. I'm not aware that he's been there otherwise."

"Just a family event for him, then."

"As far as I know. Why?"

Montufar almost answered. He was a priest, after all. She'd respected priests as spiritual guides and counsellors, among other things. Telling him everything felt right. Second nature. *But that's not why you're here*, she reminded herself. *Father Ed is an interview subject right now.* "What about you?" she asked.

"I visit St. Paul every few years. Father Dan and I normally communicate through email when there's a need."

"When was your last visit?"

"I honestly don't recall. It's been a couple of years, I think." He twined and untwined his fingers. "Why is this important, Corina?"

Interesting that he used her name rather than her rank. He was appealing to the Catholic bride, not the detective. She decided to throw him a bone, see if that softened him up. She leaned forward and lowered her voice as though sharing a confidence. "We have reason to believe there's a connection between the vandalism at the two churches. I'm trying to find that connection."

Father Ed frowned. "What makes you think that?"

"I'm afraid I can't say right now, but it could be important."

He leaned forward, too. "I can't imagine it's personal. It must be about the Church herself. Two Catholic parishes in the same general area? That's the only connection I see. Whoever is doing this is trying to rile us. The best defense is to clean up the mess and get on with business as usual. For the good of our parishioners. The last thing we need is a media circus."

     The Wages of Sin

He was almost pleading with her to keep everything under wraps, to ignore it, to go away and take it with her. "I hope you're right," Montufar said. "But I fear you're not. What if someone is out to harm you?"

He rocked back, eyes wide. "Me?"

"You."

"Why would anyone want to harm *me*?"

"You're a priest, the visible face of the Church. That might be enough reason."

Father Ed mulled that over. His voice quivered as he replied, "If God calls me to martyrdom, then so be it."

"Or maybe you have a personal enemy."

"I have no enemies, Corina. I may not be perfect, but I've only ever done my best to serve my flock. Ask anyone here."

"It isn't necessarily someone here. They also targeted St. Paul."

"I hardly know anyone at St. Paul. Not since my brother…"

Montufar perked up. Could this be the missing connection? When Father Ed didn't continue, she prompted, "Your brother attends St. Paul?"

Father Ed bit his lip. "He did, once."

"Did he move out of the area?"

"He died."

"Oh, I'm sorry. How long has it been?"

"Six years. I still can't believe he's gone."

Six years. That meant Father Ed had been at St. Augustine not quite three when his predecessor died, he became pastor, and his own brother passed away. A lot of stress packed into a short time. Maybe that was why the archdiocese hadn't moved him. "Was it cancer?" she asked, more from sympathy than a need to know.

Father Ed closed his eyes. "No. He was shot."

Chapter 9

Dumas waited until just after one o'clock to call Shelly Beck at the St. Paul office and ask about Father Walter's nephew. Beck found the information in no time. "Carlyle Navin," she said. "His mother Janice Navin is Father Walter's younger sister. Her husband's name is Alex. All three used to be in our parish, but the parents moved and now attend St. John the Evangelist."

That was the Montufar family's church. Did Corina know the Navin family? That could be a boon, although they'd have to inform Captain Morris of the personal relationship if one existed. Not that Dumas expected much would come of it. It was just another piece of background information in a case that offered little to sink a detective's teeth into.

When Montufar materialized at his desk, that changed. She had the calm of a reservoir moments before the dam breaks. Constant motion was Montufar's default setting. When she grew still, something was up. She perched on the edge of his desk and looked down at him as though studying a chess board.

"Better tell me," he said. "Before you explode."

"We have research to do."

"On?"

"Father Ed's brother."

"What about him?"

"He was shot to death six years ago."

"Shot!" Dumas leaned into his keyboard. "What was his name?"

"Mark Tyler. His body was found in Centennial Park."

Dumas searched the case files for the name and year. "Found him," he said. He skimmed the reports and read off relevant information. "The body was discovered about ten A.M. on a Thursday by a couple who'd rented Pavilion H for a birthday party scheduled to start at noon. They'd come to set up and saw someone lying on the tennis court. When they approached, they realized he was injured and called 911. The victim had been shot in the chest seven times, once piercing the heart in the left ventricle, twice the upper left lung, once the lower right lung. The rest lodged in the sternum and ribs. All the bullets were recovered in the autopsy. Twenty-twos."

He frowned at Montufar. "Twenty-twos. As grouped as buckshot. Hardly a professional job."

"Or even competent, but it did the trick."

"Seven shells recovered at the scene," Dumas continued. "Remington twenty-two shorts. No other particularly interesting physical evidence. The victim had a wallet full of cash and credit cards. Subsequent investigation couldn't identify any personal items missing." He pushed back from the desk. "Sounds like an altercation that ended badly."

Montufar gave him a crooked smile. "But you don't like coincidences."

"Never have," he agreed. "It's too convenient, him being Father Ed's brother."

"I agree. He could be our connection between the churches. According to Father Ed, Mark Tyler attended St. Paul. It's possible Father Dan knew him, although six years is on the cusp of typical service in one parish, also according to Father Ed. It might have been before his time."

"Then we find out how long he's been there."

"Here's another coincidence for you."

"Oh, joy."

"I knew you'd be excited. The location of Father Ed's death is the same area Theresa's been monitoring. Squirrel Shooter nicked someone near Pavilion H. They recovered a twenty-two bullet from the grass nearby."

Dumas didn't like that at all, but it had to be coincidence. Mark Tyler had been intentionally killed. Six years before. Squirrel Shooter looked to be a young guy taking potshots at wildlife, or more likely vegetation. They hadn't found any murdered animals.

Montufar raised an eyebrow. "No crazy ideas?"

"Not unless Squirrel Shooter once cut classes in sixth grade, made off with daddy's gun, and mistook Tyler for a really big rodent."

"I once heard of a farmer who hired college students to paint the word 'cow' on his cows before deer season opened."

"Did it save the bovines?"

"Not a hundred percent of them."

"Figures. Anyway, it's my turn now. Do you happen to know—"

Theresa Swan and Holly Ross slid into Dumas' cubicle at that moment, filling it to capacity. "We need to talk," Swan said without waiting to be asked. "We need Rick, too."

"And maybe," Ross said, with far less enthusiasm than usual, "Captain Morris."

Montufar slid off Dumas' desk. "Looks like *your* surprise will have to wait," she told her husband.

†

Peller was disinclined to pull Morris into the fray until he knew the details, so they started without her. But once the story was out, he called a break and personally retrieved the captain from her corner office. Morris settled at the table with them, Peller on her right, Montufar on her left, Dumas and Swan and Ross opposite with backs to the conference room window. Dumas, Morris noted, had absently pulled a quarter from his pocket and was manipulating it between his fingers, performing vanishes, retrieving it from thin air, all without moving his hands more than a few finger-widths above the table. She'd never seen him do any magic but coin vanishes. Maybe she should get him a pack of cards for his birthday and see how he handled that.

But to business. "From the top," she said.

Swan and Ross exchanged glances and by some invisible signal agreed that Swan would tell the story. "We interviewed Clare Fleming this morning," she said. "The rectory housekeeper at St. Augustine. She previously suggested she might be the target of the messages. She started working at the rectory five years ago, after divorcing her husband. He cheated on her, she retaliated by cheating on him, and since then she's persisted in promiscuity. That led to a job of sorts."

Morris picked up her pen, looked at it, set it down. She could feel her fingers aching to click the damn thing. Whatever was coming wasn't good.

"The rectory position doesn't pay very well," Swan continued. "So when someone offered her money to sleep with a friend as a 'birthday present,' she agreed. She's already been running around, so why not? Then he made another offer, and then another."

"Okay," Morris said. "She turned prostitute. So?"

"More than that. Her employer instructed her to chat up her partners. Simple stuff at first, then more probing. Family circumstances. Financial conditions. Where they worked and what they did. Any closet skeletons she could worm out of them."

"Hell," Morris said. "Recruitment for espionage."

Swan nodded. "Fleming's bright enough, but the adventure and the extra income blinded her. She woke up once she realized her targets were federal employees with security clearances. She's scared and wants out. She tried to extricate herself, but her handler threatened to kill her. That's why she thought the messages were intended for her."

Morris clicked the pen a few times before setting it down and giving it the evil eye.

"I don't think we have a choice," Peller said.

"Don't you."

He raised an eyebrow but held his tongue.

"How important is she to our case?" Morris directed the question at Peller. He would know the team's inclination, and debate was pointless. Because he was right. She had zero choice. As of this moment, Fleming was en route to the feds.

"Probably not very. The messages seem to be directed at someone inside the rectories. At St. Augustine, that could be Clare Fleming, but probably not at St. Paul. Yes, she's a connection between the churches, but so are Father Ed and Father Walter. The smart money is on one of the priests. Fleming's problems are likely coincidental."

Dumas looked at the ceiling. Montufar smirked.

Great. A dissenting opinion. "What?" Morris snapped.

"Coincidences are forming a line around the block," Dumas said.

"And Eric hates coincidences," Montufar added.

Fine time for the team's chemistry to brew chaos. "Let's hear it."

"Father Ed's brother could be connected." Dumas shook his head. "I don't like any of this."

Ross turned to him. "What about Father Ed's brother?"

"He attended St. Paul," Montufar said. "And he was murdered six years ago. In Centennial Park. At Pavilion H. With a twenty-two."

Swan about gagged.

"Squirrel Shooter," Morris grumbled. "No, that *has* to be coincidence."

"At least Angry Granny isn't involved yet," Ross said.

Morris gathered up her pen, clicked it a few times, and stood. "Don't even think it. I'll pass Fleming to the FBI and try to weasel us a dispensation to keep her on a long leash. Let me know if we need to pull her in."

She left a leaden silence in her wake.

†

Given the tangled mess of the church investigation, Ross didn't mind escaping to the straightforward if weird world of Angry Granny. She scanned her list of seventeen Escalades of interest for close matches to the tag number Clayton Parker had reported. True to form, nothing fit. The closest match included a reversal and two substitutions, too far off to take seriously. Still, she made a note of it. That plate was attached to one of the vehicles from the gated community, one belonging to Samuel...

...Ortiz.

Age, seventy-three.

Well, now.

That SUV was one of the no-shows, neither vehicle nor people home. Ross called Mr. Ortiz and got voice mail, so she left a message asking him to call her back. But now she was stuck waiting for a response. From Ortiz, from the MVA, from anyone. Hell with that. She dropped Dumas an email saying she'd be out chasing down a lead, grabbed her purse, and set course for North Laurel.

Not that she expected to find Ortiz hiding in his basement, but maybe a nosey neighbor could tell her the condition of his Escalade. She arrived full of hope in the land of overpriced townhouses and oversized single-family homes packed together like strawberries in a carton. The residences clustered about an artificial lake. Most of the driveways stood empty. The asphalt was riddled with cracks, as though all that money had weighed too heavily on it.

Ross pulled into Ortiz's driveway. He lived on the east side in a detached unit. His house stood on a court at the end of a one-block road backed by trees, not far from the confluence of the Middle and Little Patuxent Rivers. She paused at his front door and listened but couldn't hear the water, only the swish of traffic. Oh, well. She gave the doorbell a try, knowing she'd get no response. Then she hiked around the court and down the street, trying each house.

She found someone at a place with a red Firebird parked on the street. An elderly gentleman dressed in black jeans and a purple turtleneck opened the door a crack and peered at her. A chain dangled in front of his face between the door and the jamb, just in case she was a bad girl intent upon breaking in, tying him up, and robbing him blind.

Ross introduced herself and showed ID.

The man squinted at her photo and her face. "What?"

"I'm conducting an investigation of a traffic incident," she told him. "I was wondering—"

"I don't drive." He started to close the door.

Who owned the Firebird, then? She almost thrust her foot into the crack but stopped herself. *Use your words*, she scolded. "Do you know the Ortiz family?"

The man opened the door as far as the chain would allow and pushed his face as much into the gap as possible. His eyes shifted to the Ortiz house. "No," he lied. It had to be a lie, because he was looking right at the place.

Ross pressed on. "They own an Escalade, right?"

"How should I know?"

"What color is it?"

"Their car?"

"Yes."

"I don't know."

"It's blue, right?"

The old man nodded, then shook his head, then said, "I'm not involved."

"Involved in what?"

He started to close the door again, and Ross nearly did shove her foot in that time. She could feel her mean face taking shape. She forced a smile, probably a terrifying smile, and did her best to keep her voice professional. "Does it look like it's been in an accident?"

He thought about that, then opened the gap again. The chain, stretched taught, remained on its hook. "Why not ask *him*?"

"He isn't home."

After sneaking another peek at the Ortiz house, he shrugged.

"Who usually drives it?" Ross asked. "Mr. Ortiz or Mrs. Ortiz?"

"There is no Mrs. Ortiz. She died three years ago."

Says the man who doesn't know them, Ross grumbled to herself. "Then Mr. Ortiz lives alone."

"I don't keep tabs on him."

"Yes or no?" she snapped. Okay, that one slipped out.

"Both." The old geezer slammed the door in her face.

At least her foot wasn't in the gap. With three houses left to visit, Ross about gave up. They'd be a waste of time. Ortiz's wife was dead, his vehicle probably wasn't damaged. He might have taken up with someone else, but if she wasn't living there—not full-time, anyway—she wouldn't likely be driving his car. She'd have her own. Still, Ross couldn't leave unturned stones, so she rang the remaining doorbells.

And, of course, got nothing.

Chapter 10

On Wednesday morning, Kevin Graham began a new assignment, one he rather wished he hadn't pulled. Okay, volunteered to accept. This one was on him.

Skulking around the park in his civvies wasn't his style. Yeah, it had its points. The sun was bright, the air warm, the sprinkle of cotton-ball clouds serene. Even the people dotting the park exuded peace. Yet he felt like a fraud arriving in his eight-year-old Pontiac Sunfire, hiding in plain sight as he walked the beat in his jeans and sweatshirt. He was cop. An officer of the law. People should know it, should know he was there to protect them, should feel safer with him around.

Not that a uniform kept anyone safe. The world was a dangerous place, even without criminals. He'd learned that the hard way. Once upon a time, he'd been a young constable on the Jamaican Constabulary Force, married not quite five months, their first child on the way, proud owner of a new if small house. The next day, Hurricane Gilbert struck, the worst storm in his island-country's history. Forty-nine dead. Half a million homeless, Graham and his wife Janeil included.

She'd holed up in temporary shelter while Graham reported for duty. He fought off despair by doing his job, maintaining as much order as possible, assisting relief efforts. But the experience hit Janeil hard. She got word to one of her brothers, who had emigrated to the U.S. and was living in New York City. He helped them obtain refugee status and gave them a room in his apartment. After the requisite year was up, they applied for permanent residency and in due course obtained citizenship. Meanwhile, the family's contacts found Graham a position with the Howard County police. He and Janeil moved to moderate-income housing in Columbia, had three children—boy, girl, boy, the first two now in high school and youngest in middle school—and in time bought a house of their own. His career in the U.S. had been littered with landmines of racism and xenophobia, but he refused to be intimidated. When he put on his uniform, he did it with pride, focused on helping people, on planting himself immovable in the path of troublemakers.

And now he was slinking around a park, waiting for a pop gun to go off. Dumas owed him for this. Big time.

Theresa Swan had supplied the data on the gunshot reports, and he'd been present as the sole victim, Seth Weisselberg, was questioned and refused treatment. Given that and backroom dealing among the higher-ups, Graham was elected to walk the lakeside path back and forth, back and forth, taking his time, doing nothing but watching the clouds and the birds and the water and, without being too obvious, the passers-by. He didn't see any characters he'd brand suspicious. Old couples, young couples, small groups, loners, black, white, Asian, Latin. Nobody pointing a twenty-two at anything.

The temperature had seesawed recently between jacket and t-shirt weather. Today, some park visitors wore unzipped jackets, some carried them, some went without. Some jacket pockets might have concealed a handgun, some not, but Graham didn't have x-ray vision. Most of the bulges were likely granola bars and water bottles. He walked until his legs told him they'd had enough. Then he sat on a bench and rested, then he walked some more. And absolutely nothing happened.

Graham really, seriously wanted his uniform and patrol car back.

By three fifteen, he'd had his fill of it, and anyway, thick clouds were gathering, building to another afternoon shower. No sense getting soaked. He returned to his Sunfire and slid in, grabbed a blue flip notebook lying on the passenger seat and unclipped a black pen from its cover. He wondered how best to record a waste of time. Eh. Just be direct. He turned to the first blank page, jotted down the date, arrival time, and departure time. Then he started the note but only got "W" down before the pop of a small-caliber weapon sounded, followed by something smacking his windshield. Hard.

He squinted at the glass. A star-shaped chip had been gouged into it, low on the passenger side. He got out and circled the vehicle, checked the hood and the ground alongside it. A bullet lay beside the tire, as innocent as an acorn fallen from a tree, aside from not being an acorn. The star on the windshield was symmetrical. He guessed it had been a head-on hit.

Jaw clenched, Graham stared at the woods across the field. Sure enough, two minutes later a teenager in a black hoodie emerged from the trees, hands in his jacket pockets, eyes on the ground, making a beeline for the parking lot. Since the kid was coming his way, Graham waited. He dug some gloves and an evidence bag from his glove compartment and collected the bullet. The suspect reached the parking lot and made for the only other car present, an old Civic five spots down from Graham's. When the kid's back was turned, Graham strode after him. "Hey!" he snapped. "You owe me a windshield!"

Startled, the teen nearly tripped over his own feet. Graham was in his face before he could gather his wits. He had a Mediterranean complexion. His terror-filled eyes met Graham's glare. Graham shoved his ID in front of those eyes. "HCPD," he said. "Hands out of your pockets."

The suspect didn't move.

"Now!"

The suspect withdrew his trembling hands and held them up in surrender.

"Turn around. Lean on the car." After the kid complied, Graham did a quick pat-down and found a Ruger Mark III in his right hoodie pocket. "Well, well, what's this?" He made sure the safety was on, then set it on the hood of the car, out of the kid's reach. "Got ID?"

"In my wallet, back pocket." His voice practically squeaked.

Graham retrieved the wallet and found a driver's license. "Peter Zelly. You're seventeen, huh?"

"Yeah," Zelly said. It was more exhale than word.

"Mommy and daddy won't be happy, but good thing you're a juvie. You winged somebody the other day, you know that?"

"I didn't shoot anybody!"

"You kinda did."

Zelly's mouth worked for a moment before it found a reply. "I didn't know! It was an accident!"

"Uh-huh. Why aren't you in school?"

"I finished my classes first semester."

"If you're so smart, why're you shooting up the park?"

Zelly said nothing.

"Turn around," Graham ordered.

Zelly turned. "What happens now?"

"Now I take you in, we call your parents, and you answer our questions. We'll be keeping the gun as evidence. Just in case."

"In case what?"

"Charges are filed." Graham figured that wouldn't happen. Zelly was just a scared kid out for a metaphorical joyride. With luck, he'd learn his lesson.

Zelly nearly collapsed backwards onto his car. "Are you going to cuff me?"

Graham didn't think it necessary. Zelly posed no danger and hardly seemed brave or stupid enough to jump from a moving vehicle. "Do I need to?"

"No, sir."

"All right. But if you cause me any trouble..." Graham stepped to the side and glared at Zelly.

"No trouble. I promise."

"I'll hold you to that. Come on." Graham escorted Zelly back to his Sunfire, scratched out the "W," and recorded the kid's license information in his notebook. He bagged the gun and stowed it and the bullet in the glove compartment. Then he radioed in a report. "Tell Detective Swan," he added. "She might want to be there."

†

Detective Swan sure did. So did Peter Zelly's mother, Margot Zelly. She arrived at Northern District Headquarters in a fine fume, eyes ablaze, ears figuratively belching steam, mouth spewing curses at her son, her ex-husband, her brother, the police force, and the governments of the State of Maryland and the United States of America. Swan stared at the woman's hairline and told herself not to make annoyed faces. *The kid takes after his mother's side of the family*, she told herself. *In looks if not in temperament.* That kept her on an even keel. So far.

They—Swan, Graham, and Montufar—herded Margot and Peter Zelly into a smallish interview room. Eric Dumas raised an eyebrow as they passed, but Graham held up a hand to ward him off. More wouldn't be merrier in this case. Once Margot's temper tantrum played out enough for someone else to slip in a word or two, Swan began the interrogation.

"Do you have a license for this gun?" She slid the bagged weapon to the center of the table. They already knew he didn't, neither him nor his mother nor anyone else. God knew where it had come from.

"We don't keep guns in our house," Margot snapped, half at Swan, half at her son.

"I was asking Peter."

"Don't say anything," she commanded. "We're getting a lawyer."

Swan gave Margot a less than civil look.

Montufar cut in. "Ma'am, your son is a minor. The damage was minimal, just one man who refused medical treatment and a ding in a windshield. I'm sure Peter's learned his lesson. We're more interested in where the gun came from."

Margot crossed her arms over her chest and leaned back. "You're not charging him?"

Montufar shrugged. Graham mimicked her actions. "Depends on you," he said. He switched his stone-faced glare to Peter.

Peter swallowed, glanced at his mother and opened his mouth.

"Quiet," Margot ordered. "If you're not being charged, we can leave." She started to rise.

"Mom—"

"Quiet!"

"You never listen! That's why Dad left. He always said you never listen."

Lawyers and leaving forgotten, Margot dropped back into her seat and waggled a finger at her son. "Don't even mention that bastard. If it hadn't been for him and your uncle, you'd never have picked up a gun in the first place."

"Is that where you got it?" Swan asked, tapping the gun.

Peter shook his head.

"It's their fault," Margot repeated, in case the cops hadn't figured it out. "'Every boy's gotta learn to shoot,' they said. He didn't *want* to learn."

"*You* didn't want me to learn, Mom."

"You had no interest until they hauled you to that range and put a gun in your hand."

"We aren't interested in your domestic problems," Swan said. Margot looked ready to bite somebody. Peter slid down a bit in his chair. "Why were you shooting up the park, Peter?"

He shrugged. "I wasn't."

"Officer Graham's windshield says you were. So does a man named Seth who's leg was winged by your bullet." Swan placed two more evidence bags on the table, each containing a bullet. "You know as well as I that ballistics will tell us both of these came from that." She tapped the gun again.

"And you," Graham nearly growled, "had that." He tapped the gun, too.

"I wasn't shooting up the park," Peter insisted, although with less confidence than he no doubt wished. "I was just shooting at stuff in the woods."

"What kind of stuff?" Swan asked. She really wanted to suggest squirrels, to vindicate the nickname she'd given him.

"Fallen branches. Trash. Nothing I would hurt. I just wanted…" He heaved a sigh, glanced at his mother, and mumbled, "I just wanted to do something fun for a change."

Margot gave him the evil eye.

Swan felt for him. His mother must make his life a living hell. Did she even let him have any friends? "Where did you get the gun, Peter?"

He shrugged.

"Stole it, huh?" Graham interjected.

"Don't you call my son a thief!" Margot slapped the table for emphasis.

Graham stared at her, still as a boulder.

"I found it," Peter said. "In the woods in the park."

Montufar and Swan exchanged a glance. Father Ed's brother had been shot in the park by an unknown assailant. The weapon, also a twenty-two, had never surfaced. This gun looked to be in good shape, though, not a piece buried in the undergrowth for years. "Where, exactly?" Swan asked.

"Inside the south loop, across from Emy's Meadow."

"Can you show us?"

Margot leaned forward "You're not hauling us off on some damned---"

"It's okay, Mom," Peter interrupted. A light bulb seemed to have turned on in his head. He got it. They were interested in the gun, not him. To Swan, he said, "Yeah, I can show you."

"Perfect," Swan replied. "I'll drop you off at home after." She looked at Margot, who was seething in silence. "Unless your mom cares to join us?"

Thankfully, she didn't.

†

While his colleagues were enjoying that interview, Dumas dug further into the shooting of Mark Tyler, Father Ed's brother. Detective Lieutenant Bill Trengove, then a sergeant, had investigated that case. Dumas stopped by his cubicle and settled into the guest chair.

Trengove was on the phone. "No," he told the other party. "Absolutely not. You know why. The County won't pay me what Bill Gates pays himself." He glanced at Dumas. "We'll talk later. Work beckons. Yeah. Bye, Jean. Love you, too." He cradled the phone and squeezed his eyes shut. "You live in an apartment, don't you?"

Dumas nodded.

"You're lucky. Corina can't demand an addition."

Dumas smirked. "She might want a whole new house."

"You're not here to talk construction costs, are you?"

"No, just an old case you worked. Mark Tyler, found dead in Centennial Park six years ago, on the tennis court near Pavilion H."

Trengove ran a hand through his thinning brown hair. He was a bit older than Rick Peller with more attitude but no less sharp. "So it's torture, is it?"

Dumas cocked his head.

"That case. Brutal on several counts. Certain people wouldn't let me forget it was never solved."

"I've read the reports, but I wanted to hear it from you."

"Why?"

"Mark Tyler's brother, Father Ed Tyler, is associated with something new."

"Christ."

Dumas smirked. "Was that intentional?"

"Don't start," Trengove grumbled. "I'm agnostic, and Jean says it fits."

"Oh?"

"Because I never know anything."

Once he stopped laughing—and Trengove traded his annoyed face for his jokester face—Dumas got back to business. "Father Ed, or his church anyway, has been targeted by graffiti that could be a death threat."

Trengove raised his eyes to heaven. Or the ceiling at least. "Father Ed wasn't my favorite person."

Dumas waited, but Trengove didn't continue. "Come on, Bill, don't make me drag it out of you. This could be serious."

"I'm just pulling my thoughts out of their dusty closet. Mark Tyler was the older brother by two years. He was an information technology project manager. He'd worked for several large defense contractors."

That got Dumas' attention. Red flag number one. Clare Fleming had been unwittingly recruited to gather intelligence on such people.

"Mark's body was found six years ago on the morning of June eleventh, lying, as you say, on the tennis court near Pavilion H. He'd been shot in the chest seven times by a twenty-two. We know because the bullets were pulled out of him during the autopsy."

Dumas' eyebrows arched.

Trengove smirked. "Yeah, okay, and the casings. The perp left them for us. The gun was another matter. It never surfaced. Father Ed was devastated. I got that, but he refused to talk."

"About what?"

"About anything. Even family background. Maybe I should've taken pity on him, but he was stonewalling. Who does that? Who doesn't want their brother's killer found? And a priest, of all people."

Dumas wondered if that was really it. Peller had found Father Ed's reticence odd, too, but maybe that was just his personality. Some people coped with tragedy by refusing to face it. "The reports are silent on possible motives," he said. "Did you have any hypotheses?"

"Hypotheses." Trengove shook his head. "We had a stiff on a tennis court, killed with extreme if unsteady prejudice, aside from the lame use of a twenty-two. Why not a Dirty Harry number, if you're that ticked off?

My highly evolved detective brain says it wasn't a professional hit. The guy manages IT projects which, okay, government connection. Some people hate the government. But is that any reason to snuff an average Joe like him? I ran him by the FBI and his FSO, but nothing."

"FSO?"

"Fed-speak. Facility Security Officer. They'd know about his clearances, any reported misconduct or suspicious behavior, stuff like that. Mark Tyler was as clean as Mother Nature herself. At least, as far as anybody knows." Trengove pinched his lips. "That doesn't mean he *wasn't* up to something. Maybe he was just good at hiding it."

"You think the government connection is important?"

"How the hell should I know? He had no known drug connections, no known gambling debts, no known indications of infidelity. No known anything that would've marked him for death. Maybe he insulted somebody's mother."

Dumas mulled everything over. Trengove was right. Someone seriously wanted Tyler dead. Not a trained killer—the choice of weapon testified to that, as did the scattered hits—but someone. That plus the connection with Clare Fleming set Dumas' teeth on edge. He was missing something, but what?

Trengove was watching Dumas.

"What?" Dumas asked.

"I feel those wheels spinning in the mud. Why?"

"Father Ed's housekeeper, Clare Fleming, was unwittingly recruited by someone to gather information from people with security clearances."

Trengove leaned forward and motioned him to continue.

"We don't have a lot of details yet, but Captain Morris is alerting the FBI."

"Do that, and you'll never see her again."

"No choice. But she'll try to keep Fleming available if needed."

"Trust me," Trengove said, "you'll need her."

Dumas didn't doubt it, but for now the subject had been exhausted. He stood. "I appreciate it, Bill. I'll keep you in the loop."

Trengove looked up as someone lumbered in behind Dumas.

"Eric," Kevin Graham rumbled. "Bill. Got a bit of the loop for you."

They both raised their eyebrows.

Graham grinned in satisfaction. "We think we found your gun."

†

It was getting late, but Swan wanted this done. She texted her boyfriend Ken to let him know she might be home late, then she escorted Peter Zelly to Emy's Meadow, a pollinator garden along the trail in the southwest corner of Centennial Park. On the ride there, Zelly maintained silence save when Swan asked a question. She wanted to talk about his family, but dysfunctional wasn't her forte, so she stuck to the case.

"When did you find the gun?"

Zelly studied his fingernails. "About a month ago."

"How long have you been using it?"

"Two weeks, I guess."

"Where did you get the rounds?" Maryland law didn't allow the sale of ammunition to a minor, so unless he had a fake ID, someone must have made the purchase for him.

Zelly didn't care to answer that with more than a shrug.

He wasn't an idiot, anyway. He knew when to clam up. Swan let it go. "I guess you didn't plan on using it."

"Not really. Mom hates guns. Anyway, it was in terrible shape. It must have been out there a long time."

Exactly what Swan was hoping. But that raised another question. "How did you get it working?"

"I got help cleaning it."

"From who?"

Zelly shrugged again.

Swan suspected Zelly's father, or maybe the uncle his mother had complained about. But it didn't matter.

"I stashed it after that. I figured after my birthday, she couldn't stop me from doing what I wanted. But I couldn't stop thinking about it, so…"

"How long until your birthday?"

"Eight months." The way he said it, it might have been eight lifetimes.

"You'll survive. Just, you know, next time you decide to get a gun and go shooting, do it legally and safely. You don't want to hurt anyone." *Again*, she didn't add.

Zelly looked out the side window and nodded.

The closest parking lot deposited them half a mile from Emy's Meadow. They parked and made the trek. Zelly indicated the woods opposite the meadow and led Swan some hundred and fifty feet into the trees. They fought their way through the thick undergrowth, startling birds and four-legged critters that scampered away unseen. At the base of a particularly large tree, Zelly pointed into a tangle of vines ensnaring the trunk. "I found it about here," he said. "It was mostly covered by vines. The end of the barrel was sticking out."

Swan studied the spot, studied the woods. "Why were you here in the first place?"

"No reason. I like the park. Sometimes when nobody's looking, I duck into the trees and pretend I'm in the middle of nowhere. If you tune out traffic noise, it's easy to believe you're the only one around."

"And you just happened upon the gun. Talk about random."

"Not really." He kicked at something, half-heartedly. "I know the woods pretty well by now. If something's hiding out here, I probably know about it."

Swan motioned him to step back. She snapped some photos with her cell phone to capture the site and its surroundings, then she picked through the growth but found nothing of interest. Not that she expected to. If Zelly's find had been used to kill Mark Tyler, nothing else would accompany it. The bullets had all lodged in Tyler's body and the shells had been left where they fell. The gun had been forsaken here in the hope it would never resurface. As it almost hadn't. Zelly had only happened upon it in his quest to escape the misery of his home life.

When Swan finished her search, they returned to the path, where she took a few more photos to document the location. After, she drove him home. The Zelly residence was a modest townhome in Columbia's Long Reach village. Zelly got out. He held onto the door for a moment, then leaned in again.

"Thanks," he said.

"No problem," Swan assured him.

"For not arresting me, I mean."

She smiled. He closed the car door and proceeded inside, none too quickly.

Good luck, kid, she thought.

Chapter 11

Clare Fleming woke to knuckles banging on her apartment door. She fumbled for her cell phone and checked the time. Five-thirty AM, Thursday, May third. Who would be here at this hour? She rolled out of bed, pulled a terry robe over her nightgown, and stumbled to the tiny foyer. The rapping sounded again, more like a hammer than someone's fist. She peeked through the peephole.

Damn! Not him!

She stood as still as a corpse. The hammering repeated. Across the hall, an angry neighbor bellowed, "People are sleeping!" Her visitor gave no reply, just waited and waited and when the door didn't open pounded again.

Fleming crept to her kitchen, slid open a drawer, and grabbed a steak knife. She slipped it point-down into her pocket. Her butcher's knife would be better, but she couldn't hide that. She reached the door again just as the knocking repeated and the neighbor warned, "Cut it out, or I'm calling the cops!"

Fleming unlocked and opened the door and greeted her visitor with her best befuddled look. "Mr. Beecham?"

Mr. Beecham didn't look like a Beecham. Wide in the face with a small nose, his complexion suggested east Asia, maybe China. He had a close-trimmed black beard, wore a white button-down shirt and black jeans, and stared at Fleming with the intense gaze of a carnivore on the hunt. "Let's talk," he said as though asking her out to dinner.

She couldn't refuse. He wouldn't let her. Trembling, she led the way to the living room. Her furnishings were new, not top-quality but decent stuff, comfortable, upholstered in blues and greens. She let him sit first.

He'd paid for all this, so he got the choice of seats. He picked the sofa, she a facing easy chair. Not that she was at all easy. She arranged her robe to cover as much of her legs as possible. He watched and licked his lips.

"Okay," she said. "Talk."

He took a ragged slip of paper from his pocket, a corner torn from a notepad, and handed it to her. Fleming knew what it was and what to do. "My phone's in the bedroom," she said.

He smiled a hungry shark smile.

She rose, retrieved the device, and returned to her seat, where she entered the information from the paper into her contacts list. Once done, she returned the original to him. This was his *modus operandi*. He would burn it later. "Is that it?" she asked, knowing it wasn't. He hadn't shown up at this ungodly hour to hook her up with a new mark.

Beecham cocked his head. "What did the police want?"

How did he know about that?

"I'm sure you remember, Clare. It was only two days ago."

Stick to the truth, she told herself. *Not the whole truth, but the truth.* "There's been trouble at the church."

Mr. Beecham laughed. "Churches *are* trouble."

"Have a little respect," she mumbled.

He raised an eyebrow.

"Somebody's been leaving threatening messages."

That seemed to interest him. He leaned forward, rested his elbows on his knees, waited for more.

"Weird messages. Bible verses."

"About what?"

"Sin and confession."

Beecham's expression didn't change, but for just a moment his breath caught in his throat. "Anything else?" he asked.

"Father Walter got hurt. The cops wanted to know what happened."

"And what did happen?"

"An accident, I guess. He tried to walk without his cane and fell." Mr. Beecham didn't need to know more than that, didn't need to know about the message on his window. She didn't want him accosting Father Walter.

"You couldn't have told them this at the rectory? They had to take you somewhere?"

"Damn it! Were you spying on me?" She hadn't meant to snap. He was dangerous when angered. She hung her head. "I'm sorry. I'm just..."

"Nervous, yes. Who wouldn't be with cops intruding on their private affairs? And Claire, my precious little slut..." He reached out and tweaked her nose. She flinched at his touch. "Of course I was spying on you. My management style is hands-on." He leaned back and locked his fingers behind his head. "Why did you let them lure you to a restaurant?"

She shrugged. "I just did what they asked. To cooperate."

"Ah. Yes, you are very cooperative, aren't you?" He leered.

She clenched her fists and stared at the floor.

Mr. Beecham brought his hands back before him, leaned toward her, whispered—hissed, rather, like a snake about to strike, "You wouldn't mention our arrangement, I'm sure?"

Fleming shook her head, just a little.

"Because if you did..."

She shook her head again.

"If you did, whatever you have in your pocket wouldn't save you. What is that, a knife?" He reached behind his back and brought forth a pistol. It was a nasty thing. Fleming knew nothing about guns, but whatever Mr. Beecham toted, it would leave a mess. He was that kind of animal.

"I didn't," she insisted.

Mr. Beecham turned the gun over in his hand and inspected it. He stood. He stepped to the side of her chair and touched the business end to her temple.

Fleming whimpered.

He bent down, put his face so close to hers that he could have kissed her. Thank God he didn't. He just grinned. "Good. I like well-behaved whores."

Stowing the gun, he made for the door. She didn't follow. He didn't want or need her to follow. But he didn't leave. Not yet. "That priest. What's his name?"

"Which one?" She colored the question with a glint of sarcasm. It wasn't much, just enough to show she wasn't *all* well-behaved. Not so disobedient as to deserve death, but a bit of a brat.

"Not the cripple. The one in charge."

"Father Ed."

"Father Ed," Mr. Beecham mused, then his expression darkened. A flame of hatred flickered in his eyes. "Ed Tyler. Of course. It fits."

"What fits?"

"Don't be impertinent. You have your assignment. Do it. And no more talking to detectives." He opened the door, paused, closed it, turned back. "Clare. You didn't tell Father Ed about our arrangement, did you?"

"Of course not. Why would I?"

"Not even in confession?"

She shook her head. She hadn't told Father Ed about Mr. Beecham or the nature of her assignations, only that she had them. Over and over. But it was best not to admit that.

"I hope not, for both your sakes."

Fleming stared at her hands, immobilized by fear.

"Confession. What an abomination. One's sins should be between oneself and God, no one else."

"*You* believe in God?" She couldn't resist another bit of bad behavior. She already knew the answer. No way was this beast at all religious.

Mr. Beecham grinned. "Cheeky girl. God is a useful fiction. A great motivator. But you don't need a fictional God. I'm your god now." He made a gun gesture at her forehead. "Behave yourself, saith the lord."

He left.

Fleming shook for she didn't know how long before rushing the door and locking and bolting it. Back against the wall, she slid to the floor and sobbed for a long, long time.

†

Peller was in a strange mood that morning. As he listened to Dumas' intuitions in the break room over coffee, he grew impatient, not because his colleague's ideas lacked interest, but because he was tired of sitting at his desk while everyone else did the leg work. Yes, his brain absorbed the details, but he couldn't focus on them, not completely. He needed visuals.

"Suppose Mark Tyler was involved with someone like Clare Fleming."

"Not Fleming," Peller said absently.

"Of course not. She wasn't into spy stuff back then. But someone like her. And suppose he found out what was going on and confronted the woman."

"Okay." Although, Peller didn't really suppose. He wanted to review Trengove's interviews with Mark Tyler's family. And talk to them himself, now they had the gun. Probably had the gun. The ballistics report would tell them for sure. Either way, the family at least should know HCPD was still on the case, still seeking justice for them.

Dumas spread his hands. "She kills him."

"Why?

His colleague stared at him, probably surprised that Peller was being so slow.

"Because he knows too much?" Peller suggested, then wished he hadn't. How trite can you get?

"Because she's scared."

"She kills him with a twenty-two pistol in her quivering hand, then cleverly hides it far from the scene where it might never be found. Because she's scared."

"Exactly."

"If she's that scared, doesn't she drop the gun? Or take it with her?"

"Scared doesn't mean stupid, Rick. Not always."

It often did. But it was a hypothesis, anyway. "How do we test it?"

"No idea." Dumas took a sip of coffee.

Neither did Peller. Since they couldn't, it made no difference. "Let's leave that to the FBI."

"Seriously?"

"Seriously. They'll track down Clare Fleming's employer. Through him, they'll find any other recruits and with luck Tyler's killer."

Dumas stared into his cup. "Or her."

"Her?"

"Fleming's employer could be a woman."

Peller pushed back from the table and drained his cup. "Whatever. Let's focus on the leads we have. I'll take Father Ed's family, you take Father Walter's."

Dumas finished his coffee, crushed the cup, and took it to the trash. "You and Joan didn't have a fight, did you?"

Peller tossed his empty, too. He hadn't even talked to Joan since Sunday, which, now he thought about it, might be the problem. But he wasn't about to discuss that. "I'll run your idea by Corina, too."

"Oh?"

"To get a Catholic perspective. If you're right, Mark Tyler might've confessed the affair to Father Ed."

"His own brother?"

Peller shrugged. "If they were close, why not?"

"Why not Father Dan, or whoever was priest at St. Paul back then? That was Tyler's church."

"I suppose. But if he's the connection between the two, someone could suspect he told someone at one or the other, if not both."

Dumas wandered through his own thoughts but didn't offer further insights. "All right," he said. "Father Walter's family. I'll file a report on all the boring questions and useless answers. I know you're champing at the bit to read it."

"Must've been a good honeymoon," Peller muttered to himself as they parted ways. He stopped by Montufar's desk and told her Dumas' speculations, and his own. "Would Mark Tyler have made confession to Father Ed?"

Montufar nearly laughed. "Not likely. It's not forbidden, but priests hearing confession for family members? That's frowned upon. For one thing, it can lead to major embarrassment. Tyler would have gone to another priest, and if not, I expect Father Ed would have sent him elsewhere."

"Where?"

"Any priest would do. Probably one at St. Paul. That was his church. Besides, there was no priest but Father Ed at St. Augustine at that time. A deacon served with him, but deacons can't hear confession."

"Suppose Tyler talks to his brother first, then confesses at St. Paul. Someone knows he's talked to both priests and believes they both have knowledge of his affair with a woman connected to an espionage ring. The graffiti is a warning to both to keep their mouths shut." Peller shook his head. "No, that's too complicated."

Montufar raised an eyebrow.

"You disagree?"

"Not exactly, but if the perp knows anything about Catholicism, which I suspect they do, they know about the seal of the confessional."

"They have no reason to worry about Father Dan, or whoever was at St. Paul at the time."

She pointed at Peller in acknowledgement, then added, "Tyler died six years ago. Father Ed says six years is on the cusp of how long priests typically serve at one church in the D.C. archdiocese. Father Dan may not have been at St. Paul at that time."

"But Mark Tyler might have told Father Ed outside of confession."

"Yes, but that still only explains the attacks on St. Augustine."

Peller felt a headache coming on. "It would be so much easier if Father Walter was the target," he grumbled. "But he wasn't around then, either, and I don't suppose retired priests hear confession anyway."

"They do. Retired doesn't mean the same thing for priests as for most people. When you think retirement, you imagine never working a case again."

"I don't know. That might be boring."

Montufar laughed. "I should've known you'd say that. Retired priests are still priests. They can say mass, take confessions, everything. Physical condition might prevent an older priest from performing some duties, but taking confession isn't physically strenuous."

"Well, Tyler's killing has to tie in somehow."

"Maybe not. We don't know he was having an affair with a *femme fatale*."

"That's Eric's intuition," Peller reminded her.

She gave him her stern cop look. "Don't use my husband against me, Rick."

Peller laughed. "I wouldn't dream of it. As it happens, I'm off to find some facts for you now."

And off he went.

First order of business was a review of Bill Trengove's interviews with the Tyler family. At the time of his death, Mark Tyler had a wife, a son who was a junior at University of Maryland Baltimore County studying information technology—*just like dear old dad,* Peller thought—and a daughter who was a high school senior. Trengove interviewed all three, plus Father Ed, Mark's younger brother. They proved uninformative interviews.

The wife, Bianca, knew of no reason anyone would want her spouse dead. He'd been a loving husband, a model father, and a hard worker. He had a few neighborhood friends he played golf with on occasion. Bianca gave Trengove their names. The son, Ben, had nothing but good to say about his father, while the daughter, Mary, was too sunk in grief to say much at all, although Trengove surmised she had a strong bond with her father. Those golf partners had nothing but praise for Tyler, knew of no enemies, could make no sense of his killing.

Father Ed didn't want to talk about it. Trengove's notes on the latter interview were unusually terse. Peller figured his colleague found Father Ed's reticence more than a little irritating. Peller got that, having talked to the priest himself.

Normally, time dulled memories and degraded evidence, but it could have one positive effect. Once people had sufficiently reflected on events, they sometimes discovered hints of buried truth. Hoping that might be the case here, Peller called Bianca Tyler. When he identified himself, there was a frightened, hopeful pause.

"Have you found something?" she asked, voice quivering.

"We have," Peller said. "I don't want to raise your hopes too much, but it could lead to identifying your husband's killer."

Another pause, then she said, "Tell me." A command, not a request.

"We think we found the weapon."

She choked down a sob.

"We're waiting for the ballistics report," Peller continued. "But it's the same caliber as the weapon your husband was shot with, and it was found discarded in the woods of Centennial Park, where it had been for some time, based on its reported condition."

"In the park? Why didn't you find it before?"

"It was a good distance from the crime scene and well-hidden. A teenager tramping through the woods uncovered it. If it is the same weapon, the killer stashed it where nobody would look."

Tyler didn't say a word.

Peller could imagine the barrage of hope, fear, grief, and anger assaulting her. He'd experienced the same confusion of emotions when new facts concerning Sandra's death emerged. "Mrs. Tyler," he said. "Six years ago, you didn't know of any reason your husband would have been killed. Has anything occurred to you in the time since?"

"I…" Another long pause. "You can't know what it's like."

"I actually do," he said, soft and gentle. "My wife was killed six years ago, too." *Six years next month*, he added to himself. *And I'm still dazed, taking one blind step after another, no clear destination in mind.* "You've been over it a thousand times, a million times, wondering how it could have been prevented, wondering if only you had changed this or that, would he still be here? And the answer is always no. Because you can't change anything. There isn't much you would have changed, anyway. A mistake here and there, maybe, but nothing that would have prevented this."

He heard her draw a long, unsteady breath. He waited.

"Lieutenant, I…yes, you're right. But it was worse than that. I suffered over a year of depression. I'm still seeing a therapist. Some days I feel barely functional." She drew a shuddering breath.

Peller gave her space to compose her thoughts.

"Ed and Mark were close once," she continued, "but after Ed found his calling, they drifted apart. No, that's not quite right. They weren't estranged. They just didn't have that much in common anymore. They got together at family gatherings. Birthdays, holidays. You know. But they never called each other. They never just visited. We normally attended St. Paul, but on rare occasion we'd go to St. Augustine. Mark and Ed would hi, but that was it. Sometimes I wanted to slap the pair of them." She laughed a little, but not a happy laugh.

"How frequent were those visits?"

"Two, maybe three times a year at most."

Not much, but another potential connection between the two churches. "Did Mark and Father Ed have a disagreement?"

"In a way. In college, Mark lost interest in religion. That sounds weird, I suppose. He didn't lose his faith, not really. He just didn't see it as very important. His intellectual pursuits took precedence. In some ways, he was still very much Catholic, at least a Christmas-and-Easter Catholic. Some of his opinions came straight from the Vatican. But others…some would call them heretical. I think Ed felt betrayed, and Mark thought Ed shouldn't have become a priest. He sometimes said it wasn't a good use of his brother's talents. But Ed had a calling that he couldn't deny. They're both very smart, really, just in different ways."

An interesting dynamic, possibly explaining why Father Ed kept his mouth shut when Trengove interviewed him. But did it play into Mark's death?

"Right before he was killed," Bianca went on, "Mark and Ed spent the weekend together at a rental home in the mountains. It was Mark's idea. He told me he wanted to reconnect with Ed. It was out of the blue, but it sounded positive. I didn't question it. When Mark got back, all he said was they had a good time hiking and talking. He was unusually vague, but I didn't give it much thought, and then he was dead, and..."

Peller could imagine. Death pushed everything else aside for months.

"Two years later, my therapist said I should ask Ed about that weekend. She said it would be good for me to hear something positive Mark did in his last days. So I asked, but Ed wouldn't talk about it. He said it was too painful. I tried a few more times, but he's not the most open person to begin with, and eventually I gave up."

"Do you think that weekend had something to do with Mark's death?" Peller asked.

"I don't know. How could it? But if it does, and it's something bad..."

She didn't need to say more. Some people felt compelled to dig until every moldering secret was unearthed. Others didn't want their polished memories stained. "I'll be as discreet as possible," Peller promised.

"Thank you, Lieutenant."

After writing up his notes on the interview, Peller leaned back, hands locked behind his head, and read them over three times, Bianca Tyler's words murmuring in his ears. Something wasn't right. Mark Tyler decides to reconcile with his brother "out of the blue," and four days later he's dead. Another of those coincidences Dumas wouldn't like. They were piling up so fast, Peller couldn't ignore them.

He had to convince Father Ed to talk.

†

Dumas, meanwhile, made a call of his own. He had three possible interview subjects: Janice Navin, Alex Navin, or Carlyle Navin. Alex was only related to Father Walter through marriage to his sister Janice, so he could wait. Dumas flipped the half-dollar he used for magic practice, heads for Janice, tails for Carlyle. Tails it was.

Hmm. Maybe he should make it two out of three. Janice was likely closer to Father Walter, being his sister.

He flipped again. Tails again.

Fine, whatever.

He called the number Shelly Beck had given him for Carlyle and got voice mail. So much for coin-based decision-making. He left a message, then started to call Janice, but something niggled at him, some small detail he'd forgotten to check on. What was it? Oh, right. He needed to ask Corina something.

About ninety seconds after Peller vacated Montufar's cubicle, Dumas took his place. He sat in the guest chair, legs stretched and crossed at the ankles, and gave his wife a smile. She returned it with an "I'd rather be alone with you than here" twist, which momentarily derailed his thoughts. Why had he come here? Oh, right.

"You don't know the Navins, do you?"

Her smile evaporated in puzzlement. "I don't think so. Why?"

"They attend St. John."

Montufar thought about it but came up empty. "Let me call Eduardo," she suggested.

Dumas waited while she placed the call. Eduardo took his time answering. "Hey big brother," she said at last. "Oh, you know. Vandalism, road rage, phantom gunshots in the woods. Slow day. Can I put you on speaker? Eric wants to ask you something. Thanks." She punched the button and added, "You're on." To Dumas she said, "Make it short. He's at work."

"Hey there, new little brother," Eduardo said with a healthy dose of cheer. "You want the inside scoop on some embarrassing secret about Corina, right?"

Montufar put a hand to her mouth and suppressed a laugh.

"Some other time," Dumas said. "Today it's just business."

"Okay, shoot. Not literally, though."

"Do you know the Navin family? They attend St. John."

"Navin. Maybe. Let me think."

Dumas watched the phone. Montufar watched Dumas. He only noticed her gaze on him a second before Eduardo answered, which was a bit of a shame, really.

"Yes, I've met them once or twice. I can't say I know them. Husband and wife, forty-five or fifty years old I think, one or two grown children. Maybe. I never met the kids. Why? Are they in trouble?"

"No trouble," Dumas assured him. "Their names popped up in connection with an investigation. I'm about to talk with Janice Navin. She might have some helpful information. I thought it might break the ice if I could drop your name."

"Feel free to drop it. Just don't break it." Eduardo laughed. "She might remember me, but probably not in any detail."

"Eduardo," Montufar chided. "You're the sort people always remember."

"Touché. When are you guys coming over for dinner? Sylvia's begging to cook for you again."

"Yeah, and to find out when the baby's due. I'm afraid she'll have to wait a while for that."

"No stork deliveries during an investigation," Eduardo teased. "Got it."

After they said their farewells, Montufar disconnected and arched her eyebrows at Dumas.

"Baby," Dumas said. "That's a thing already, huh?"

"What did you expect?"

"A little lead time, anyway. I gotta get used to wearing this ring." He held up his hand, as though she didn't know what he was talking about.

"Go conduct your interview, Sergeant."

"Right away, Sergeant."

He was in a good mood when he dialed Janice Navin's number. Navin answered on the fourth ring, and he introduced himself. In the puzzled silence, Dumas interjected, "You don't know me, but my wife and I attend the same church as you. You don't happen to know the Montufar family, do you?"

"The name's familiar," Navin said. She sounded like she expected a scam pitch to follow.

"Corina Montufar is my wife. We just got married."

Silence.

"Never mind, not important. Just curious. I'm investigating incidents of vandalism at a couple of Catholic Churches lately. I understand you're Father Walter Simmons' sister."

"Yes, I am. Is he okay? He took a fall a few days ago, and—"

"He's fine," Dumas assured her. "Up and about against doctor's orders, from what I've heard."

She laughed. "Thank God. I was afraid...how can I help you?"

"The incidents involve both St. Augustine and St. Paul. I'm doing some routine follow-ups on connections between the two. Your brother is one of them."

"What do you mean?"

"Just that he lives at the one and sometimes visits the latter."

"What's wrong with that?"

"Nothing, Mrs. Navin. He's just one of the connections."

Navin was quiet for a moment, probably trying to read between the lines, but she came up empty. "Okay. What do you want to know?"

"Can you think of any reason anyone might want to harm your brother?"

"Harm him! No, of course not!"

That felt too emphatic. Or was it just her personality? Dumas wished he could see her face. "I'm not accusing him of anything. I want to protect him. If he needs protecting?" He lifted his pitch into a question to prompt Navin, if she had anything to admit. But either she didn't or the invitation didn't work.

"Walter's the sort of guy everyone likes. Nobody in the world could have a reason to hurt him."

The direct approach having flopped, Dumas switched gears. "He attended mass with you at St. Paul last summer, right?"

"Yes. We have a family picnic every summer. We always go to mass together then."

"You and your husband no longer live in that parish, though?"

"We moved some years ago. As you said, we attend St. John now."

"So why not take Father Walter there?"

"We would have if we had hosted the picnic. It was our son Carlyle's turn. He still lives in the St. Paul parish."

"I see," Dumas said. "Are he and Father Walter close?"

"Somewhat. They don't see each other much, but they enjoy playing chess when they're together. Walter takes an interest in Carlyle's career."

"Oh? What does Carlyle do?"

Navin didn't answer right away. Maybe she thought Dumas was getting too personal without good cause. But she didn't clam up. Not yet. "He's a software engineer."

Another computer guy. What the hell? "What company does he work for?"

"I can never remember the name. Some small contracting outfit."

"Government contracting?"

"Why does this matter, Sergeant?"

Dumas laughed. It sounded forced even to his own ears. "Honestly? I don't know. I'm admittedly fishing. Any little detail might be relevant."

"Then let me be blunt. Whatever's going on, Walter has nothing to do with it. He's a good man and a good priest. Everybody likes him. Take your fishing pole elsewhere."

She cut the connection before he could respond.

Nice. Dumas tapped in his notes, then reread them. Another computer guy. Okay, there were a lot of them out there. A lot of government contractors, too. D.C. was just down the road, after all. But why were they clustering around this case?

Chapter 12

"I'd call this irregular," Trengove told Peller as he navigated the roads to St. Augustine in his gray—stealth gray, he called it—1997 Accura Integra. "Granted, ninety percent of your work is irregular." He glared at the cars surrounding them as though longing to ticket the lot of them for just being there.

Peller smiled, half at the comment, half at the thought. "Don't exaggerate. It can't be more than fifty."

"It could be. Morris likes you."

"You make her laugh, though. Don't discount the value of that."

"I don't. It's the only reason she hasn't kicked my butt clear to Wyoming."

"You're exaggerating again," Peller told him. "As for this stunt, it's not so irregular as it might seem. You investigated Mark Tyler's murder, after all."

Trengove shot him an irritated glance. "You could've sent Corina with me. Or do you honestly think two lieutenants will intimidate that priest more than one? My mean face didn't faze him last time, and you don't have a mean face."

"Sure, I do."

"Not as mean as mine."

Peller had to give him that. Trengove always looked ready to bite someone's head off, even when he was in a good mood. Genetics had done that to him. His round face had a strangely weather-beaten look, as though he'd spent his life riding a sun-scorched range or piloting a trawler through Nor'easters. One glance at him could send a suspect's heart into palpitations.

Trengove leaned on the horn as someone cut him off, then he changed lanes and accelerated by the offending vehicle, which slowed to make a right turn. "I could be relaxing at my desk," he grumbled. "I do have other cases. Did you hear what Andy Newton's doing?"

"I try to stay out of your lane."

"Some idiot crashing through farm gates out in the west end of the county, beyond Lisbon. No pattern to it. Just rustic structures of opportunity. Probably some drunk teenager who thinks it's fun to smash things."

"And you'd rather be doing that than this?"

"Yes, actually."

When they arrived, they parked near the church and walked through the courtyard. Peller indicated the Mary statue. "The first message was there, the second on a window on the far side of the rectory."

"And the crab basket?"

Thumbing over his shoulder, Peller said, "back there, alongside the church."

Trengove did a three-sixty rotation while walking, taking in the surroundings. "How does Mark Tyler's murder fit in?"

"Not sure yet, but it does."

"Why?"

"Because Eric says so."

"Makes as much sense as a crab basket on a saint's head."

"Corina says that's symbolic."

"The murder wasn't." Trengove sounded particularly grim. "That was fear. I'd put money on it."

Peller agreed, and he figured that fear and Clare Fleming's had the same root. But that didn't provide any connection to the vandalism.

They reached the door and rang the bell. A moment later, Fleming peeked out. "Oh, Lieutenant Peller!" She almost melted with relief. "Come on in." She motioned her guests inside.

"This is Detective Lieutenant Bill Trengove," Peller said. Trengove nodded, his hand rising and falling as though to tip a nonexistent hat. "We'd like a few moments of Father Ed's time, if possible."

"Sure, come on in."

Fleming led them to the living room and got them settled, then vanished into the back. The stairs creaked as she ascended to the priest's office. A moment later, Father Ed came down and greeted the detectives with a weak smile. "I haven't seen you in a while," he told Trengove.

"A few years," Trengove acknowledged without enthusiasm.

Fleming trotted down and vanished into the kitchen, giving Peller another relieved glance. He wondered what was worrying her now.

Father Ed lowered himself into the easy chair. "I don't mean to complain, but this is becoming obsessive. We've had no further incidents. I think the vandal's had his fun and run off."

"Do you," Trengove said.

Father Ed looked away.

"That's not why Lieutenant Peller dragged me out here. We may have found the gun used to kill your brother."

Peller studied Father Ed's reaction. The priest's eyes widened in surprise. He leaned forward as though begging for information, then sank back. Peller recognized that momentary glimmer of hope. He'd seen it time and again in grieving relatives informed of a break in their case. Mostly, it had been genuine. But Father Ed snuffed it the moment it ignited. What did he fear?

"Do you know who killed him?" Father Ed asked.

Trengove shook his head. "Not yet, but it's a step forward."

"Okay. Thank you."

The detectives stared at him. He folded his hands in his lap, twined and untwined his fingers, didn't or couldn't ask what was on their minds.

"One other thing," Peller said. "I spoke with your sister-in-law Bianca. She told me you and your brother had grown distant after you entered the priesthood."

Father Ed shrugged. "Mark chose one path, I chose another."

"But you didn't often visit or even make phone calls. Not for many years."

"We both got busy, I guess."

"It was more than that, Father. According to Bianca, four days before Mark was killed, the two of you took a weekend trip to Western Maryland. Mark said he wanted to reconnect with you. He never told Bianca much else. She said he was uncharacteristically vague."

Trengove gave Peller an annoyed glance but didn't ask when that tidbit surfaced.

For rather a long time, Father Ed stared at his hands while somewhere in the house a clock ticked and outside a breeze stirred the leaves. A clattering from the kitchen signaled Fleming at work cleaning or cooking. Peller waited, his patience greater than Trengove's. The latter started drumming his fingers on the arm of the couch.

When Father Ed spoke, it was almost in a whisper. "Gentlemen, what passed between my brother and I was personal."

"He died four days later," Trengove said without mercy. "Shot repeatedly in the chest by someone in a panic, someone I think your brother threatened."

"Mark would never threaten anyone."

"He could seem a threat," Peller said.

Trengove leaned forward. "Look me in the eye and swear before God what he said to you had zero to do with his murder."

Father Ed sank into the chair. He didn't look Trengove in the eye, didn't swear to anything.

"That's what I thought," Trengove said. He stood and grimaced at Peller. "I'm stepping out before I do something I'll regret. You can pry it out of him."

Peller watched Trengove stalk into the kitchen. A hint of conversation drifted out. Fleming laughed. Whatever Trengove was up to, Peller would find out later. He turned his attention back to Father Ed. "Lieutenant Trengove is right, Father. It has bearing. You know it does. Why would you obstruct the investigation of your own brother's murder?"

"Because he *is* my brother. Because our differences notwithstanding, he was as good a man as any. His family should be allowed to remember him that way."

"Why wouldn't they?"

Father Ed rose and went to the kitchen door. "Could we have some iced tea?" he asked. Fleming's voice assented, and a moment later he returned with two glasses. He offered one to Peller. Peller didn't really want anything, but he accepted it and took a sip to be congenial. Father Ed drained half his glass in one long gulp.

"Did he ask you to take his confession?" Peller assumed not, given what Montufar had said.

"No. We just talked."

"Then you can speak freely about it. I'll keep it as confidential as possible." A weak promise, given it was part of a murder investigation, but Peller hoped it would suffice.

"Mark asked for spiritual guidance. At least, that's how I took it. He didn't phrase it that way. He said he needed advice."

"He was having an affair," Peller guessed.

Father Ed gaped, but only for a moment. "Police and priests. We see the same things over and over, don't we?" He took another long drink. "Did you know twenty percent of married men and thirteen percent of married women report having an affair? I'm surprised it's that high, and that low. Either way, it's not uncommon. But I was shocked Mark had fallen into that trap. He'd always been a devoted husband and father."

And was it ever a trap, Peller thought, but he didn't interrupt.

"He and his coworkers sometimes met after work for food and drinks. That's where he met her. A young woman, about thirty, pretty, outgoing. She chatted him up. He thought she worked for his company. That's why he talked to her. But no. Her name was Amelia Jenkins, a bookkeeper with her own little business. She always wanted to get into computers but never got the chance, so his line of work fascinated her. She asked if he could help her find training and job placement. That hit Mark right where he lived. He loved helping people. Next thing he knew, he was seeing her once a week over lunch, then one day they drove to a park and…and…had relations. In his car."

Father Ed finished his tea and set the glass aside. He made a face at it, as though it contained a hint of poison. "It went downhill from there. He saw her once or twice a week. Took her to motels. Amelia started asking questions about his job, the procedures they followed, how facility security worked. The security questions scared him. That's when he realized her interest wasn't personal. He came to me for advice."

"What did you tell him?" Peller asked.

"What do you think? I told him to stop seeing her, report her to the appropriate authorities, and get to confession."

That would be a priest's answer but maybe not entirely correct. The government might have wanted to use Mark Tyler to get to the woman's handler. "Why not have him confess to you?" Peller asked. "You already knew the details. It couldn't get any more awkward."

Locking his hands together again, Father Ed stared absently at the wall behind Peller. "I couldn't offer him absolution."

"Why not?"

"Because I couldn't forgive him myself. I failed him in that. He'd betrayed Bianca, his kids, even me. I always believed his fundamental goodness would lead him back home to the Church, but when he told me what he'd done…" Father Ed closed his eyes. A few tears leaked out.

"It led him back to you," Peller said. "That should count for something."

"It does." The priest wiped away the moisture and opened his eyes again. They had a distant look now. "After the worst of the grief ran its course, I did forgive him. I pray for him every day. It pains me that I couldn't do it while he was still with us."

Was this the reason for the graffiti? Father Ed knew about Amelia Jenkins, but not through confession. He could be a threat to her. But then, why attack St. Paul, too? "Did Mark have contact information for Amelia Jenkins? Address? Phone number?"

"Give me a minute." Father Ed rose and vanished ups the stairs. His steps fell heavy on the treads as he made his way up and back down. When he returned, he had a cell phone in hand. He rummaged through its contents until he found what he was looking for. "There's a phone number for an 'AJ'. It looks like he never used it. No call history, no texts. I suppose he kept it cleared out." He showed Peller the number.

Peller snapped a photo with his own phone. "Why do you have this?"

"Bianaca gave it to me. I offered to contact anyone who might need to know of his passing." He dropped into his chair, leaned his head back, closed his eyes. He looked half dead himself. "I didn't want her stumbling on anything incriminating. Besides, she was in no shape for calling relatives and friends. When you lose a spouse..."

"Been there myself," Peller said. "The first things you must do are always the last things you want to do."

"Do you really think you can find out who killed him?"

Peller already knew. Mark Tyler confronted Amelia Jenkins. She panicked and killed him. Everything he had fit, but it was all circumstantial. He still needed solid evidence. "I hope so," he said. "We'll keep you posted." Getting to his feet, Peller nodded toward the kitchen. "Let me get my partner away from the food, and we'll be out of your way."

Father Ed finally cracked a smile.

†

"I was *not* eating," Trengove grumbled. "I was being polite. When a chef asks your opinion, it's rude to decline."

"And it was such a good carrot cake," Peller agreed. Clare Fleming had offered him a sample, too.

"Ah-ha," Trengove said, triumphant. "I rest my case."

No use denying it.

They were on their way back to HQ, making their way south on the two-lane Old Washington Road, passing aging homes shaded by aging trees. The neighborhood reminded Peller of his hometown of Lockport, New York. The familiarity put him at ease, almost made him forget the tangled mess he was investigating. Almost.

"What did you talk about, besides baking?" Peller asked.

"Was there anything else to talk about?"

"You don't leave an interview just because someone's ticked you off. Everyone ticks you off. Even me. Yet here you are, driving me back to the office."

"I'm sure as hell not leaving you in charge of my car."

"You could walk off with the keys."

"Then how would I get back? And don't say a cab. The great County of Howard pays us the same wage."

Peller laughed.

"We talked about her predicament," Trengove said. "Or rather, I grilled her about it, and she said next to nothing."

"Distracted you with that cream cheese frosting, did she?"

Trengove tilted a look of rebuke toward Peller. "You think I'm that gullible?"

"She probably knows the old saying. The way to a man's heart..."

"I hope you and Joan get things figured out soon. You're becoming intolerable."

That was a conversation-killer. Neither said anything until they were breezing by the ivy-draped sound barriers along Route 100. Only then did Trengove return to the real subject. "Fleming has cause for not talking. If she talks, she's dead."

"Thus her request for protection," Peller said. "We already figured that out."

"Fortunately, I'm a charming fellow and got a bit more. She's not only afraid for herself. She's afraid for Father Ed. She asked me to protect him, too."

Peller tried to slot that tidbit into the maze of the information. At first, it felt like a piece from the wrong jigsaw puzzle. Then he realized what it meant. "Mark Tyler's AJ worked for the same handler as Fleming. The handler thinks Father Ed might lead us to him."

"Bingo. Or bingo-ish. Who's AJ?"

"Amelia Jenkins, the woman who tried to weasel information out of Mark Tyler. She was probably using a pseudonym, but I have her phone number."

"How many women's phone numbers are you carting around these days?"

"Father Ed found it on his brother's phone."

"Likely story." Trengove glared at a driver who flew by in the right lane, probably doing thirty over the speed limit. "Somebody should shoot out that guy's tires."

"Why does Fleming think her handler knows enough about Father Ed to be worried?"

"He asked the priest's name and acted strange when she told him."

"He's connected Father Ed with Mark."

"I'd say so."

Peller didn't like the sound of that. "I don't suppose she mentioned her handler's name?"

Trengove rolled his eyes. "Obviously not, but she wouldn't know his real name. She did say he's Asian. Then she clammed up and fed me carrot cake so I'd forget."

Asian made sense. Most geopolitical actors coveted U.S. secrets, but none more than China. "I guess that's a bone we can toss to the feds," Peller said.

"Sure," Trengove agreed. "That narrows it down to, what, a third of a million people in Maryland? Assuming he/she/it is local."

"Okay," Peller conceded. "Maybe not a bone. Maybe a training treat."

Trengove laughed. "Rick, I do believe you've been hanging around me too much."

"Maybe so. But since we work for the same department, I'm stuck with it."

"Aren't we both."

†

The requested insurance claims info dropped into Holly Ross' inbox late on Thursday. Another strikeout. None of those Escalades had been involved in matching accidents. But ten minutes later, she received a call that more than compensated. A new Angry Granny attack had been reported, and best of all…

"Suspect all but in custody," the dispatcher told her. "Care to make a house call, or should we bring her in?"

"Let her wait," Ross said. The woman deserved it. Besides, while the responders would have documented everything, she had a hankering to see the offending vehicle *in situ*. Sometimes eyeballs were better, or at least more satisfying, than a camera. "What's the twenty?"

"Laurel Woods Elementary."

A school. Great.

The dispatcher gave the address and added, "That's a few blocks down Laurel Road from the Emerson complex."

Ross recognized the location. Emerson was a cluster of federal offices not far from the earlier incident in the strip mall. "Yep. She's staying close to home. Is the vehicle in the parking lot or on the street?"

"Sounds like she scored hits in both."

Even better. "This I gotta see. Tell them I'm en route."

"Ten-four. Just remember what curiosity did to the cat."

Everybody had to be a comedian. Ross headed into the wilds of Howard County.

Her destination, like most elementary schools, huddled in the middle of a residential area. Townhomes and single-family houses surrounded it. The schoolyard was edged with trees. Behind, a stand of woods spread beyond the athletic fields. The building wasn't much to look at: low, red brick, a parking lot and marquis in front. Pretty much a clone of every other school its age. But today it wore its educational attire with a difference: four police cruisers boxing in a powder blue Escalade on the street just beyond the parking lot exit, while the furious driver screamed through her open window in solid English with a thick Mexican accent, berating the lot of them for their incompetence.

"*They* hit *me*, you morons! Any fool could see *I* am the victim! Arrest *them*, why don't you!"

And so forth and so on. She looked to be in her sixties. Her dark hair, going a bit gray, was cropped short. A pair of silver-rimmed glasses perched far out on her nose, allowing her to sneer over them at the officers.

Ross slipped from her car. One of the officers, noting her arrival, motioned her over with the enthusiasm of a wounded soldier cheering the arrival of reinforcements. "Officer Bennett," she acknowledged when she drew near.

"Detective Ross. Thank God. What do we do with this..." Bennett glanced at the woman, who was spewing nonstop vitriol at his colleagues. "Lady." He made a face, suggesting he wished he could use a less complimentary term.

Out of character for him. Bennett was slow to judgement and even slower to anger. Ross had been in academy with him and liked him. She could see him "growing up" to be another Kevin Graham, if only he could develop a mean face. But he didn't seem to have one. Not yet. Maybe this incident would change that. "Who did she hit?" Ross asked.

Pointing to the parking lot, Bennett indicated the last four vehicles before the exit. "Gray Civic, black Camry, white Mazda, black Impala. Bing, bam, boom, right down the line. Strafed every rear bumper. Tore off the Imapala's. Then she pulled onto the street and sideswiped that blue Mazda. The driver swerved to avoid getting t-boned. No injuries, at least."

"Her defense is they all hit her?" Ross put a hand to her mouth to cover an almost-laugh.

Bennett grimaced. "Yeah."

"Okay, let me have a go at it." Ross approached the Escalade. The clustered officers retreated a few steps, all as relieved as Bennett at her arrival.

The irate driver, realizing in mid-tantrum that someone new was on the scene, twisted to throw a few invectives at Ross. But the appearance of such a slight woman, a woman with a Native American look in her eyes and hair and skin, threw her off. She stared, mouth open, and waited.

"Hi," Ross said. "I'm Detective Holly Ross. What's your name, ma'am?"

The woman closed her mouth. She glared at the officers clustered behind Ross. "I don't know anymore. They took my license."

Ross hadn't expected that sort of answer, but she could run with it. She turned and held out her hand. One of the officers passed the license to her. "Carlotta Becerra," she read. "Mrs. Becerra?"

"At least *someone* here shows some respect. Give me that." Becerra held out her hand.

Ross glanced back at the officers. "Done with this?" she asked.

They all nodded, so she returned it to Becerra. "What brings you here today, Mrs. Becerra?"

"My grandson goes to school there." She thumbed at the building. "I came to pick him up, but those stupid teachers let him go home with someone else. They should have told me! I not only wasted my time, all these cars hit me!" She waved around as though implicating every vehicle in the neighborhood. "And now these fools are arresting the wrong person!"

Ross wasn't sure which was more disturbing, Mrs. Becerra blaming parked cars for the collisions or the school releasing her grandson to someone else. "What's your grandson's name?"

Mrs. Becerra made a face. "Roger." Obviously, that wasn't the name she would have picked.

"Who did Roger go home with?"

"His stupid father."

A certain amount of insanity was the lot of police officers everywhere, but Ross was starting to suspect it dogged her more than her colleagues. She'd have to compare notes on that with Theresa Swan. "You didn't know he was picking up Roger?"

"Of course not! Would I be here if I did? He works late all the time. In those big buildings." She motioned in the direction of the Emerson complex. "*All* the time these days. But the one day my daughter asks me to pick up Roger, that's the day he decides to be a dad for a change. Except he doesn't tell me! Totally irresponsible. Rotten to the core. He has no business being a father."

Family drama was the worst. No cop liked to walk into a domestic dispute. They always posed a threat of violence, and any officer on the scene could get caught in the crossfire. But this was different. Weirdly different. "Mrs. Becerra," Ross said as gently as possible. "Those cars you hit in the parking lot—"

"They hit *me!*" she insisted.

"Were their drivers in them at the time?"

She clamped her lips shut and looked away.

"Were they in motion?"

"They were badly parked," Mrs. Becerra insisted. "Butts hanging out in the lane."

"I see. What about the car you sideswiped when you pulled out onto the road?"

"He wasn't there when I started to pull out."

"He was there when you finished."

"He was speeding."

Ross didn't doubt it, but that didn't make Mrs. Becerra any less reckless. "I'm afraid," she said, "we're going to have to arrest you. Your vehicle's been implicated in several similar incidents."

Mrs. Becerra turned narrowed eyes on Ross and squeezed the steering wheel until her knuckles turned white. "I'll sue you," she snarled. "My son-in-law may be stupid, but he's got money. He can afford a top lawyer."

"Then he can also afford your bail," Ross said. "Just do yourself a favor and stop running into other vehicles. If you don't, you or someone else might get hurt, and then you'll be in real trouble." She turned to the officers. "All yours, boys," she said. She winked at them.

They looked like they'd rather be anywhere else.

Ross returned to her car and watched the arrest from a safe distance. Mrs. Becerra continued her tirade as they cuffed her, read her rights, and put her into one of the squads. Ross wondered what Mrs. Becerra's son-in-law did for a living to make that much money working for the government. Maybe he was a manager. Or a contractor with a security clearance. Cleared contractors were always in demand, she'd heard.

The pieces only fell into place halfway back to headquarters. Ross should have gotten the son-in-law's name and contact information. It looked like she'd have the pleasure of another conversation with Mrs. Becerra once she'd been processed.

Chapter 13

On Friday morning at nine A.M., Dumas pulled into the north parking lot of the Plum Tree Apartments, about three miles west of St. Paul, turned off the engine, and studied the buildings. They looked nice on the outside. Three floors, brown brick, clean lines, well-maintained grounds adorned with trees large and small. As for the inside, he'd soon find out. The complex's website suggested they were comfortable, maybe a bit pricey but not outrageous. Residents left generally good reviews. The place must be worth it, and hey, Carlyle Navin was a software engineer. Those guys made money sufficient to the purpose. Unlike cops.

Navin hadn't yet returned Dumas' call. Likely he'd already gone to work, but a quick check couldn't hurt. The apartment complex wasn't even ten minutes from HQ. Dumas exited his vehicle and strolled to Navin's building, buzzed the apartment number, and waited, hands stuffed in his jacket pockets. When he got an answer, the voice threw him. It wasn't Carlyle Navin. It was a woman.

"Who is it?" The fog of interrupted sleep tainted her voice.

"I'm sorry," Dumas said, "I may have the wrong apartment. I'm looking for Carlyle Navin."

After a curiously long pause, she repeated her question: "Who are you?"

"Detective Sergeant Eric Dumas, Howard County Police. I need a word with Mr. Navin, if he lives here."

The woman might have evaporated. Dumas checked a note on his phone. This was the apartment number he'd received from Shelly Beck, unless he'd entered it wrong. "Ma'am? Are you still there?"

"Yes, sorry. I, um, I just…never mind. Yes, Carlyle lives here."

Dumas figured she'd tried to rustle a good lie, but it evaded her. "May I come up?"

"Yeah, but...yeah, okay." A buzz sounded. The door clicked open. He pushed into the lobby and noted the bank of mailboxes, some with names and some without. Navin's last name was there, right where it should be. He mounted the stairs, knocked on the door, waited longer than expected. The woman ought to have been already peering through the peephole.

The door slipped open far enough for a pair of wide brown eyes to stare out. Dumas displayed his ID. "May I come in?"

She pulled the door open. She was on the short side, about five feet even. She craned her neck to look up at Dumas' face. Her body was wrapped in a light blue terry bathrobe, her feet bare.

"Sorry if I woke you," Dumas said. "I do need to speak with Mr. Navin, though. If he's here."

"Carlyle's working." Maybe she hoped that would make Dumas go away.

"Are you Mrs. Navin?" He had no information on Navin's relationship status, but she must be wife or girlfriend.

Or not. "No, I'm...no. We aren't together. Just roommates. Share the rent." She tried to hold Dumas's gaze but couldn't. She looked back over her shoulder. "Anyway, he's working."

"Where does he work?"

She shrugged.

"Does he work from home?"

She glanced back again without answering. That probably meant yes.

"Ma'am, it's really important I talk to him."

She swallowed. "Is he in trouble?"

Dumas had an impulse to push past her and find Navin himself, but he couldn't. No warrant, no probable cause, however strange the woman's reluctance. Time to turn on the charm. He smiled. "What's your name?"

"Mary."

"Hi, Mary. I'm Eric."

"You said that already."

"That was a while ago."

Mary cracked a smile. "Only a few minutes."

"Listen, Mary. Carlyle isn't in trouble. I just need to ask a few questions about an investigation we're conducting. Some of his family members might be peripherally connected, that's all. This is just routine stuff. To cover the bases, you know?"

Mary exhaled in relief but still didn't volunteer his whereabouts.

"How did you and Carlyle meet?"

Her eyes shifted away. "Um. At...church."

Dumas wondered why she bothered lying. She didn't have the knack. "I see. Which church?"

"Uh." Mary winced, no doubt realizing her mistake, but she bounced back quickly. "St. Peter's Episcopal."

Dumas recognized the name. An Ellicott City church. She'd picked a likely venue, aside from the fact that Navin's family was Catholic. "You must need your morning coffee." He gave her another smile. "Again, I'm sorry for waking you. Is Carlyle here, then?"

She thought for a moment, then relented. "He doesn't like to be... well. Yeah, he has an office in the spare bedroom."

"Can I wait on the couch while you get him?"

"Sure."

She led him into the living room, pointed without enthusiasm to a light blue sofa, and slunk into the back. Dumas gave the room a once-over. The furnishings suggested a discount store, but they were in mint condition. The sofa, a couple of swivel chairs of a similar color, a couple of glass-topped black metal tables of uninspired design. Navin and his friend had a modest TV on the wall, a few pop art prints in cheap frames, and one small bookcase stuffed with science fiction.

When Carlyle Navin showed up, he was alone. Although half a foot taller than his roommate, he was on the short side, skinny, dressed in black jeans and a black t-shirt, his golden hair a disarrayed mop. He wore black-framed glasses which he took off on entry. "Mary said you're a detective," he said. His voice was flat, devoid of emotion, devoid even of interest.

Dumas rose and showed his ID again. "Detective Sergeant Eric Dumas," he said. "Thank you for speaking with me, Mr. Navin."

Navin cocked his head. "About what?"

"Let's have a seat and I'll get into that."

"Sure."

Once they were settled, Navin leaned back, crossed his legs, and waited. A rather cooler customer than his roomie.

"I'm investigating incidents of vandalism at a couple of churches, one of them being your own, St. Paul."

"I haven't heard about that."

"You probably wouldn't have."

"So why are you here?"

"Because similar incidents occurred at St. Augustine, where your uncle, Father Walter Simmons, resides."

Navin pursed his lips and stared at Dumas, unflinching.

"We believe the incidents are connected."

"You think my uncle is involved?"

"He might be the target."

That disturbed Navin. He uncrossed his legs, frowned at the floor, shook his head. "That's ridiculous. Why would anyone want to hurt him?"

"Exactly the question. He lives at St. Augustine. He occasionally attends St. Paul with family. That makes him a possible link between the two."

"My uncle," Navin insisted, "is a good man. A harmless man. He has no enemies. It's ridiculous."

Dumas waited.

"It's not him. It can't be."

"Okay." The detective relaxed and draped an arm along the back of the couch. "Mary tells me you met at church."

Navin blinked. Good. It was news to him.

"Has she attended St. Paul long?"

"A while, yeah."

Not just good. Perfect. They hadn't agreed on a story. Was their relationship platonic, or had that been a lie, too? "What's her last name?"

Navin's control cracked. "You've wasted enough of my time. I need to get back to work." He sprang to his feet and waited for Dumas to leave.

Dumas took his time standing. "If either of you know anything about these incidents, you'd do well to tell me." He pulled his card from his wallet and passed it to Navin. "We tend to find out what we need to know, one way or another."

"There's nothing to tell," Navin insisted.

Oh, but there was. Who was Mary? What were these two hiding? As Dumas stepped out the door, he glanced back. Mary lurked in the darkened hall beyond the living room. He couldn't see her face, but he could feel her tension. She was afraid. Terrified.

Of what?

†

"Bless me, Father, for I allegedly have sinned. That's our condition, yes? We live, so we must have sinned. The only escape is death."

Father Ed raised an eyebrow. "That's not quite the form."

"Oh, I'm sorry. I'm supposed to say how long it's been since my last confession. I have never made confession. I don't intend to start today."

The penitent—apparently not so penitent—had called ahead and asked for confession behind a screen. Father Ed had no idea who he was talking to. He took up position in the reconciliation room ten minutes prior and waited, and at exactly ten thirty the man began to speak.

"No reaction, Father?"

"I'm surprised. Why ask for confession if you don't mean to make one?"

"To maintain confidentiality. Your lips are now sealed, are they not?"

An interesting question. If the request for confession was a ruse, did the seal of the confessional apply? Likely not. "That depends," he said. "If you wish to share a confidence, I'll keep it confidential if I can."

"A weak commitment," the unpenitent said. "But let's start there and see what happens."

"All right. Why are you here?"

"I am here about your brother."

A chill crawled up Father Ed's spine. "What about him?"

"What do you know about his death?"

The voice was unfamiliar. Father Ed had been trying to place it, but it wasn't any parishioner he knew, wasn't any of the detectives he'd talked to. Not that they would have pulled a stunt like this. He'd never met this man before. "He was shot," he said. "The police never found his killer."

"Why was he shot?"

"If anyone knew that, the police *would* have found the killer."

The other laughed. "Such confidence. But then, you are a man of faith."

"My faith is not in the institutions of men."

"Sound. But you shouldn't put it in imaginary beings, either."

"'The fool has said in his heart, there is no God.'"

"Psalm fourteen, verse one," the unpenitent said. "I've heard it. Did the killer confess to you? That would have been torture. Knowing who had done it, not being able to tell a soul. If I'd been the killer, I certainly would have come to you."

"Are you the killer?"

"God is the killer. He allowed it to happen. Answer the question."

Father Ed said nothing, neither to answer nor to respond to the mockery. There was evil here. Great evil. He knew better than to debate with the Father of Lies.

"What about your brother?"

"What about him?"

"Did he confess his sins to you?"

"One doesn't generally act as confessor for family members."

"That's not an answer."

"You've asked no question I *can* answer. Even without the seal of the confessional, some things are confidential."

"I like that. It implies that whatever you know—and you do know something—it will remain a secret. Even from the police. Yes?"

That cold sensation returned with a vengeance. Whoever he was, this man was involved in Mark's death. He knew the police were asking questions.

"Silence means assent. Good. I would *so* hate to watch a priest die."

Laughter.

Footsteps.

Father Ed was alone.

He told Corina Montufar he was willing to accept martyrdom. He asked himself if that was the truth. He prayed for the strength to accept whatever God willed for him.

Then he returned to the rectory and called his sister-in-law.

†

Peller called a meeting as soon as his team arrived. Coffees in hand, they took up residence in the conference room, and the boss quickly reviewed their status.

"Peter Zelly, a.k.a. Squirrel Shooter, got a slap on the wrist in exchange for showing us where he found his twenty-two, which we now know is the weapon used to kill Mark Tyler."

Swan made a face. "If you can call his mother a slap on the wrist."

Peller hadn't met the woman, but he'd heard the story. "We also have Carlotta Becerra for various road rage incidents."

"Parking lot rage, mostly," Ross amended. "With luck, she'll get some counselling."

"One would hope," Peller agreed. "I hate to think what might have happened on the highway. Your report mentions her son-in-law Rodrigo Paniagua. What's that about?"

Ross got the name in a follow-up conversation that was barely noted in her reports. "Maybe nothing, but according to Becerra, Paniagua makes big bucks working a government project. Given what we know about Clare Fleming, Mark Tyler, and Carlyle Navin, I thought it worth following up. As recently noted, Eric doesn't like coincidences." She winked at Montufar.

At least everyone was in a good mood. Peller allowed himself a smile while Dumas propped his head on his fist and gave Montufar a long-suffering look. "Paniagua bailed her out yesterday evening, yes?"

Ross nodded. "I had a quick talk with him. He affirmed he has a security clearance but naturally wouldn't talk about his work. When he picked up his son from school the other day, he forgot to inform grandma. He says she's normally a very kind lady and doesn't know why she's—to use his term—gone wacko lately."

"Dementia?" Dumas asked. "It's odd Paniagua would refer to Becerra as a kind lady, given how she talked about him. Was she snapping and snarling and smashing things because she was mad at the whole world, or was it something about him?"

It was an interesting question, but Peller couldn't see how they could work with it. "We don't have cause to dig into Paniagua's business," he said. "Not so far. But we might pass the info to the FBI and let them do what they will with it. Speaking of that, Captain Morris had a meeting with them yesterday and shared our progress to date. They're focused on Clare Fleming. We're to keep our distance from her, but everyone else is fair game for now. Which brings us to the fun stuff. Eric?"

Dumas drummed his fingers on the table for a moment, then he cleared his throat as though about to make a speech. But all he said was, "I'm puzzled."

"Uh-oh," Montufar whispered. "Here we go."

"I spoke with Carlyle Navin this morning. He claims no knowledge of the church vandalism and insists his uncle the Father can't be the target. He's a cool customer, hard to rattle, but he's lying through his teeth."

"About which?" Peller asked. "Or both?"

Dumas shrugged. "He has a roommate, a young lady named Mary, no last name volunteered. She claims they're just friends sharing the rent. They allegedly met at St. Peter's Episcopal."

That jolted everyone. Montufar snapped, "What?"

Dumas nodded. "Navin said they'd met at his church. It may have been someplace else entirely, though. Mary made that up on the spot. She gets points for imagination, but zero for delivery."

Montufar frowned at the table. Peller knew that look. Everyone did. They all gave her space to think. "Jacey's graphology report said one writer was emotional, passionate, and creative, the other even-tempered. The first was a take-charge person on a mission, the second balanced but with secrets. The first was the leader, the second the follower. Is that right?"

"Basically," Peller said. Montufar had phrased some of it differently but caught the essence.

"It could be them," she said. "Mary could be the leader, Carlyle the follower."

"Leader?" Dumas half-laughed but choked it off when Montufar raised an eyebrow at him. "The woman can't even tell a decent lie. She shoots from the hip."

"But Carlyle doesn't. And I'll bet she's got him wrapped around her finger."

Peller would have told her she was speculating wildly, but that wasn't her style. Based on Dumas' report, the personality profiles could fit. Plus, Navin attended St. Paul, and his uncle was a possible target of the graffiti. On top of that, something else niggled at Peller. He thought he knew who Mary was, but he couldn't pull her from the shadows of his memory.

"But why?" Swan asked. "Why would Navin attack his own uncle's church, his own uncle's *window*? That message must've frightened Father Walter. That's probably why he fell and hurt himself."

Father Walter hadn't admitted to that, but Peller agreed.

"That might not have been Carlyle's doing," Montufar pointed out. "Maybe Mary vandalized St. Augustine and Navin St. Paul."

"His own church," Swan objected.

They could speculate all day about that. They needed more data. "Let's find out who Mary is before we go too far down the rabbit hole," Peller said. "Let's see if she's connected to someone we've already interviewed." *That must be it*, he thought. *Why else would the name feel familiar?* "Let's also see if Mary and Carlyle will volunteer handwriting samples. If they aren't the vandals, that would eliminate them, while a refusal would be suggestive. Then we'd just need to find probable cause for a search warrant."

"That shouldn't be hard," Dumas predicted. "Whatever they are, they aren't pros. They were damn clumsy with a cop in their living room. I'll talk to Janice Navin again. Maybe she knows who Mary is."

"I'll follow up with Carlotta Becerra and Rodrigo Paniagua," Ross suggested.

She looked a bit too eager. Given her history, that might not be a good thing. "What's to follow up?" Peller asked.

"Her health, her mental condition." When Peller didn't respond, she added, "Don't worry. I'll be careful. I just want to make sure she's okay."

He supposed he couldn't stop her from being concerned. If that's what it was.

"I guess Theresa and I get a breather," Montufar said.

Alas, she'd jinxed the pair of them. Peller's cell phone jangled. It was Bianca Tyler. He signaled the team to wait and took the call.

"Lieutenant Peller? I need to talk."

"What's up?"

"Not on the phone. In person. Somewhere...private."

Her voice quavered. Peller wondered what was wrong now, but no doubt she would just repeat the request. "Okay. Where?"

"Rockburn Branch Park. The parking lot behind the elementary school."

"You got it. When?"

"One hour. But Lieutenant, would you mind sending someone else?"

Peller leaned back. That was odd. "I suppose not. Mind telling me why?"

Tyler didn't answer, didn't even say, "Because."

"No matter. I'll send a couple of my colleagues."

"Thank you. I really appreciate this."

Call over, Peller raised an eyebrow at Montufar.

"Who are we meeting?" she asked.

"Bianca Tyler, Mark Tyler's widow. At Rockburn Branch Park. She doesn't want to see me."

"I guess it's us, then," Montufar told Swan. To Peller, she added, "What did you say to put her off?"

"No idea. You can ask when you get there."

Swan leaned toward Montufar and said in a not-quite whisper, "He must be losing his touch."

Peller laughed. "Did I ever have one?"

†

When Peller returned to his desk, he found Geri Franklin waiting in his guest chair, legs crossed at the ankles, eyes focused on the blank panel along the back of the cubicle. He looked at it himself. He couldn't imagine why it commanded her attention unless it concealed some evidence of a crime, but there was nothing, not even a stain from slopped coffee. He settled into his chair and waited.

When she turned her emotionless gaze on him, he felt like *he* was under investigation. He met her eyes with his own brand of stare, the one he used on recalcitrant suspects.

"You'll be relieved to know the injury to the dog was done post-mortem. No clotting, no other vital reactions evident. So says the lab." She pointed at his computer. "Unless you already saw the report."

"Haven't, no."

"One other interesting thing. The cut wasn't just clean. It was precise, likely done with a scalpel or similar instrument. Nothing conclusive, but there are indications of a double-edge bevel. The initial cut was deep and straight, done with a steady hand."

Peller frowned. "Are you suggesting a doctor did it?"

Franklin shrugged and returned her attention back to the wall. "Doctor. Veterinarian. Med student. Carpenter with a doctor relative. Who knows?"

"We don't have any of those on our list."

"You don't have a list at all."

If it hadn't been Franklin, Peller would have taken that as criticism. With her, it was just a fact.

She added another, although one from the left field wall. "Maybe it was Ozzie."

"Ozzie?"

"Ozzie White."

"Why would we suspect him?"

"He's very good with a knife."

Peller cocked his head.

"Oh yes, he's quite the chef, given he hasn't had any formal training."

"He cooked dinner for you?"

"And breakfast. His cinnamon pancakes are divine." She winked. She actually winked. Then she sailed off to her next destination, leaving Peller staring at nothing.

She was joking, right? Except joking wasn't her style. If she was serious …

Never mind. That wasn't a lead Peller cared to pursue.

†

Folded in woods, surrounded by upper-middle-class homes, the quiet of Rockburn Branch Park was broken only by the distant squeals of children on the school playground. The parking lot to which Montufar and

Swan had been summoned sat empty save a white Toyota RAV4 halfway back. When they drove in, Bianca Tyler stepped from the vehicle.

She wasn't what Swan expected. To her, "Bianca" suggested a tall, slim blonde, pale, smiling, sunlight glinting off her hair and skin and teeth, all of them sparkling like in a silly movie. Tyler wasn't that. She was short, curvy, chestnut hair, worry lines tying her eyebrows together. Her fists were clenched tight at her sides as though holding onto the air.

The detectives approached, and Montufar asked, "Mrs. Tyler?"

Tyler nodded.

"I'm Detective Sergeant Corina Montufar. This is Detective Theresa Swan. Lieutenant Peller sent us."

"I hope I didn't offend him by asking for someone else."

"No. It just surprised him. Do you mind telling us what that was about?"

Tyler waved a hand toward the back of the lot. "Can we walk?"

Montufar nodded, and Tyler led the way to a pair of handicapped parking spaces in the rear. Beside them, they found a trailhead and a curious boulder in a circle of pavers bearing the sign, "Welcome to The Rock." Swan nearly laughed. How obvious. A well-aged two-story house stood in the distance, unmarked, maybe a structure forgotten since the Civil War.

Tyler led them down the paved trail, which turned to crushed stone cutting through the woods. She didn't speak until they were out of sight of the parking lot. "Ed called this morning," she said. "Someone asked for confession, but that wasn't what they wanted."

"What did they want?" Montufar asked.

"To threaten him."

It was a warm morning, but Swan felt a chill in the air. "Concerning Mark's death," she guessed.

"Yes. They threatened to kill Ed if he spoke to the police."

Now it made sense. Peller had interviewed Father Ed a couple of times. The priest must have asked his sister to sneak this news to them, keeping Peller out of it. The park was safe. She could be sure she hadn't been followed.

Montufar figured it the same way. "He asked you to let us know."

"Not exactly. He told me he couldn't mention it to Lieutenant Peller. That was his way of asking me to do it without asking. Ed doesn't know who threatened him or how they knew the police had been talking to him, so he took precautions. He's guarded even when not threatened."

That was one way of putting it. Swan had heard about his obfuscations. "The individual who threatened him isn't a church member, then?"

"Ed didn't recognize the man's voice. The guy knew something about the sacrament of confession, but that doesn't mean he's Catholic."

"This person was focused on Mark's death?" Montufar asked. "Nothing else?"

"That's what Ed thought. There was no mention of the vandalism."

"How much do you know about that?"

"Ed told me someone had been leaving threatening messages. He said his visitor didn't mention that, only Mark's death."

They came to a small wooden bridge over a meandering, rock-strewn stream. Rockburn Branch, the park's namesake. They paused to watch the water bubble by.

"I can't lose Ed, too," Tyler told the stream. "I can't. But if there's any chance of justice for Mark..."

"We'll do everything we can," Montufar promised. "For both of them."

"Why did Mark die?"

Montufar leaned on the wooden rail and stared into the water. She looked calm, but she must have been as conflicted as Swan. How could they answer without hurting Tyler further? "We can't say too much right now. It's a complicated investigation. We don't want to compromise it. For your sake. For Mark's and Father Ed's."

Tyler flicked a dead leaf from the rail into the water. "Then you know why."

"Maybe."

"Okay. For now, I'll take that as progress and be patient." She straightened and turned back the way they had come. "You ladies wait here for fifteen, twenty minutes. It's a relaxing spot. My therapist recommended it to me."

Once Tyler vanished around a curve, Swan crossed to the other side of the bridge and gazed into the woods. "How do we break it to her?"

"We hope we don't have to," Montufar replied. "If we're lucky, that falls to the FBI. But if not, we do our jobs. As Rick once had to tell me, we can't change the facts. Whatever happened, happened."

"From all we've been told, Mark was such a good man. Almost Superman."

"There's no Superman, Theresa. Everyone makes mistakes. A few mistakes, even big ones, don't make someone a bad person. We don't know what pressures Mark Tyler was under. Not yet, anyway."

Swan knew that. All of it. But she found no comfort there.

Chapter 14

Dumas' earlier phone call with Janice Navin didn't end on an up note. She wouldn't jump for joy when he knocked on her door, especially not once he asked about her son and his female roommate. He decided to bring a peace offering, not a standard tactic in his repertoire, but her cooperation was crucial.

What kind of peace offering, though?

He chuckled when the notion came into his head: *You're a cop. Bring donuts.*

Sure, why not? He could use another cup of coffee, anyway. He stopped at a drive-though and got two large cups of joe in a carrier, plus a bag with two double chocolates and two glazed. Then he drove to the Navin home, a comfortable, above-the-middle middle-class home in the well-wooded neighborhood of Kendall Ridge in eastern Columbia. There were no sidewalks here. Though everyone had driveways, many vehicles slumbered by the curbs. At the Navin place, no means of transport was in evidence. With luck that didn't mean Janice was out. Or at work. She had been home this time of day when he phoned.

He rang the bell and waited. And waited. And waited. He rang again and waited some more. He was about to give up when the deadbolt clicked and the door opened halfway. The storm door remained closed, presumably locked.

Janice Navin squinted at Dumas. She was on the short side, with ringlets of blonde hair. She wore dark jeans and a floral pattern blouse. Despite her domestic appearance, she possessed an air of prison guard. She said nothing. Maybe she was hoping for a sales pitch so she could slam the door in his face.

"Mrs. Navin, I'm Detective Sergeant Eric Dumas of the Howard County Police. We spoke on the phone yesterday." He showed her his ID.

"I remember. I thought we covered everything."

"Something came up. I was hoping we could talk a bit further." He held up the coffee and the donut bag. "I brought snacks." He smiled hopefully.

Navin stared at him as though he was a squid that had dropped from the sky onto her front lawn. Then she almost cracked a smile, though she struggled to contain it. "Okay. But just for a few minutes." She unlocked and pushed open the storm door.

The interior of the place was nice. Nothing special, but nice. Neutral walls, neutral curtains, neutral furnishings on a hardwood floor. She led him from the foyer through the living room into the dining room, where a table seating six sat unadorned save a napkin holder and salt and pepper shakers. She motioned him to one of the chairs and settled opposite, arms folded on the table, gazing at him as if conducting a job interview. Dumas passed her a coffee and unpacked the donuts. Navin accepted the offering. They spent a few moments focused on food.

"I talked to Carlyle," Dumas said.

Navin paused, coffee cup raised to her lips. She stared over the rim, then set the cup down. "Why?"

"Same reason I talked to you. To find out if there was any possibility your brother might be—"

"I told you, Walter has nothing to do with anything you're investigating."

"Carlyle said the same," Dumas admitted.

"Then why are you here?"

Dumas took a sip of coffee and inspected a glazed donut. "Who's Mary?" He took a bite while Janice Navin scowled at him. When she didn't answer, he continued, "I met her when I went to Carlyle's apartment."

"I don't know any Mary."

"Your son is living with a young lady named Mary. I didn't get her last name. She says they met at church."

"My son lives alone, Sergeant. I don't know what this game is, but—"

"The game is simple," Dumas interrupted. "I bring you coffee and donuts, and you tell me about Mary. If you honestly don't know her, fine. He might not have told you. But I have a problem."

"And what's that?"

"They both lied to me. I asked a few simple questions, nothing at all incriminating, and they lied. Badly. So badly, it was painful."

Navin pushed her chocolate donut to the middle of the table and set the coffee beside it. "I think you should leave."

"You're not interested?"

"No."

"Mary says they met at St. Peter Episcopal Church. Carlyle says it was at St. Paul Catholic. I'm pretty sure they didn't meet through either. But so what? Why the deception? It worries me."

"You're making this up."

"Why would I do that?"

"I don't know."

"I don't, either. Are you sure you don't know who Mary is? If not, I'd think you'd want to find out before your son lands in trouble." *If he hasn't already*, Dumas added to himself.

Navin's hands were quivering. Too late, she tucked them into her lap to hide her agitation. "That makes no sense. I've never heard of this person. The last time I was at Carlyle's apartment, he was living alone."

"When was that, Mrs. Navin?"

"Three, four weeks ago, I guess."

That was long enough. The first vandalism occurred two weeks back. Mary could have recruited Carlyle, moved in, and planned the attacks with him after Mom's last visit. Janice Navin's agitation testified she was telling the truth. She didn't know about Mary.

"For what it's worth," Dumas said, "Mary claims their relationship is platonic. They're just sharing the rent."

"Carlyle doesn't need financial help. He's been living there for a year and a half with no problem."

Which also fit Dumas' expectations. Software engineer. Good income. He put his business card on the table next to Navin's rejected coffee and donut. "I believe you. I'll see what I can find on Mary from other sources. Meanwhile, if you think of anything or learn anything about her, please let me know. Your son's domestic arrangements are his own business, of course, but Mary...something's not right there. I'm just trying to protect Carlyle—and your brother—from harm."

She said nothing, didn't escort him to the door, didn't give any sign of having heard. Dumas let himself out. It looked like mommy's little boy was about to get an earful. Once he did, it would be worth paying the kids another visit.

†

Getting Rodrigo Paniagua's attention was rather like coaxing a panda out of a bamboo forest at lunchtime. Ross obtained his cell and office numbers easily enough. He was required to provide them when he posted bail for his mother-in-law. But that was the easy part. Ross sent texts and voice mails hourly from the moment the morning meeting ended until mid-afternoon without response. Some part of her whispered she was being too aggressive again, but she had no intention of waiting a week for Paniagua to give her five minutes of his time. This was, after all, about his mother-in-law's well-being.

He finally returned her call just after three o'clock. "I've been in meetings all day," he said by way of excuse. "What can I do for you?"

"I was worried about Carlotta. How is she doing?"

"That's very kind of you. I wouldn't have expected that from the police."

"It's an unusual situation. I wish we hadn't had to arrest her, but she was so angry, I don't think she knew what she was doing. She was becoming a danger to herself and everyone around her."

"For what it's worth, she's calmed down. Some, at least. We've asked her not to drive herself anywhere for a while."

"I'm glad to hear that. Is she facing a health issue? That might explain her recent aggressive behavior." Ross avoided specifying mental health, but with luck Paniagua would pick up on it.

Except he didn't, or if so, he didn't let on. "Not that I'm aware of. She isn't one of those people who tell the world about her ailments, but as far as I know, she's been in good health. She sees her doctor regularly and takes a few maintenance meds. Nothing you wouldn't expect for a woman her age."

"When did you first notice a change in her behavior?"

Paniagua thought for a moment. "I can't say. I've been uber-focused on work lately. I didn't realize she was being so aggressive behind the wheel. I'm not sure I even noticed the damage to her vehicle."

Ross wondered what could have occupied his attention to that degree. "I don't mean to pry," she said, although she certainly did, "but has anything changed in the family recently?"

That ruffled his feathers. "I don't see where that's any of your business, Detective Ross. My mother-in-law has legal counsel. Her defense isn't your job. In fact, your job is just the opposite, isn't it?"

"Not necessarily. If there are extenuating—"

"I'm not answering any further questions. If you want her lawyer's contact information, I'll give you that, but nothing more." He cut the connection before she could ask for it.

"Obviously you didn't mean it," Ross muttered.

Time for plan B. She set course for Carlotta Becerra's home. Becerra lived with Paniagua, his wife Olivia, and their grandson Roger not far from the elementary school where she had been apprehended. The route was twisty. Ross bobbed south, then west, then north to a dead-end street lined with the newest and nicest homes in the area. They weren't particularly large, surprising given the money Paniagua allegedly made. Maybe he wasn't the ostentatious type. Still, it was a quiet, pleasant neighborhood of brick façades, well-kept lawns, and flower gardens. The land prices might have been through the roof.

Carlotta Becerra and family lived at the end of the street. Her banged-up powder blue Escalade rested now in the driveway, in need of minor body work and a new paint job. No, Paniagua hadn't missed all *that.* Not unless he was blind.

When Ross rang the bell, Becerra answered. Upon recognizing Ross, her grim visage morphed into sunshine, as though her best friend had dropped by for a long-overdue visit. She hustled Ross inside, settled her on the couch, and insisted on getting her some coffee. Ross couldn't have refused if she wanted to. Once they were suitably caffeinated, Becerra said, "I'm so glad you came. Everything has been crazy. That *lawyer.*" She made a face. "All his questions. He says I should see a neurologist. He thinks I'm a nutcase."

"He's just trying to protect you," Ross said. "You've been very angry. From what people tell me, that's not like you."

"Angry! Who says I'm angry?"

"Rodrigo, for one."

She pinched her lips and looked away. "Idiot."

"He says you're usually a sweet lady."

"Hmph."

Ross couldn't help but smile. "You aren't?"

"I'm nice to nice people."

Ross wondered if Rodrigo Paniagua's abrupt termination of their call masked something darker than impatience. "He seemed okay to me. He didn't like it when I asked questions about the family situation, but I expect he was just being protective."

"Why did you ask that?"

"I was worried about your health."

Becerra picked up her cup, frowned at the coffee, set it down. "My health is fine. I run circles around them all. Except my grandson." She smiled, then sank into irritation again. "It's Rodrigo's fault. He not protective of any-one but himself. Don't tell my daughter, but it's all his fault."

"What's his fault?"

"That I'm so tense. So angry. He's never home anymore. He works late all the time. He doesn't pick up Roger from school."

"He did the other day," Ross pointed out.

Becerra ignored that. "*You* know what it means when a man isn't there for his family anymore. He's seeing another woman."

"What does Olivia think?"

"She's blind. Stupid. She accepts his excuses."

Rodrigo Paniagua's personal behavior wasn't police business. Montufar would have told her so. Peller already had. But was that absolute? He was a government contractor. What if he was another Mark Tyler? What if he was seeing another Clare Fleming? At the very least, Ross should pass Becerra's speculations to the FBI. Except the feds were only focused on Fleming thus far. Maybe she needed to dig a bit further, first. Just so she didn't waste the Bureau's time.

She wished Theresa Swan was here so they could talk it through. "You should tell this to your lawyer," Ross suggested. "I don't know how it might work toward your defense, but the more he knows, the better he can help you."

Becerra shook her head. "I'd hurt Olivia or make a fool of myself. I'd rather people thought I *was* a nutcase."

For what it was worth, Ross didn't think that. Not anymore.

†

When his cell phone jangled, Carlyle Navin was deep in thought, rummaging through a mass of code in search of an obscure bug that was intermittently crashing one of the websites his team maintained. He suspected a timing issue, some asynchronous process taking longer than expected, but he hadn't tracked it down yet. Every time he thought he was closing in, it slipped away. His brain needed a break anyway, so he grabbed his phone, glanced at the caller, and answered.

"Hi Mom. What's up?"

"Who the *hell* is Mary?" Janice Navin demanded.

Carlyle pressed a hand to his forehead. First that detective, now his mother. He warned Mary, warned her right from the start, but she was hell-bent on justice—revenge, more like—with or without him. She wouldn't have stood a chance without him. Even she knew she needed someone logical and even-tempered to bank her fire, and he was the only one who could. Or would. He cared about her, couldn't bear to watch her throw herself off a cliff. "You've been talking to that detective," he told his mother.

When Mom was on a mission, she couldn't be deflected. "Who's Mary?" she repeated.

"Just a friend. She needed a place to stay. I had an extra room, so why not?" Not that she'd find that remotely adequate, but he had to say something, and that was the story Mary had given the cops.

"Where did you meet her?"

At least he knew that much. Mary told Sergeant Dumas they'd met at church. Carlyle didn't know why she'd said that, but so long as they stuck to the story, they'd be safe. "At St. Paul," he said.

Turned out he was wrong. "Mary said you met at an Episcopalian church."

Carlyle about gagged. Why would Mary have said *that*? It wouldn't deflect attention from St. Augustine and St. Paul for long. The cops would dig into their backgrounds, discover they both had deep Catholic roots. How stupid could you get?

"They know you're lying," his mother continued. "Whoever she is, something's not right about her. Tell me the truth. If you need a lawyer—"

"For God's sake, Mom! She's just a friend. She needed a room. That's all. We aren't dealing drugs. I'm not holding her hostage, or vice versa. We certainly didn't kill anyone."

Mom breathed into the phone but said nothing.

"I'm an adult, you know. I've been an adult for a while. If I want to live with a woman, it's my call. And she's just a friend. I'm not sleeping with her." One big lie, but he sure wasn't telling her about that. Not yet. "We aren't hosting orgies. She just needed a place to stay."

"I'm not asking about your sex life. You're lying to the police, and that's ignorant and dangerous. Who is she? Why is she *really* living with you?"

If he told her, would she tell Dumas? No, not intentionally, but an unguarded moment, a slip of the tongue... Best to keep it simple and semi-truthful. "She's like anyone else. She's a vet tech. She doesn't make much money. She does her job, I do my job, and that's it. We met about a month ago. We were both out for a walk and our paths crossed. We said hi and started talking. One day she told me she was looking for a place to stay and asked if I knew anywhere affordable." A gross oversimplification, but Mom didn't need to know the details. He just hoped she'd be satisfied with it.

"And you just invited her to move in with you."

"Not exactly, but more or less."

Mom pondered for a moment. "Why didn't you tell the police that?"

"They talked to Mary first. She said we met at church. I don't know why. I didn't want to contradict her, but I didn't know she said an Episcopalian church." Which was beyond stupid. Even *he* couldn't fathom why he kept on playing to Mary's lead. People forget things, get facts crossed up. He could have told them the truth, could have said that church came later. Or no, not really. Not an Episcopal church. *Damn, it, Mary,* he thought. *What's wrong with you?*

"If the police come around again," Mom instructed, "don't say anything. Don't talk to them without a lawyer."

Carlyle pinched the bridge of his nose. A lawyer's meddling was the last thing they needed. That could wait until—unless, rather; best to stay positive—they were charged with a crime. "We don't need a lawyer, Mom. Nothing's going on. Mary probably got scared when a detective showed up."

"Scared of what?"

"How should 1 know? Cops make some people nervous. Don't worry, okay? Everything's fine."

He said it, but he should have known better. His mother could read him too well. "It is not," she insisted. "I'm calling Mr. Bedi. Don't say a word to the police unless he's with you."

Mr. Bedi. Great. Carlyle could only understand every third word the man said. The guy spoke impeccable English, but between his accent and his automatic-rifle pace, he could be indecipherable. His parents had used him for a long time, mostly for real estate transactions and their wills. He also handled small claims and occasional accident and injury lawsuits. Whether or not he was any good with criminal cases was an open question.

"Understood?" Mom asked.

"Fine, whatever. But 1 don't see the point."

She exhaled. Hard. To make sure he got her frustration and disappointment. "What's her name?"

"Mary. You already know that."

"Her last name, damn it!"

No matter what he said—truth, lie, or nothing—he was sunk. He chose the least of three evils. "I'm sorry, Mom. 1 really need to get back to work. Bye." And he cut the connection. He'd pay for that later, but until he figured out how to get Mary and himself in the clear, he'd have to accept the fallout.

Why had he let Mary talk him into this? Why hadn't he made her forget the whole business?

Because he couldn't. He couldn't make her stop, and the only way to protect her was to join her madness. He hadn't done a good enough job, but how could he? She had but one thought in her entire brain and pursued it like a bloodhound.

He leaned forward, cradled his head in his hands, stared at the code filling his monitor.

Huh.

So *that's* what the problem was.

†

Clouds crowded the sky as Dumas ate a fast food burger in his car and let his thoughts wander through the details thus far assembled. He had to admit, it was quite the jumble. If it were a jigsaw puzzle, he would have suspected a manufacturer error. Pieces from two or three or even four pictures all mixed together, all cut differently, no possibility of assembling anything.

Mary was the keystone. He was sure of it. Except how could she be? How could someone so seemingly impetuous have dragged someone as cautious as Carlyle Navin into a vandalism spree? And why?

Sure, they were both young. She was good-looking, he was a nerd and probably attracted to her. She might have cajoled him into living together. They might even be sleeping together. But so what? Why would they vandalize a church? Two churches? Carlyle, at least, should never have agreed to such acts. And Mary—what could have driven her down that road?

Dumas wanted to toss the idea out the window, but he couldn't. They fit the profile, and they were lying like Lucifer if not a tenth as well. He and Montufar both thought them likely suspects. In his book, that made it at least seventy-five percent certain they were the culprits. So again: assuming Mary had reason to vandalize the churches, why would Carlyle play along?

Maybe Mary worked in the same racket as Clare Fleming? No, she hardly seemed the type. From what Peller had reported, Fleming could project self-confidence even when scared out of her wits. She probably lured men in before they knew what was what. She only confessed out of fear for her own safety. But Mary? She couldn't tell the whitest of lies without tripping over her tongue.

Could Mary have a grievance against the Church? That was Father Dan's assessment of the vandal. But none of the detectives agreed with that. This was personal.

Okay, suppose Mary was targeting an individual, someone who had wronged her. Although some messages implied a threat, taken together they could be a plea for honesty. For openness. For confession. Father Walter had invoked the seal of the confessional, and one of the messages had appeared facing inward on his window. Dumas could cobble together a coherent scenario from that. Except…why vandalize St. Paul? Why would Carlyle agree to attack his own church?

Which brought Dumas back to where he started. Mismatched puzzle pieces. Peller was right. They needed something concrete. They needed handwriting samples. If guilty, Carlyle and Mary wouldn't surrender them until pressured. Really pressured. Which meant Dumas needed…

Finished eating, he crumpled up his sandwich wrapper, stuffed it into the fry holster, and dropped that into the bag. Then he called dispatch. "Request Officer Kevin Graham for assistance at the Plum Tree Apartments in Ellicott city." He gave the street address.

The dispatcher acknowledged and added, "This is a very specific request for a Friday. You know that, right?"

"I'm going fishing. I might need help wrestling in a big one."

"Ten-four. I'll tell him to bring a net."

When Dumas arrived at the apartments, Graham was already there, waiting in his squad car. He lowered the window as Dumas approached. "Together again, eh mon?"

"Just like old times."

"Not quite. Last time a detective called, she had me looking for a little ol' bullet in big, big field and some dumb kid in the woods. What's it today?"

"Same in spirit. Two persons of interest, Carlyle Navin and Mary Last-Name-Unknown live up there." Dumas pointed to their building. "Allegedly platonic relationship, just sharing the rent. He's a software engineer. I have no idea what she is, but every time she lies, her nose elongates."

"Elongates." Graham raised an eyebrow. "I'm reporting your language to your wife."

Dumas ignored him. "There's a theory they might be our church vandals, but so far, it's way circumstantial. Rick wants handwriting samples from the two, either volunteered or by court order. I'm offering them a chance to play nice."

Graham nodded. "And I make non-cooperation feel not so nice. Let's do it."

At the building's entrance, they found someone had propped the front door open with a brick. So much for security. They ascended the stairs to Navin's place. Dumas knocked. They waited. And waited. He knocked again.

"At work?" Graham wondered.

"Navin works from home. No idea what Mary does, other than sleep late."

"It's afternoon, mon."

Dumas cracked a smile. "Point. Last time I came by before lunch." He knocked again.

This time the door flew open to reveal Navin, fists planted on his hips, eyes spitting fire. "How did you get up here?"

"One of your neighbors disabled the security system," Dumas said. "Can we come in?"

"I'm working. What is it now?"

"I need your help. It won't take long."

Navin grimaced at Dumas and gave Graham a once-over. The officer's grim visage and sheer size convinced him not to argue. He stood aside and waved the pair in. Dumas proceeded to the living room and without invitation sat where he had before. Graham elected to stand next to him, arms folded over his chest. Navin took a seat facing Dumas and, with one last glance at Graham, said, "Get on with it."

Dumas had to admit, despite his unease, Navin could maintain his cool. "Is Mary here?"

Navin shook his head.

"Where is she?"

"Why?"

"Because we're asking," Graham snapped.

"I don't have to tell you anything."

Dumas nodded. "True, you don't. But that would raise suspicions."

"You know what happens when you raise suspicions?" Graham asked.

Navin matched Graham's expression. "You know what happens when cops exceed their authority?"

Not a bad bluff, except he had no clue how the game was played. Dumas leaned forward. "Look, Carlyle, we won't beat you up. I don't work that way. On the other hand, I could have you detained. Thus..." He thumbed at Graham.

"Not without cause," Navin said.

"Cause is easy," Graham said. "Pick any driver on the road, and within a few minutes I can find cause to pull 'em over."

"Maybe you didn't notice, but I'm not driving."

Dumas and Graham exchanged a knowing glance, then Dumas said, "Where's Mary, Carlyle?"

"How the hell should I know? I'm not her babysitter."

"What are you? What's she to you?"

"She's a friend. That's all."

"What's your friend's last name?"

Navin pressed his lips tight.

Dumas sighed and shook his head. "Okay. Here's the deal. I want Mary's last name, either from you or from her. You have my card. One of you can call me when she's available. I also want handwriting samples from both of you."

That rattled him. "Handwriting samples? Why?"

"You can give me yours now, or I can get a court order compelling you to provide it. It would be easier all around if you'd just do it."

"Get out."

"Bad move, mon," Graham warned. "Real bad move. Makes us think you got something to hide. Then we look harder, and when we find something..." He shook his head. "Cops, prosecutors, judges, wardens...nobody cuts you any slack."

For just a moment, Navin's control cracked. Dumas could feel his panic, but he squashed it and laughed. "What do you think I did? Killed somebody?"

"I don't think anything," Dumas said. "I'm just testing hypotheses. If you've done nothing wrong, you have nothing to fear. Get a paper and pen and let's get this over with."

But he had something to fear. He knew he was damned no matter what he did, so he said nothing, did nothing, just stared at Dumas. Dumas spread his hands and waited.

Graham cleared his throat.

Dumas shook his head and rose. "I really hoped you'd cooperate. But..."

With a grin that suggested he was enjoying the outcome, Graham told Dumas, "Guess it's the hard way, mon. Let's go get that warrant."

When Dumas put his hand to the doorknob, Navin called, "Wait."

They paused without looking back.

"What do you want me to write?"

Dumas turned. Graham set his fists to his hips and shook his head at the floor as though accusing it of stupidity. "Get something to write with," Dumas said.

Navin vanished into the back land returned with a piece of printer paper and a pen. He went to the dining table and awaited instructions.

"All the digits from zero through nine," Dumas said.

Navin bent over the paper and complied. "Is that all?"

"Also, the following sentence: 'Every time Janice is lost, Paul and Richard find her.'" He had constructed that ahead of time. It included all the letters that appeared in the graffiti.

Navin frowned. "What?"

Dumas repeated it slowly, one word at a time, while Navin wrote. Then he held out his hand and Navin delivered the paper. "Appreciate it," he said. "What about Mary's last name?"

"You'll have to ask her."

"How can you not know?"

"I can't give out personal information without her consent. That would be an invasion of privacy."

Nice deflection, but not unexpected. Dumas gave the ceiling an imploring look. Graham turned and eyed Navin. "You wanna do it the hard way, huh?"

"You can ask her yourself when she's home."

"When's that?" Dumas asked.

Navin shrugged.

"He claims not to know," Dumas told Graham.

Graham grinned at Navin. "Suit yourself. Next time you see us, you're not gonna be happy."

They didn't give Navin a chance to respond. They were out the door and down to the parking lot in no time, maintaining silence until they reached their vehicles. Once there, Graham leaned against his squad car and gave the complex a thorough examination. "Nice place," he said. "Too bad that kid's here to muck it up."

"He's too defensive," Dumas said. "That's for sure. Mary's the linchpin in this case. I can feel it."

"Linchpin." Graham shook his head. "You're on a roll today. Good thing the little lady's not here to listen to that talk."

"Yeah, she'd threaten to confiscate my thesaurus again."

"Seems you keep getting it back."

"So far." Dumas nodded at Navin's building. "Assessment?"

"Same as yours. I don't have all your data, but this Mary character's gotta be important. You know *anything* about her?"

"Just that her name is Mary, she and Navin allegedly met at a church neither of them attend, they're just pals unless they're lovers, and she's a terrible liar."

"I'll bet she's connected to one of those priests," Graham said.

"Why?"

"Everyone else is."

That was true. More or less. Dumas pondered it. "Navin is Father Walter's nephew. Mark Tyler was father Ed's brother. Father Dan... nobody's connected to him, as far as we know, although he and Father Ed have occasional contact. I guess I could ask them each how many thirty-something Marys they know, but that would be a lot. The name may not be as popular as it used to be, but it's still up there on the list, isn't it?"

"How should I know? Ask Corina. She's the web search guru." Graham opened his car door. "I should get back to work. Don't want irate taxpayers complaining."

Once they went their separate ways, Dumas made for HQ. He couldn't get Graham's suggestion out of his head. Neither could he fit Mary into the overall picture. But if she wasn't involved, why lie? What was she hiding? Truth be told, it could be any of a hundred things, from her relationship with Carlyle to a drug habit to a crime unrelated to the church incidents. Whatever it was, Carlyle was protecting her. But he'd made a mistake. He'd given them the handwriting sample. If it matched either of the graffiti incidents, that alone would provide probable cause for a search warrant.

Chapter 15

Peller was pulling into his driveway when his cell phone, until then slumbering peacefully in the holder suctioned to his windshield, went off. Joan Churchill's name, number, and face smiled at him on the caller ID screen. He parked and turned off the engine before answering.

"I have a treat for you," she said. "Pick a restaurant, and I'll tell you over dinner. I'll even drive."

She had such a sparkle in her voice that he couldn't decline, although after this week, he really needed a month off from everything. His brain felt like a vehicle stuck in the mud. He was missing something—they all were—but he couldn't see it. There was so little physical evidence in this case, nothing to look at, nothing to mentally rotate and disassemble and reassemble, nothing to trigger recognition or reveal a pattern. Well, maybe one thing. Pressured by Dumas and Graham, Carlyle Navin caved and provided a handwriting sample, but even that felt wrong. Navin was too smart to be tricked and probably too stubborn to be pushed. And the sample itself? Inconclusive, as far as Peller could tell. It no more than superficially matched the previous graffiti. He sent the sample post haste to Jacey Alexandre, but he didn't expect results before Monday noon.

He pushed all that aside. Joan awaited his choice of restaurants. "Since you're driving," Peller said, "Elkridge Furnace Inn."

Churchill didn't respond. Peller almost laughed. He could imagine her gaping.

"I had their filet once," he added. "It was amazing."

"Yeah, and I'd have to sublet my apartment to afford it. Good thing I didn't say I was buying."

"Are you?"

"No way. Separate checks."

"You're driving—"

"And it *is* a drive."

"—so I'll pay."

"Deal." Churchill laughed. "We should go into politics. We could bring back the fine art of negotiation."

"That's the last business I want to enter." Peller was still in the truck. He wondered why. What was the point of a mobile phone if you couldn't go mobile? He climbed out and went into the house while Churchill proposed to pick him up in ninety minutes. And to see about a reservation, just to be sure they got a table. It was Friday night, after all.

Once he was off the phone, he went up to his room to select a suit. Elkridge Furnace Inn wasn't quite as expensive as Churchill implied, but was a suit kind of place, or at least it had been eleven years and twelve days ago. April seventeenth. He and Sandra were celebrating their fifteenth anniversary. He had worn a navy pinstripe suit, she a stunning sky-blue sleeveless dress. He didn't remember much beyond how beautiful she had been that evening in the low light.

Why the hell had he picked *that* place? Maybe for the memory, maybe the location. Elkridge Furnace Inn sat a mere five minutes from St. Augustine. This could be a disaster.

Or something wonderful, Sandra whispered.

Maybe. Maybe not. He'd find out soon enough.

Peller no longer had that navy blue pinstripe, but he had something similar in charcoal. He donned it, inspected himself in the mirror, wondered how he'd gotten so old. *How do I look?* he asked Sandra.

She said nothing, but maybe she smiled.

Churchill arrived on time, wearing a long, yellow, floral print dress. Eight o'clock approached as they arrived at the restaurant. Peller would have been starving had he not been so nervous. On the drive, they didn't talk much beyond, "How was your day?" and the usual empty answers that suggested nothing wrong save the chaos of every office. She asked how Father Walter was doing. He said so far, so good. He asked if her customers were behaving. She said yes, except when they weren't. Upon arrival, Peller offered Churchill his arm and led her in. Their table was waiting.

The Elkridge Furnace Complex dated to 1751. An ironworks facility on the Patapsco River, its water-powered bellows had fanned a charcoal-fueled fire for production of nails and horseshoes. Technically, that made it a criminal enterprise. English law prohibited finished production in the colonies. During the Revolutionary War, the facility upped the ante by manufacturing cannons and bayonets. In the nineteenth century, economic ups and downs afflicted the furnace until a pair of floods in 1868 and 1873 destroyed most of the buildings. Only two structures remained, one being the owner's residence, a fine two-and-a-half story Federal/Greek Revival. In time, the house became the Furnace Inn, providing restaurant and indoor/outdoor facilities for weddings and other events. The décor remained nineteenth century luxury, with ornate chandeliers, fireplaces, and elegant carpets.

They ordered iced tea, Peller's straight up and Churchill's strawberry flavored. He told her to get whatever she wanted, but she forewent alcohol in his company. She absorbed the surroundings and melted in the luxuriance. "It reminds me of Christiana Campbell's at Colonial Williamsburg," she said.

"Not too far removed, historically," Peller said. "The cuisine is different."

"Hmm, cuisine." She skimmed her menu once, twice, thrice. "Hard to decide." Then she peeked over its top edge and smirked. "You said you're buying."

"I did."

"Let's see. What's the most expensive entrée?"

"The filet or the Delmonico."

"Filet it is. Oh, look, you can get a crab cake on the side."

Peller raised an eyebrow. "Can you eat all that?"

"I have a fridge. Or didn't the detective notice?"

"He noticed. Go for it."

After they ordered and the menus were taken away, Churchill cradled her chin in her hands. "You said you were here before. When was that?"

He was afraid that might come up. He shouldn't have mentioned it. But he couldn't obfuscate, not with her. "I brought Sandra here for our fifteenth anniversary."

She reached for his hands. He gave them to her. "I know it won't ever stop hurting," she said. "You had a beautiful life together."

He nodded. It was comforting to find someone who didn't push him to "get over it" and "move on," as though one could ever cut themselves off from their past. Maybe those who hadn't experienced the loss of a life partner didn't realize what a cavern it left in one's soul. Or maybe they did and only said such things to insulate themselves. People had burdens enough of their own.

Peller squeezed Joan's hands. "I've been thinking about the house," he said. "I haven't changed a thing since—"

"I know. You told me once or twice." In truth, it had been far more than twice.

"Maybe it's time," he finished.

"What would you change?"

He rattled off his ideas: repainting, expanding the rose bed, turning Jason's bedroom into an office. She listened with a gleam in her eye, as though she had notions of her own. But all she said was, "That's wonderful, Rick. I'd be happy to help. Planting roses sounds fun. I've never done much gardening. And speaking of that, I said I had a treat for you. This weekend the Potomac Bonsai Society is holding its annual spring show at the National Bonsai and Penjing Museum in the National Arboretum. I want to go, and you're invited."

"That's three organizations in one."

"Is that a yes?"

"Sure, why not? Are you driving again?"

"Given the cost of this meal, I might be your chauffeur for the next three months."

Peller's cell phone vibrated. One look at the caller was enough to kill the mood. "Sorry," he told Churchill. "I need to take this."

She sighed and waved him on.

"Hi Jacey. Why are you still at work?"

"Your fault, Rick," Jacey Alexandre accused. "You keep handing me interesting problems. This is payback time. Wait, are you at a restaurant?"

She must have heard the clanking of plates and the murmur of conversation. "Yes. And my companion's giving me the evil eye."

"Revenge is sweet. That sample you gave me. Clever. It has all the letters and numbers that appeared in the messages. Was that your handiwork?"

"Eric's."

"Ah, the one who pulls rabbits out of hats. He did it again."

Peller noticed Churchill arranging her napkin in her lap. Impatient, and with good cause. He held up a finger to ask her to wait just a moment. "Give me the short version," he told Alexandre.

"The new sample is consistent with the others from St. Paul based on indications the writer tried to disguise their handwriting. That tends to introduce inconsistencies, and underlying similarities always slip through. The details will be in my report. You'll have that Monday morning."

"Thanks, Jacey. That's welcome news."

Churchill made a slashing motion across her throat. Peller had his good news. It was time to end the call.

"Which part?" Alexandre asked. "That I found one of your vandals, or that I'm sending you more paperwork?"

"Both. I have to go before I'm lynched."

"Must be a steaming hot date if she's more interesting than this. Bye!" She disconnected before Peller could respond.

He pocketed his phone. "Sorry about that," he said. "It could have waited until Monday."

Churchill shook her head. "Do all you cops work twenty-four seven?"

"Only the obsessed ones."

"Sounds like you need to get a life. Good thing I'm here." She winked at him.

It was the sort of thing Sandra might have said.

He had a feeling she was winking at him, too.

†

"I don't know about this," Theresa Swan mumbled.

Holly Ross didn't, either, but she wasn't about to let on. At least this plan wasn't as rash as certain others she'd formulated. She wouldn't bully anyone, wouldn't put herself or her colleague in danger. They would only watch, and if nothing happened, then nothing happened. But if something did...

"We might need authorization," Swan added. "We shouldn't be here." She turned in the passenger seat and eyed Ross, who was behind the wheel, attention focused on the car in front of them, a black Toyota Highlander driven by Rodrigo Paniagua, Carlotta Becerra's son-in-law. Swan knew because she got the make, model, and license from the MVA, and she burned the plate number into her brain. They'd waited until nearly six o'clock, watching the Emerson complex exit, until Paniagua drove out and made for a destination other than home.

The stake-out proved tricky. There weren't any pull-offs near the facility, no parking lots, nothing but a striped shoulder just before the exit to westbound State Route 216. If Paniagua turned the opposite direction on exiting the complex, the detectives might miss him. But of greater concern was the guard station, which had a clear view of the detectives as they sat there, doing nothing. Feds got nervous if they thought they were being watched. And those guards had serious weaponry.

Ross had a plan for that. Before parking, she drove to the station and identified herself and Swan. "We're looking for a suspect we believe will be driving by in about an hour or so. We'll be parked right out there while we wait. Just wanted to give you a heads up."

Following a credentials check and protracted discussion among the guards, the women were given the green light and directed to the exit.

They got lucky. Paniagua's vehicle emerged and made for the state highway. Ross put her car in gear and followed at a discreet distance, keeping a couple cars between herself and their target. Travelling fifteen miles an hour over the speed limit, he drove northwest, crossed over I-95, over U.S. 29, and turned into a sprawling commercial complex in Maple Lawn packed with shops and eateries. It felt roomy. Broad streets, broad sidewalks fronting buildings of red brick and tan stone. Classical street lamps. Every restaurant offered outdoor seating with greenery dripping all around.

Paniagua found street parking in front of an Irish pub called O'Callaghan's. Ross pulled into a parking lot half a block down while Swan kept an eye on their target. He took his time getting out, but he had no suspicion he was being watched. He didn't seem too aware of his surroundings, anyway. His vehicle beeped when he locked it. He checked his cell phone, tucked it into his trouser pocket, and strolled into the pub.

"He's meeting a woman," Ross predicted.

"Or having an after-work drink," Swan countered. "Either way, we keep our distance."

"Don't worry. I just want to see what he's up to. If it's what I think it is, we'll give the FBI the intel and let them handle it."

"If you try anything else, I swear I'll cuff you."

"Deal. Let's go."

Inside, the place was packed. Of course it was. Friday. Between the basketball and baseball games playing on overabundant wall-mounted TVs and everyone talking over each other, it was a wonder the servers could hear orders. Paniagua was at the bar, receiving a beer from the bartender. The seats on either side were empty. Ross pointed to a pair of stools further down. She and Swan took those.

"Are we on or off duty?" Swan asked.

"Yes," Ross told her.

"That doesn't help."

They both got colas. Better safe than sorry.

Swan had her back to Paniagua. She kept it that way. Ross, though, had her eye on him. Alas, he did nothing interesting. The stools flanking him remained unclaimed while he sipped at his drink and watched the Orioles take on Cleveland at home. The game had just started when the detectives arrived. It looked to be a long one. Two and a half scoreless innings passed, then Baltimore's Jay Payton hit a home run in the bottom of the third. The noise level in the pub rose on the heels of that belt before returning to its normal roar. Paniagua remained alone, nursing his drink.

"Told you," Ross said. "How about we go home?"

And that's when something happened. Just not what Ross expected.

A bearded man settled into the seat on Paniagua's left, ordered a drink, and set a mailing envelope on the bar. He said something. Ross couldn't see the newcomer's face. He kept it tuned toward the TV. Paniagua glanced at him and said something back.

"Theresa." Ross nodded at the pair. Swan turned to look.

The newcomer smiled at Paniagua, a shark smile, and then the detectives could see him. He had a broad face, a small nose, a neat black beard. Ross guessed he was of Asian ancestry. He was dressed casual but conservative in a light button-down shirt and dark jeans. He pushed the envelope toward Paniagua.

Paniagua pushed it back and returned his attention to the TV.

Ross glanced at Swan. Her colleague watched the exchange with a poker face. She might have been focused on the ball game, for all anyone knew.

The stranger grinned his shark grin again—Ross decided to call him the Shark—and spoke as he eased the envelope back to Paniagua.

Paniagua snapped a rebuke that was swallowed up in the background noise.

The Shark took the envelope back. He opened it as though inspecting a fragile letter from a long-lost relative, chattering the whole time. He extracted a three-by-five photo, set it face down on the bar, slid it to Paniagua.

At first, Paniagua did nothing, but as the Shark prattled on, he grew increasingly agitated. Finally, he snatched up the photo and, without looking at it, tore it to pieces and threw it in the Shark's face. The bits fluttered to the bar.

"Hell," Ross muttered. She started to rise.

Swan caught her arm. "Wait."

Ross dropped back into her seat.

The Shark laughed. He gathered up the bits of torn photo from the bar and his lap and returned them to the envelope. He spoke again, still with that predatory smile fixed to his face. No fear, no agitation. He held the good cards and knew it.

But Paniagua had an ace up his sleeve. He grabbed the Shark's shirt front and shoved him off the bar stool. The Shark toppled backwards, taking the stool and the one next door with him. The crash caught the attention of the closest customers. As the Shark scrambled to regain his footing, Paniagua dropped onto him and pummeled his midsection. A doorman shoved his way through to the scuffle, but Paniagua was already up and running for the exit, the envelope in his grasp. The doorman almost pursued but did a double-take. He kneeled beside the Shark and pressed a hand to his abdomen. "Call nine-one-one!" he bellowed. "Call nine-one-one!"

"Damn it," Swan and Ross said in unison, and a moment later they were beside the injured man, flashing IDs. The Shark was bleeding from a gut wound, while the doorman tried to squelch the flow with a bunch of cloth napkins someone had rushed over.

"Go," Swan said. "I'll stay with him."

Ross bolted for the door, parting the crowd with cries of, "Police! Move aside!"

She blew through the doors, almost knocking over a young couple just arriving. Paniagua's vehicle was already on the move, down the street and turning a corner. She was going to lose him. She rushed to her car and pursued anyway. As she rounded the corner, she saw him turn west onto 219. At least, she thought it was him. The vehicle's size and color were right. She radioed for backup, giving the location, direction, and vehicle information. Thank God she had the license memorized.

Flooring the accelerator, Ross weaved around the moderate traffic, hoping for a safe spot to slap her Kojak light onto her car's roof, but she had to keep both hands on the wheel and eyes on the road. The last thing she needed was to cause an accident.

She gained on Paniagua, but as she came up on his left, he must have realized she wasn't just an aggressive driver. He cut her off and widened the gap. The lanes collapsed to one each way. Paniagua leaned on his horn. There was almost no shoulder here. A few drivers veered out of his path, others didn't. He swerved into the oncoming lane to get around them, nearly causing more than one head-on collision. Somehow, everyone escaped.

"Stop driving like a crook," Ross snarled. The traffic thinned as they blew by a synagogue. Ross lowered her window, grabbed the light, switched it on, and slid it onto the roof. Magnet grabbed metal. Now Paniagua knew who was after him and didn't like it. They were topping a hundred miles an hour on a two-lane semi-rural road, dodging other vehicles as they came upon them. *We're going to die*, Ross told herself, but she didn't cut Paniagua any slack.

She radioed her position after they ran the red light at state route 108, leaving behind a mass of squealing brakes and screaming horns. Sirens sounded behind and, maybe, ahead. The cavalry was coming. She hoped they could box Paniagua in and convince him to stop.

Between the trees, the curves, and the hills, she couldn't see that far, but the sirens got louder as they closed on Brighton Dam Road, then flashing lights came into view and Paniagua realized he couldn't escape. Brake lights flared. He fishtailed to a stop beside a line of pines. Ross nearly rammed him from behind but veered into the grass to avoid the collision. Part of her wished she *had* hit him. It would've served him right, except the paperwork would be horrid.

His door popped open. He sprang out and made for the trees. Ross nearly pursued, but he fell and seemed unable to regain his footing in the mulch or pine straw or whatever padded the slight slope beneath the boughs. Maybe he'd sprained an ankle. That would be apropos, too.

Since he wasn't going anywhere, she waited for the uniformed cops to arrive, weapons drawn, and extract him from the shadows. Once he was cuffed and seated in the grass by the road, she approached. "Thanks, guys," she told the officers. "That was one hairy ride." She stood over Paniagua, giving him the full benefit of her angry face.

She said nothing. He offered nothing.

"What the hell?" she asked.

Still nothing.

"Detective Holly Ross. We spoke on the phone earlier."

"Lawyer," he said.

"You are not."

"I want my lawyer."

"I don't blame you. Who was that man at the bar?"

"A vulture."

Ross sat in the grass, cross-legged, and stared at him.

"I don't know his name," Paniagua said.

"Blackmailer, right? He had photos of you and some hot young thing. Where's the envelope?"

"What envelope?"

"The one you ran off with."

"I want my lawyer."

"No wonder your mother-in-law was so wound up. She was right about you."

"Don't drag her into this."

"*I'm* dragging her into it?"

"I want my lawyer."

Ross stood. "Take him in," she told the nearest officer. "Get him his damn lawyer." To Paniagua she said, "I'll be seeing you."

She stalked back to her car, slid in, left the door open so the warm breeze could touch her face. She watched them herd Paniagua into a squad car. They searched his vehicle, then called a tow truck to remove it. It all took time.

"You all right, Detective?"

Ross looked up. A nameplate met her eyes. Officer Jeff Bartholomew. She looked farther up and found a young, angular face. A concerned face. Only then did she realize her hands were shaking. No, not just her hands. Her entire body. She drew a long breath to calm down. "Yeah," she said. "I thought..."

He nodded. "Thought you were going to crash."

"Die, more like."

He smiled. "You did good."

"Thanks."

"Want me to drive you back?"

Might not be a bad idea, but no, she didn't want a crutch. Instead, she forced a laugh and ribbed, "Are you hitting on me?"

He looked thoughtful, as though about to confess. But then he grinned. "You're out of my league, ma'am. I just want to make sure you're safe."

"I'll be fine," she said. "Thanks."

He winked and returned to assist with the rest of the operation.

"Out of your league," Ross mused. "That's the nicest thing a guy's ever said to me."

†

Paramedics packed the victim's wound to staunch external bleeding and loaded him into the ambulance. In their wake, O'Callaghan's slouched back into its Friday night routine as though nothing had happened. Most of the customers didn't know, anyway. They'd only seen the EMTs enter with their gear and exit with a patient. Could've been nothing, just a choking victim or a heart attack.

Left without transport, Theresa Swan bummed a ride in the ambulance. The victim was dazed from the fall, a possible knock on the head, and blood loss from the stab wound in his abdomen. He was barely responsive. Swan searched him for ID while waiting for the paramedics and found a driver's license in the name of Warren Beecham, age forty-one, with an address in Takoma Park, where Maryland bumped into D.C.

Beyond the victim's wound, Swan found only two pieces of physical evidence. She requested a plastic bag and kitchen gloves from the manager, then snapped pictures with her cell phone and collected every shred of torn photo she could find. There weren't many. A few had fallen to the floor, but Beecham had packed most of them into the envelope with which Paniagua absconded. She also photographed and bagged a bloodied steak knife she found under a bar stool. The manager identified that as belonging to the restaurant.

Upon arrival at the ER, Beecham was triaged and rushed into surgery, leaving Swan to do the requisite admissions paperwork. Beecham wasn't just a victim, not in Swan's eyes. He'd become a suspect in a web of crimes ranging from vandalism to blackmail to espionage. None of it made sense, but she wasn't taking chances. She had his personal information, if it was real. Her intuition told her no. When the doctors were done, she would need full details on Beecham's injuries and, if possible, access for questioning.

Swan debated calling Montufar, but it was Friday night. *Somebody* might as well have a quiet evening.

Forms taken care of, she settled in to wait. Surgeries for this type of wound could range from simple to complex, depending on the internal damage. It might be an hour or four hours. No way to tell. She texted Ken to let him know where she was and that she was vechicleless.

RU ok? he replied immediately.

I'm fine, she assured him.

Should I pick U up?

Not yet. Might be a long night.

Should I sing to U?

Noooo!

He sent her an *LOL* and a link to a music video instead.

Chapter 16

The bonsai show was stunning. In addition to the Japanese, Chinese, and American pavilions where the National Arboretum's collection of works by prominent masters of the art was displayed and cared for, the Potomac Bonsai Association had assembled an exhibition of trees styled by the local artists of the Association's member clubs.

Peller and Churchill wandered the displays and watched demonstrations. Whether straight or twisted, full or spare, aged to perfection or battered by the elements, each tree seemed to tell a story. Peller was most drawn to those whose roots twined about great rocks. Churchill liked the forest plantings, particularly *Goshin*, the famous work by Japanese-American artist John Naka, composed of eleven Foemina junipers representing his grandchildren.

They also browsed the vendor tables without buying. Trees, pots, tools, supplies—all would be wasted on them.

"I can't keep a cactus alive," Churchill joked.

"House plants were never my forte, either," Peller admitted.

"They aren't house plants," a bearded, graying fellow standing next to them said. He was bent over, studying a four-hundred-dollar tree. "You keep them outdoors, for the most part. Tropicals come in for the winter, of course, but hardy trees need the winter cold to stay healthy."

"That's even worse," Churchill told him. "I live in an apartment."

"You could keep them at my place," Peller joked. "They could die outside, where they're happy."

She play-punched his shoulder.

"You can learn," the bearded man said. "I've been doing this for thirty years, and I'm still learning. Just start small. Join a club. They'll help you get going."

"We'll ponder that," Peller said. They moved on, and once they were out of earshot, he told Churchill, "I guess we should have started thirty years ago."

"We didn't know each other thirty years ago, Sherlock."

Peller about choked.

She laughed. "Hey, you're the one who said it."

"I only meant—"

"I know."

He thought he heard Sandra laughing. *Lighten up, Sherlock*, she commanded.

Not you, too.

Churchill took his hand. "Come on, there's a display of viewing stones. I want to see that."

The stones, called suiseki in Japanese, were chunks of rock that evoked a natural scene or object. Often, they resembled mountains. Others suggested lakes or rivers, still others animals. Nature had fashioned them, not human hands. Neither cut nor polished, they were collected and placed in a wooden stand crafted to fit, or in a tray filled with sand. Peller found the effect calming. It almost transported him to the Rocky Mountains towering over Denver.

They spent the whole morning at the show. By then they were starving, so they found a nearby restaurant for lunch then returned for a drive through the arboretum's gardens and collections. Many of the dog-woods were in bloom. Churchill wanted to walk among them, so they wandered the paths for over half an hour, stopping at an Anacostia River overlook. The river crept by below the trees. The moment felt ancient, timeless, as though they had passed through a portal to a thousand years before.

Peller didn't realize he had put his arm about Churchill's waist and pulled her close until her breath tickled his cheek. It felt right. For the first time, it felt right.

And that, of course, was when his cell phone went off.

†

Captain Whitney Morris liked her weekends. Most of them. On Saturdays and Sundays, her husband Doctor Daniel Morris enforced, as much as possible, a relaxing regimen designed to let them decompress. He took a dim view of high-stress jobs even though they had each claimed one at an early age. "In my defense," he sometimes told people, "I was an ignorant kid when I decided to tackle med school."

Captain Morris didn't think he'd been *that* ignorant, and his devotion to her and her health was sweet, if occasionally annoying. Like now.

He was giving her the evil eye over the dinner table while on her cell phone FBI Special Agent in Charge Miriam Pack spoiled Morris' home-made pasticcio with a tirade loud enough to be heard in the next room. Underneath the rant, water splashed. A lot of water. In an echo chamber. When Pack paused for a breath, Morris asked, "Are you in the shower?"

"I was, until I heard what your cowgirls did! What the hell kind of operation are you running? What part of 'hands off' don't you get?"

"Let's not jump to con—"

"I'm not jumping! I'm standing here dripping wet because of *your* detectives. Reign them in, Morris. Now. I don't want them anywhere near my guy."

"Sounds like they kept your guy from dying," Morris snapped.

"Don't sugar coat it. They were off the rails, and you know it."

She didn't know anything but what Pack had told her around fits of snarling and cursing, and that wasn't much. "I'll get on it," Morris said. "But you need a chill pill."

"I'll prescribe her one," Daniel muttered. Thankfully, Pack didn't hear.

"What about that phone number for AJ?" Morris asked. "That should have been of some value."

"It's no longer in service. The damn thing was prepaid, so no address on file. Plus, it's long out of service. It was activated six and a half years ago. The last payment was six months later. After that, nothing."

Interesting. AJ got the phone half a year before Mark Tyler's death and ditched it right after. Was she the killer? Had someone been closing in on her? Not HCPD. They didn't even know she existed until Father Ed handed over his brother's cell phone.

"No redemption there," Pack added, possibly to twist the knife. "Keep your guys out of my way."

The call ended on a less than cordial note, after which Morris set her phone down and chewed the air while glaring at her cooling pasticcio as though it had caused the fracas.

"So?" Daniel asked.

She picked up the phone and all but smacked Peller's contact icon. "I have to handle this," she said.

He pushed back, crossed his arms over his chest, and watched her handle it. Peller answered on the third ring. "We have a situation," Morris told him.

The nature of the situation must've been baked into her voice, because he asked, "You ticked off the FBI already?"

"Not I. Holly and Theresa."

"What happened?"

"According to Pack, they followed Rodrigo Paniagua to a bar, where he met with and stabbed a person of great interest in the Clare Fleming case. The victim is now at Howard County General in fair condition. Paniagua is in custody following a high-speed chase."

"Holly and Theresa?" Peller asked, alarmed.

"Fine, I hope. I haven't talked to them."

"How did the FBI find out?"

"They had a tail on their guy."

"Why didn't they step in and take charge?"

"God knows, Rick. Maybe Pack chewed me out because her people screwed up. We probably did them a favor, but you know how it works. Get our side of the story from Theresa and Holly and report back to me. Keep it low key. I just need the facts, particularly why they followed Paniagua and under what authority. If any."

She could hear him wince. Holly Ross wasn't known for restraint. "Got it," Peller acknowledged. "I'll let you know."

When Morris put her phone down, Daniel eyed it. "I swear, I'm going to confiscate your battery."

She gave him a weary smile. "Sometimes I wish you would. But who would hold the county together?"

"Let Rick be the workaholic. He likes it."

"Not really. He just doesn't know what else to do with himself."

Morris pushed her phone aside, partly to distance herself from it, partly to keep Daniel from making good on his threat.

†

Given how scattered the team was, they agreed to meet in a Burtonsville eatery halfway between Columbia and the National Arboretum. The establishment had a family restaurant feel, smallish, brick, and named for route 198 beside which it sat. It served American fare and featured live music, although they arrived early enough to miss both the crowds and the entertainment.

That was fine. They needed space to talk. Peller got them a table for six, and now they were all there: himself, Dumas, Montufar, Swan, Ross, and one interloper. He couldn't leave Churchill in the car while they ate. She had a conspiratorial gleam in her eye. All-area access excited her. Before they went in, Peller instructed her to be a silent partner. She made a zipping motion over her mouth and winked.

Once food was ordered, Peller dove into the incident. He didn't mean to put Ross in the hot seat, but she squirmed as though he had. It had, after all, been her idea.

"I wasn't planning on getting involved," she said. "But even Carlotta Becerra knew Paniagua was up to something. Plus, Eric was right. There are too many government contractors circling the vandalism case to be a coincidence." She glanced at her Sergeant as though begging for support.

For a moment, the look in Churchill's eyes suggested she might give Ross a hug. Thankfully, She didn't.

Dumas nodded. "There are," he said. "And you weren't exactly out of line, but given the sensitivity of the situation, you should've run it by me. Besides, what if he did meet up with a woman? You couldn't do anything. It might have been a run-of-the-mill affair. Nothing illegal, not even reasonable suspicion."

"But he didn't meet up with a woman," Swan pointed out. "He stabbed a suspected spy. Even if Paniagua wasn't passing secrets, the knife-work was illegal."

"And the FBI didn't bat an eyelash," Ross added. "Who knows if they were even there? We sure didn't see them."

Peller listened to the back-and-forth, absorbed the information without rendering judgement. "We'll assume they were, if only because Pack said so. They might have been gathering intel and weren't prepared to make a move. And when you two jumped in..." He spread his hands.

"The feds didn't have to," Montufar finished. "Convenient in one sense, but it doesn't look good to anyone's superiors. If the press gets wind of why Paniagua and Beecham were meeting, we'll all look like idiots."

Ross folded her hands on the table and studied them. "I swear, I only meant to watch. If anything surfaced, I would have turned it over to the FBI. But come on, for all we knew, Paniagua was just going out for a drink."

"Which hardly links our case to the FBI's," Peller said. When Ross pinched her lips, he added, "I'm not criticizing, Holly. Legally, you did nothing wrong. Everything happened in public, so Paniagua and Beecham can't claim any expectation of privacy. But we're skirting the edge of a federal investigation, and we know it. We need to tread carefully."

Montufar, eyes narrowed, stared across the restaurant at nothing.

"Uh-oh," Dumas teased.

"Beecham," she muttered.

"Don't keep us hanging, dear."

"The FBI was watching him in connection with Clare Fleming. He's her handler."

Peller picked up his fork, looked at it, put it down. "They didn't say so, but it's likely."

"On the surface, it looks like he set up Paniagua with a woman and then tried to blackmail him into providing classified information. He could have done the same with Mark Tyler, and that could have led to Tyler's death." When Peller raised an eyebrow, Montufar smirked. "I know, but run with me for a bit. Beecham badly misread Paniagua. He might have misread Tyler as well. And that connects to the vandalism because Mark Tyler is Father Ed's brother. But how does it connect? What about Beecham's network could lead to Mary and Carlyle scrawling messages on church walls?"

Dumas snapped his fingers. "Right. Mary's connected to someone in Beecham's network. She knows what Beecham is up to, but moreover she knows that one of the priests knows."

Swan gaped at him. "How would one of the priests know?"

"Through confession. Father Walter mentioned the seal of the confessional."

"Oh, come on," Ross objected. "Mary's barely an adult. She'd have to be hip deep in Beecham's swamp to have all that information. Does that make sense? And what about Carlyle Navin? What motive could *he* possibly have?"

"Nothing we know of," Peller said, "aside from pleasing Mary." He still hadn't dug her out of memory, but her identity was in there somewhere. He was certain of it. He must have skimmed over some fleeting mention of her somewhere. In an interview. In a report...

Wait. He almost had it.

Churchill raised her hand as though in grade school and broke her vow of silence. "Is it just a coincidence," she asked, "that the first message was left at the feet of Mary?"

Everyone looked at her as though hypnotized. The spell was shattered by a crash of glass in the kitchen and accompanying raised voices. Peller's almost-insight slipped away. Damn it.

"No coincidence," Montufar said. "Everything here means something. It's all symbolic. Mary—Carlyle's Mary—is calling someone to confession. The inward-facing message on Father Walter's window wasn't only so someone on the inside could read it; it's reflection, looking inward. The message on the garage door at St. Paul is like a billboard, announcing something to the world."

"The crab basket?" Dumas asked.

Montufar thought, then did a search on her phone and read the results. "Matthew 5:14 – 16: 'You are the light of the world. A city set on a mountain cannot be hidden. Nor do they light a lamp and then put it under a bushel basket; it is set on a lampstand, where it gives light to all in the house. Just so, your light must shine before others, that they may see your good deeds and glorify your heavenly Father.'" She looked up. "We were wrong. These aren't death threats. These are pleas for truth. Honesty. Light."

Peller could see that, except for one thing. "What about the dog genitalia?"

"I don't know," Montufar admitted. "But I'm sure it meant something to Mary. Something that fit the theme, at least in her mind."

Swan folded her arms on the table and leaned on them. "All that to get a priest to open up?"

"Sure," Ross said. "If she's desperate enough. Maybe one of her friends or relatives is in Beecham's employ."

That would tie everything together, but again, caution was in order. "Let's not get ahead of ourselves," Peller said. "We need further evidence. We need to discover Mary's identity and connections. As for the Paniagua incident, my report will confirm Holly and Theresa weren't out of line. They didn't know he was meeting Beecham. They did their duty when things turned ugly. End of story. The Captain will be on board with that. We'll let her fend off the sharks."

"Poor lady," Churchill said.

Peller raised an eyebrow at her second violation, but the rest nodded agreement.

†

By the time Peller pulled into his driveway, killed the engine, and clambered out of his truck, he was beyond exhausted. Churchill was still with him, as fresh as ever. And Jerry Souter was rocking on his porch, eyeing them with amusement, though only those who knew him well would get that. It barely deviated from his default expression.

May as well get it over with. Peller offered his arm to Churchill and said, "I'd like you to meet someone." He escorted her across the lawn, up the steps, and into Souter's presence.

Souter looked up at them, as serene as a warm summer day, with all the curiosity of a sleeping dog. "Name's Jerry," he said. "You must be Joan." He rocked forward and extended his massive hand. It swallowed hers up, but his grip was so gentle, they might not have touched.

"Hi, Jerry. Rick's told me about you."

"He left a few war stories for me, I hope. Sit a spell." Souter motioned to the rocker beside him, the one Peller usually occupied. Churchill settled into it, while Peller leaned on the wooden porch railing. "Mind the splinters," Souter told him. "I gotta refinish that one of these days."

"I'm used to flesh wounds." Peller winked. Mere deflection, that. He felt he should say something else, something about Joan, but his mind was blank.

Souter didn't need his chatter. He rocked and gazed at the neighborhood, content with silence.

Joan was another matter. She squirmed a bit in the chair. She looked at Peller. She looked at Souter. Then she laughed. "Do I pass the test?"

Souter cracked the barest of smiles. "Don't see how you could fail. I leave judgement to higher powers. He's the one you gotta convince." He nodded at Peller.

"Don't start with that, now," Peller replied lightly.

Leaning toward Churchill, Souter added, "He's not all bad. He's just had a rough spell."

Rough spell. That was an understatement.

"I know," Churchill said. "But he's tough, too. Kind of like you, I think."

Souter shrugged. "I don't know about that."

"You're still here."

"That's just good genes. My family lives long. You want anything to drink?"

Peller waved that off. "We just came from a stimulating dinner-and-crime event. I'm for an early night."

"He doesn't tell me much about those crime events," Souter confided to Churchill. "Only enough to let me interfere with his judgement."

She laughed. "I got away with that tonight. It might be the last time."

"Nah. He needs a bit of interference now and again. You keep on."

Peller suspected Souter wasn't talking about criminal investigations. He wasn't sure whether to object or ignore it or embrace it. People had indeed interfered in his personal life over the past couple of years. A lot. He'd resented it, often tried to push by them as though he hadn't noticed, and yet here he was on this porch with Churchill, a prelude to another night under the same roof with her. Only this time it would be his roof. His and Sandra's roof. It felt...

...strange, anyway.

It's your roof, Sandra whispered in his ear. *I have a bigger roof now.*

He didn't want to hear that, although in some measure he did.

Churchill and Souter were both eyeing him. Peller pushed away from the railing, brushed off his hands, and said, "Let me know if you want help refinishing this thing."

Souter gave him a military salute.

"I hate to cut this short, but I really am tired."

"Go home, old man."

Churchill rose from the rocker and touched Souter's shoulder. "It was great to finally meet you," she said.

"Likewise."

She hooked her arm through Peller's and waved toward his house. "Come on, Sherlock. Let's get you home."

Peller pinched his lips and glanced at Souter.

"I'm a military man," Souter assured him. "I keep operational secrets."

Great. "You did that on purpose," he whispered.

Churchill smiled and led him down the steps.

†

Peller's mind liked to play tricks on him. A particular trick, at least. When he was relaxed, when he'd left work a million miles behind, it would pick at a loose bit of mortar, some small detail that, once dislodged, caused a cascade of bricks to topple, revealing whatever had been walled up behind.

It happened again Sunday morning. Twice.

He woke from a deep sleep alone in the quiet of his room, a faint odor of sausage wafting up from the kitchen, an occasional clank of cookware signaling Churchill making breakfast. The woman loved to cook and was good at it.

He tucked his hands behind his head and gazed at a stripe of morning sunlight spraying onto the ceiling through a small gap in the curtains. It would be a nice day according to the last forecast he'd seen: bright, warm, light breeze. A good day for yardwork. Maybe it was time to start on that rose bed expansion. Churchill wanted to help, and well, she was here, so why not?

Peller sat. Churchill's clothes were slung over the footboard. That was odd. They hadn't gone back to her place before coming here. She didn't have extra clothes with her. What was she wearing down there in the kitchen? In fact, what were her clothes doing in his room at all? He'd given her Jason's old room for the night. Not that he saw her go. They sat on his bed for a time, talking, before he flopped back and closed his eyes, and the next thing he knew, it was morning. He was still dressed. Rumpled, but dressed.

He rose and shoved aside the curtains. He blinked into the sudden light, then studied Churchill's clothes again. Something occurred to him, but not the answer to that puzzle. He grabbed his cell phone and hurried downstairs while searching the web for Biblical references to canines. And there it was.

"Joan," he said as he came into the kitchen, focused on what he'd found. "Listen to this."

Dressed in a light-weight chestnut nightgown, she was at the stove scrambling eggs. She turned and smiled.

"This is Phillipians 3:2," Peller said, then he did a double-take. He gaped at her, scriptures forgotten.

Churchill looked down at herself. "I'm sorry," she said. "I hope you don't mind, but I needed something, and it was in the top dresser drawer."

She was wearing Sandra's nightgown. Sandra's favorite nightgown. Peller hadn't given away any of her clothing. He had nobody to give it to and at the time couldn't part with it. Maybe he should have later, but every time he thought about it, he hedged.

"I should have asked first," she said. "I'm sorry. You fell asleep, and..."

"It's okay. You look great in it." Which she did.

There's hope for you yet, he heard Sandra tease.

He refocused on his phone. "Listen to this. Phillipians 3:2. 'Beware of the dogs, beware of the evil workers, beware of the false circumcision.'" He looked up to find her half puzzled, half amused.

"I need to run it by Corina, but I think this could be the connection to the...you know."

"I know. I heard about it yesterday. But that wasn't circumcision. That was castration."

Peller suspected it was close enough for Mary's purposes, if Mary was behind it.

"Rick." Churchill bit her lip. "Is Mary the sort of person who would do that to a dog?"

Who could say? They knew nothing about her. Jacey Alexandre's profile suggested someone on a mission, a crusader. Who knew what such a person might do? "According to the lab report," he said, "the animal was already dead."

"Even so."

"We have to find her. That's the only way to resolve this."

"Assuming she's the vandal."

"Yes." He sat at the table and reread the passage. Another incongruity struck him. "You're asking good questions for an outsider. I thought you were in customer service."

Churchill laughed. "It's a people position."

The mental cogs were still turning. He couldn't stop them. "Mary must be connected to either Father Ed or Father Walter."

"Not Father Dan?"

"I doubt it. The more I think about it, the more I think the St. Paul incidents are secondary. St. Augustine is the main attraction. The connection between the vandalism and the espionage ring has to be Mark Tyler."

"People form networks. What if there's more than one connection?"

That was possible, but one thing at a time. He started to call Montufar.

Churchill stepped to his side and relieved him of his phone. "It's Sunday, Sherlock. The only work you're doing today is around the house."

Peller gave her a long, slow once-over. One more anomaly occurred to him, one that should have occurred a lot sooner. It would have, had the Bible verse not surfaced from the depths of his memory. "Joan," he said.

"Yes?"

"Did you change in my room?"

She shrugged. "That's where the nightgown was. And you were asleep."

"I might've woken up."

She handed his phone back and winked. "You might've."

Whether he was shocked or pleased or both, the distraction gave one more fact time to steal from the shadows into his consciousness.

He knew who Mary was. And he knew how he knew.

Chapter 17

Monday, May seventh. A cold front swept over central Maryland in the small hours of the morning. Rain hammered on roofs. Thunder shook people and dogs awake. Peller's rose bed expansion, planned and dug the previous afternoon with Churchill's help, became a sea of mud. The commute was horrid, even though the storm had largely passed before the workforce mobbed the streets.

Peller presented his Biblical discovery to Montufar in the break room while she filled her coffee cup.

"I asked my dad about that once," she said. "I was upset dogs were portrayed so badly in the Bible. I think I was maybe twelve at the time." Cup full, she added sugar and swirled the drink with a stir stick. She sampled the steaming liquid before continuing, "He said dogs back then were street animals, not house pets. They were considered unclean. The references to them in the Bible are always along those lines. To compare a person to a dog is to call them unclean, probably wicked. Among the Jews, circumcision was a sign of belonging to God's people. But outward signs can be misleading. In modern terms, calling yourself a Christian and going through the motions doesn't mean you're living a Christian life, or even that you believe the Church's teachings."

"I see," Peller said. "Then whether the dog genitalia are a reference to this specific verse or the concept generally, the message fits the theme."

Montufar nodded, took another sip, made a face at the cup. "Is this a knock-off brand?"

Peller glanced at the box of pods next to the coffee maker. "Yep. Maybe someone stiffed the fund."

Montufar took another drink anyway. "What's the plan?"

"For the case or the coffee?"

She gave him one of her annoyed cop looks. She'd become famous for them and could wield them equally to intimidate suspects and amuse colleagues.

"Another talk with Father Ed and Father Walter," Peller said.

"What about?"

"I know who Mary is."

Montufar nearly slopped coffee on herself. She set the mug on a table. "Who?"

"Mark Tyler's daughter. Father Ed's niece."

"How do you know that?"

"A line in Bill Trengove's report. He listed the family members, including the children, Ben and Mary."

Montufar retrieved her mug and took a careful sip, her eyes never leaving Peller's face. "Okay. I'll come with you."

He was grateful for the backup. He didn't normally need it for something this simple, but Montufar's connection with the Church might help. He nodded at her mug. "After you finish. I wouldn't want to deprive you of such a delicious beverage."

"Right," she said. "You just want me fully caffeinated."

"So long as it helps."

"Sometimes," she admitted. "Sometimes."

†

About the time Peller and Montufar walked out, Captain Morris got off the phone and called Ross, Swan, and Dumas into her office. She'd rather address the whole team, but this couldn't wait, and Holly Ross was the one for whom the bell was tolling. Once they were seated, she clicked her pen a few times before realizing it, set it down, and sighed.

"Must be good," Dumas said.

"If by good you mean rotten. I just spoke with Agent Pack. She's not my favorite member of the human race right now. As she sees it, everything is our fault, including the weather and the price of milk. The *best* worst part is, no matter how incompetent we are, she suddenly needs our help."

"Joy," Swan muttered.

Ross leaned forward, no doubt sensing she was in the eye of the storm and ready to prove she could ride it out. Morris didn't often worry about her team, but that woman was too eager sometimes. "Warren Beecham slipped out of the hospital around four A.M. Walked out through emergency with the help of a security guard."

Dumas almost laughed. "Wasn't he hooked up to monitors?"

"He's clever. He must have dressed while connected, then pulled the plugs and hurried out with the cables. They were found on the floor outside the ward."

"Points for brains. How did he find his way out? That hospital's a rabbit warren."

"He told a security guard he was lost. Claimed he'd brought his wife into emergency the previous evening and needed to get home to bring her things. The guard escorted him out."

Dumas put a hand to his forehead. "Great."

Swan smirked. "Don't blame the guard. In his street clothes, Beecham wouldn't have looked like an escapee."

"Meanwhile," Morris continued, "after grilling Paniagua for several hours, the FBI decided to leave him in our custody. The story he's sticking to—which Pack rightly doesn't believe—is that Beecham insulted him and he blew a gasket. He says he'd never met Beecham before the incident."

"That's dumb," Ross said. "Beecham passed him an envelope. Paniagua ran off with it. It's in our reports."

"Unfortunately, no such envelope was found."

"Paniagua had plenty of opportunity to ditch it before he was arrested," Swan said.

"Yes, but since we don't have it, it's a moot point. Holly's testimony isn't sufficient. Not to call up ghosts from the past, but in Pack's view, a defense attorney could easily cast suspicion on anything she says."

Ross bit her lip.

Morris shrugged. "Which is why Pack wants you, Holly, to follow up on that envelope. You pursued him, and you interviewed him a couple times. See if you can track it down or convince him to confess the truth. They're prepared to offer immunity if he helps take Beecham down. Which means his assault charge is in our hands until it isn't."

"That's not how it works," Dumas pointed out.

"It is now."

He crossed his arms over his chest and made a face. Dumas never liked deals that made serious charges disappear, and stabbing someone in the gut in a crowded restaurant was serious by any definition. But neither he nor Morris were calling the shots, and they all knew it. The FBI had given them a crowbar and expected them to use it.

Ross, anyway, had no misgivings. "I got this."

"Maybe take Kevin with you," Swan suggested. "He's on a roll."

Morris about said no. They had to handle this themselves.

Ross beat her to it. "Won't be necessary. I almost have a rapport with Paniagua. It'll be enough."

Morris raised an eyebrow. "Almost?"

Ross shrugged. "The first half of our first conversation was fine. I think I can get him back on our side."

Dumas made a face.

"Spit it out," Morris told him.

"Assuming he was on our side in the first place. He tried to kill Beecham in front of everyone. With the restaurant's steak knife. That's not premeditated. Whatever was in that envelope blindsided him."

"You're saying he didn't know he was being blackmailed until that moment?" Swan asked. "But if he was seeing someone like Clare Fleming..."

She didn't need to finish. Had that been the case, Paniagua would have known Beecham's game. If he wasn't in a cooperative mood, he should already have talked to his FSO, who would have relayed it to the FBI. Maybe that was why they hadn't moved in. But then why the homicidal outburst?

He should have pretended to play ball with Beecham. Ergo, Dumas was right. Paniagua wasn't helping the feds. It felt like a drug deal gone wrong, but with state secrets instead of cocaine.

Ross wasn't fazed. "He dumped the envelope somewhere along miles of road, maybe in pieces. It might have disintegrated in the rain or blown away on the wind. Finding it is dicey. But no problem. I'll get him to talk."

Although the others didn't share her enthusiasm, they had little choice. "Do it," Morris said.

†

The trees dripped on the walkways as Peller and Montufar made their way from the parking lot to the St. Augustine rectory. A few errant rays of light breached the billowed clouds, but the sky remained ominous. The forecast had a schizoid quality, calling for rain on and off, mixed with partial sunshine.

Peller rang the bell, expecting Clare Fleming to answer. Instead, Father Walter was there, cane in hand, his face a bit paler than before. "Ah," he said. "More questions."

"I'm afraid so."

The priest opened the door wide and motioned them in.

"We'd like to speak with both you and Father Ed, if possible."

Father Walter nodded, got them settled, and offered them coffee or tea, which they declined. He then called up the stairs for Father Ed. When the younger priest came down, he too looked haggard. "I do wish you hadn't come here," he said. "You know why."

Montufar nodded. "Message received. But things have grown more serious. We need straight answers if we're going to protect you and your parishioners."

Father Ed motioned them into the kitchen. "Let's talk out here," he said. "I need to be active, and things need doing. Clare called in sick late last week and hasn't been heard from since. That's not like her. I can't get a replacement until Thursday."

Probably the FBI's doing. Agent Pack hadn't said a word about Fleming recently.

The detectives followed Father Ed into the kitchen, with Father Walter bringing up the rear. They settled around the table, all save Father Ed, who puttered at the sink, halfheartedly rinsing dishes and loading them into the dishwasher.

"We need information on someone of your acquaintance," Peller said.

"If possible," Father Ed replied. "Please don't ask for anything I can't give."

Turning to Father Walter, Peller continued, "You have a nephew, Carlyle Navin."

Father Walter narrowed his eyes but failed to either confirm or deny.

"We've talked to him," Montufar added. "And his roommate."

Father Walter rubbed his chin. "He doesn't have a roommate. At least, he never mentioned one."

"A young woman named Mary," Peller said. "Father Ed's niece."

Father Walter frowned. Father Ed froze, a dripping plate in his hands. After a moment, he replaced it in the sink and groped for a towel to dry his hands. "This is news to me," he muttered.

"And to me." Father Walter grabbed his cane and leaned on it as though he couldn't stay in the chair without it. "But what has it to do with spray paint?"

Peller watched Father Ed, whose back was still turned. "Good question. How long have they known each other?"

Neither priest answered. Father Ed kept his eyes on the sink, while Father Walter studied the tabletop.

Peller glanced at Montufar. Getting the signal, she rose and went to Father Ed's side, leaned on the counter, tried to make eye contact.

He didn't oblige.

"Please, Father," she said. "If you know anything, tell us. People have gotten hurt."

He turned in alarm. "Mary?"

"Mary and Carlyle are fine so far, but it may not stay that way."

The priests looked more pained now, but they maintained their silence. Peller decided to deploy his nuclear weapon. "Carlyle wrote the messages at St. Paul. His handwriting matches. We believe Mary wrote the ones here."

Father Ed stumbled toward the table. Montufar caught his arm and helped him into a chair. Father Walter looked like he'd bitten into a worm-ridden apple.

"That's not possible," Father Ed said. "Why would they do such a thing? They're family!"

"We believe the messages are a plea for help," Montufar said. "For truth. Mary's father—your brother—was murdered. She thinks someone here or at St. Paul can ID the killer."

"I already told you what I know. Or had Bianca tell you. If Mark made a confession, it wasn't to me, and it certainly wasn't to Father Walter. He wasn't here until three years later."

Peller turned to Father Walter. "No. Mark Tyler couldn't have confessed to you."

Father Walter shook his head.

"But someone else did."

The old priest was so still, he might have died. Father Ed gaped but couldn't find words. Even Montufar was stunned by Peller's leap of logic.

"Who was it, Father?" Peller demanded.

"The seal of the confessional is absolute," Father Walter muttered.

Father Ed buried his face in his hands.

Montufar's eyes lit up. She got it. "You've said that before. Someone did confess to you. About Mark's murder. That's what Mary is after."

Father Walter had all but become one of the statues dotting the ground, cold, silent, unmoving.

"AJ," Peller told Montufar. "Amelia Jenkins. She confessed to killing Mark Tyler."

The priest-statue said nothing, but he didn't have to. His silence confirmed Peller's conclusion.

Father Ed collapsed on the table and cried.

Montufar put a hand on his shoulder. "But how did Mary know?"

"Excellent question," Peller said. "And it can't be good that she does. Not with Beecham on the loose."

†

Whenever Ross entered an interrogation room, she felt she'd stepped onto the set of a TV cop drama. Drab walls, one-way mirror, bare tables and chairs that looked half a century old. Now, Paniagua sat at that table fidgeting. He eyed her while she folded her hands before her. She hadn't brought any notes. She didn't need them. All she had was her smile, which might calm him or unnerve him. Either could work.

"Good morning, Rodrigo," she chirped. "That was quite a ride the other day."

He half-smirked, half-grimaced.

"Let's start at the beginning. Warren Beecham, age forty-one, from Takoma Park, Maryland. Who is this guy, and why does he deserve death?"

"Who?"

"You know who. The guy you stabbed in the gut."

"I didn't know his name. Never saw him before. He just showed up and insulted me for no apparent reason."

"Must've been some insult."

Paniagua nodded.

"Like what?"

"Is it important?"

"If it was worth a man's life, it must've been."

He shifted as though he hadn't expected her to out-logic him. Probably he hadn't. Most men didn't. "I was out of line. I'll admit that."

"I'd call that out of line, yes. First-degree assault. Maximum penalty, twenty-five years."

"I have a good lawyer. He's already working on this. He also told me not to say anything without him present."

Ross cocked her head.

"I don't plan on going to prison. My family depends on me, you know."

"You mean your wife and kids and your sweet mother-in-law who got so bent out of shape over your affairs that she smashed up a quarter of the vehicles in North Laurel in her mental anguish?"

"I wasn't having affairs."

"Just working late."

"Yes."

"And stabbing foreign agents in the gut."

Paniagua frowned. "Foreign agents?"

Ross leaned forward and lowered her voice. "Come on, Rodrigo. I saw him slip you that envelope. I saw him take it back. I saw you shred that photo and throw it in his face. I saw you stab him and bolt, envelope in hand. He didn't insult you. He tried to blackmail you. With photos of you and another woman, right?"

"There were no photos. There was no envelope."

"You know there was. I can testify to it. Also, we have a few fragments of the one you tore up. The court will believe me."

He smirked. "Then where is this envelope?"

Ross sighed, sat back, returned to normal volume. "Beecham's in the FBI's sights. When they catch him—and they will—the truth will come out. This will go so much easier for you and your family if you cooperate."

Paniagua chewed that over. "Are we talking immunity?"

"Maybe."

"How soon?"

"That's not up to me."

"But it's legit. The FBI wants to deal."

Ross nodded.

He was interested, she could tell he was, but he was hedging. Why? It should be an easy choice: his affairs out in the open and him in prison, or cooperation and everything hushed up. But he didn't make that choice. He tottered on the edge, unable to make the leap.

"You aren't a bad guy, Rodrigo. You just got caught up in some bad things. The women did, too. The FBI isn't after you or them. They want Beecham. He's the real bad guy." Which might have been a stretch. The feds took traitors down with extreme prejudice, no matter the excuse. But Captain Morris said the FBI was offering Paniagua a deal. If it was a lie, it at least wasn't Ross' lie.

"The women." He perched his elbows on the table and steepled his fingers before his chin. Maybe hope had erased all memory of his lawyer's instructions. "They get the same deal? Talk and walk?"

Oh, good, there *were* women. She shrugged. She had no knowledge of those details, nor did she care. Why should Paniagua, unless he'd formed a relationship?

"Fine," he decided. "I'll tell you. But I want guarantees. My family can't find out. My name can't be released to the public. And I want out of here as soon as I've made my statement."

Good luck with that, Ross thought. "That's the FBI's call, but I'll see what I can do. Meanwhile, why don't you start from the beginning? Maybe we can use your testimony as leverage." *We*, she silently added. *You and me, allies in the fight for justice.*

He wasn't allying himself with anyone. "The deal for the story," he insisted. "I don't say a word until I have that in writing and my lawyer approves it."

So much for that approach. Ross checked the time on her cell phone. It was still early. "I need some coffee. You want anything?"

Paniagua shook his head.

"I'll make a call. But Rodrigo, I gotta be honest. You've already proven yourself a flight risk. No judge in the country would let you out, at least not until we've verified what you tell us." She didn't add that he might be needed on the witness stand. He wouldn't like that, given he didn't want his family in the loop.

He didn't reply, so she left him sitting there and made her way to the nearest break room, poured herself a cup of coffee, and called Captain Morris. "He wants to deal," she reported, "but he demands impossible conditions." When Morris asked, she gave details.

"Tell him not to hold is breath," the Captain replied. "What do you think?"

"He's playing a game. He's too eager to get out of here. We don't want him anywhere near another knife."

"You think he knows where to find Beecham?"

"Maybe. Or maybe he wants to take out other witnesses. Maybe the women involved in the scheme."

"If so," Morris said, "he'd give us any half-credible line to get out."

Ross agreed. Paniagua wasn't what they'd assumed. She didn't know what he was, but he wasn't just a victim. "If only we had that envelope," she mused. "Wait, I have an idea."

"Oh?"

"Half an idea. I'll let you know once I see how it works."

"Holly..."

"Don't worry, Captain. I'll behave." She laughed.

Morris didn't, but she neither did she pry.

Ross tucked away her cell phone and returned to the interrogation room, coffee in hand. After seating herself, she took a long, slow sip, eyeing Paniagua over the rim of the cup. She could feel his impatience, his tension, but he wasn't going to ask.

"I'm curious," she said.

He still didn't ask.

"That envelope."

"What envelope?"

"Come on, Rodrigo. I saw the damn thing. You know I did. I'll grant you, we'll never find it, but I gotta know. Where did you ditch it?"

Paniagua laughed. "Why, so you can pick it up?"

"It rained. Hard. The ink ran down to the river and the paper turned to mush. Even if I found it, it would be useless."

"So why ask?"

"Curiosity. You could have dropped it in the trash on your way out, of course. If so, it's probably in a dumpster or even a landfill by now. But I don't think you did. You were hell-bent on escaping the scene. I think you must've tossed it out the window somewhere between the restaurant and Brighton Dam Road."

"If there had been an envelope, that's probably where it would be."

"A big area. Be more specific."

He was trying not to grin at her. It must've been a really good dumping ground. But where? Any spot would have done. The entire route had been houses, trees, shops, a few fields. Nothing special, but nothing special was necessary. Whenever he realized he needed to lose the evidence, he could have.

Oh, wait.

Whenever he needed to.

Ross leaned back and laughed. "I'm such an idiot."

Paniagua looked like someone had let the air out of him.

"When I bring it back, you and I are having another talk. Only this time, you'll cooperate. Won't you?"

Chapter 18

Dumas was going nuts with anticipation. With Peller, Montufar, and Ross out on their appointed rounds and no word back on anything, he could but pour over the notes and evidence to date, drawing hypothetical connections between the dots, puzzling over the all-too-many coincidences, getting nowhere.

Except…

One possibility lodged in his mind, and he couldn't shake it loose. If he was right, it could be bad. Really bad.

He bolted from his cubicle, nearly taking out another detective who happened to be passing by. "Sorry!" he called over his shoulder. He ambushed Theresa Swan in her cubicle, where she, too, had been mulling things over while waiting for news. Dumas didn't say a word. He dropped into the guest chair and bit his lip.

She scrunched up her face. "You, too, huh?"

"Yeah."

"Paniagua."

"Beecham."

"They're in it together."

There it was. Dumas pressed a fist to his forehead as though trying to squeeze out something useful. "But who's working for whom?

"Who do you think?"

"You got me. All we know is, Beecham showed Paniagua something, and he blew a gasket."

"More than one," Swan said.

"Does that tell us anything?"

"Not that I can see."

"Me, either."

"The way it looked to Holly and I, Beecham was pressuring Paniagua. But was that the boss handing his underling a foul assignment, or was it the underling turning the tables on the boss?"

It could have been either. Or neither. Everyone assumed Beecham was blackmailing Paniagua to get access to government secrets. Maybe he was. But if not...

"Too bad that envelope disappeared," Swan said. "That would have told us."

"Yeah, but Mother Nature probably disposed of it. That leaves us only one option."

Swan waited. When he didn't explain, her expression turned severe. "No, Eric." She waggled a finger at him. "That's the FBI's turf. Remember what happened over the weekend."

"But if we could find Beecham..."

"Sergeant Dumas, please. No."

She rarely addressed him so formally. Accompanied by that scowl, it was almost comical. Dumas wished he could snap a photo for posterity. "Okay, look. We have three scenarios. One: Beecham tries to recruit Paniagua through blackmail. Two: Beecham already owns Paniagua and assigns him a task he can't stomach. Three: Paniagua owns Beecham, who tries to change the power dynamic by blackmailing him. It almost doesn't matter which is the truth."

Swan picked up the thread. "Right, because whatever it was went south, and now the feds want to play ball with Paniagua to nail Beecham. Paniagua's the one everyone wants to believe."

Dumas nodded "If the guy has any brains at all, he'll snap up that deal. Nobody will even listen to Beecham's story. Stabbing him might not have been anger at all. It might have been brilliance."

"But Beecham isn't an idiot. He knows the score. He slips out of the hospital before the feds get to him." Swan frowned at Dumas. "Where does he go?"

"Safe house, maybe. Except..."

"Potential witnesses. AJ's long gone, but Clare Fleming, Father Ed, maybe Carlyle Navin and Mary Whoever-She -Is."

Dumas pointed at her in acknowledgement.

"Damn it," Ross muttered. "He doesn't need to know for sure who's involved. He can just wipe the slate clean." She grabbed her purse from under her desk. "Okay, I'm convinced. Where to first?"

"Rick and Corina are already at St. Augustine. I'll give them a heads up. We'll cover Carlyle and Mary. Shall I drive?"

"I'll do it. I've been studying Corina's technique." Swan winked at him.

"Heaven help us all," Dumas said with a grimace.

†

Early that morning, Warren Beecham found himself somewhere he never would have thought, seated in dew-laden grass, back propped against a tombstone, waiting for the sun to illuminate the resting places of the dead. He felt like one of them. He could soon be, if he wasn't careful.

How had it come to this?

It started, of course, with his mother. She had been an old hand at Yanchuan patchwork. She learned it from her mother, who learned it from her mother, who learned it from her mother, and so on through uncounted generations. Who knew how far back the tradition stretched? It didn't matter. As a child, he watched his mother work cloth and thread, piecing together mismatched scraps of fabric to create something whole and beautiful. Young Beecham was fascinated at how patterns emerged from apparent chaos. That had been the trigger. He soon realized people's lives, too, were a patchwork of elements. If you collected the bits of a person's life, you could understand them, predict them, even manipulate them. You could control almost anyone. Family. Friends. Enemies. Anyone.

Beecham wasn't really Beecham, but by now he'd all but drowned himself in the role. He had become Beecham, and Beecham was no traitor. Not in his own mind, not really. It was all a game. At least, he hadn't set out to betray his country. He'd been born in Modesto, California, the son of immigrants who had become citizens. His father studied mathematics at Stanford and worked at Lawrence Livermore National Laboratories before deciding he'd rather teach. He maintained his government connections, though, which helped when his son entered college and then the workforce. Beecham learned to manage government IT projects before jumping ship to private contracting, where the money was better. And then he discovered a more lucrative career still.

It was April, 2002. The nation was laser-focused on Islamist terrorism when a pretty Chinese woman sidled up to Beecham at an upscale pub and made small talk. He could see in her eyes she was playing him, but he liked it. He liked the challenge. He liked her mind. She sought to draw him out, he sought to draw her out. They played chicken with each other's lives, giving nothing up, learning nothing. Damn, she was good. He wanted another sparring match, so he asked to see her again. She slipped him a coy smile and melted into the night. He figured that meant yes.

She didn't disappoint. There followed another night, and another, and another. He made no headway with her, nor did she with him, and two weeks to the day later, he admitted as much. "Who are you?" he asked point blank.

"Who are you?" she returned.

"You already know, I think."

"I know enough to know I want you."

With some women, that could have meant anything from a night in bed to a life together. But she desired neither fling nor romance nor even friendship. She coveted his skill, while he craved her intellect. "You have me," he said without knowing what might follow.

She handed him a folded scrap of paper torn from a notebook. "Read later," she said. "I'll be in touch."

It was that simple, that elegant. He didn't care what that paper said, didn't care that she had ordered a meal of classified information. He served it up. She asked for seconds. He brought them. And on and on it went.

Beecham never learned her real name. She called herself Lihua, nothing more. He passed her secrets for six months, amassed a small fortune in payouts, socked it away in an array of accounts at different financial institutions, touched none of it. Sudden affluence would be a red flag. He could live it up later, once he retired. At the rate he was going, that wouldn't be long.

And then one day, Lihua blew away like a spent blossom on the wind. He mourned her loss, but her disappearance felt appropriate, for that's what Lihua meant. Pear blossom. After, Beecham worked for several handlers, all men, all far less interesting than her, but he did his job and in due course was allowed to recruit and run others. He knew how to assemble scraps of people's lives, how to determine who to approach and who to avoid. His successes were small but steady. Finally, he was granted his own operation, and not just anywhere. The big time. The center of the western universe. Washington, D.C.

Beecham ran his game on the fringes. Some of the federal government's juiciest targets lay outside the Beltway, and he had a plan for infiltrating them. He set up shop and plucked blossoms in Lihua's memory. That's how he thought of his women. Beautiful blossoms, just like her, if not a tenth as clever. He gave them direction and control until they, too, were spent and blew away on the wind. He mourned the loss of none of them. They were simply means to an end.

Probably that's where he'd gone wrong. Whatever compassion he had as a child withered on the vine, poisoned by greed. Not for money, though. For power. He devoured the weak to get his fix, and it was too late for rehab.

The sun peeked over the horizon. Hidden from the rectory by a line of trees on a descending slope, Beecham shivered in the wet grass, winced at the pain in his gut. It might have been stupid to leave the hospital, but staying would have been far worse. The feds would have been all over him. So he snuck out, phoned for a cab, had the driver drop him off at the nearest car rental agency. There, he secured a silver VW Jetta under the name William Ross, a name as unnoticeable as the vehicle. And all that to accomplish one thing: to silence that damned priest and his damned housekeeper before anyone connected him to them.

He abandoned the Jetta in the neighborhood across Old Washington Road from St. Augustine. That seemed logical. It was a short walk to the church for a healthy man. Alas, he was far from healthy. The wound hurt, and with each step, he felt his body ripping open. The sutures held, but he couldn't move fast. Fortunately, he made the walk in the morning twilight. Nobody driving by paid him any heed.

His back pressed against the tombstone, Beecham focused on his breathing, willing away the pain, willing order into his crumbling world. But order wouldn't form spontaneously from the chaos. It needed a push, which was why he'd come. Clare Fleming and the priest had to be silenced. Fleming could ID Beecham. Father Ed…who knew what he knew? Who knew what he might say to the cops? Better safe than sorry. His brother could have told him something. Or Amelia Jenkins, the damned fool. It would be just like her to unburden her soul to Father Ed even though she wasn't Catholic. If she had, would the rules even apply to her? Probably not. Either way, it wasn't safe to leave the priest alive.

Beecham wanted Jenkins dead, too, but not because she was a threat. She was merely too pathetic not to kill. Oxygen was wasted on her. She hadn't even run that far. She should have gone to Wyoming, or Alaska, or hell, even a beach on Maui. But no, she stayed nearby. Beecham tracked her down several times, in Maryland, in Virginia, in West Virginia, but each time dumb luck favored her and she slipped through his fingers. He'd had enough of that. He hoped to lure her back using someone she trusted. Paniagua. But the moron turned on him. The feds probably already had him in custody. At least it would be Paniagua's word against Beecham's, and of the two of them, only one had stabbed someone in the gut and fled the scene.

Shafts of sunlight burrowed through the crowns of the eastern trees, crept along the tombstones, steamed away the dew. Still Beecham waited. Waited for the priest to rise. Waited for him to eat breakfast, to celebrate morning mass, to return to the rectory for a quiet day of whatever the hell priests did when they weren't waving wafers.

And then that damn detective showed up again, this time with an accomplice.

Hell with it. May as well be hanged for a sheep as a lamb. Beecham checked his thirty-eight. If they didn't leave soon, he would add a pair of cops to his list.

†

Peller and Montufar were nearly out the rectory door when Dumas called with the latest. "All right," Peller said. "Give me a status when you get to Carlyle's. And let me know if Holly makes any progress with Paniagua." He tucked his phone away and grimaced.

"Now what?" Montufar asked.

"Beecham's on the street. Eric thinks he might come here or pay Mary and Carlyle a visit."

"We're in for a long day, then."

"Who's Beecham?" Father Walter asked.

Peller nodded at Father Ed. "I think you met him. The pseudo-confession you had Bianca relay to Detective Montufar."

Father Ed closed his eyes. "He killed Mark?"

"Amelia Jenkins almost certainly killed Mark. But Beecham was controlling her, so in that sense, he's responsible. Father Walter probably knows more than I do." He glanced at the older priest, who said nothing.

For once, Father Ed met Peller's gaze. "Don't pressure him. If our places were exchanged, I wouldn't speak, either."

As frustrating as it was, as little as he liked it, Peller acquiesced. They had their rules, just as he did. They had to play by them. "As you wish. But Beecham might not be so understanding, and he may be on his way here. Corina, check the house. Make sure all entrances are secured. I'll scout around outside."

Montufar nodded. "Do I have your permission to check all the rooms?" she asked Father Ed.

He affirmed.

Peller left, locking the front door behind him. The day was warming, the sky half flooded with wisps of cirrus, possibly portending another downpour later in the day. The air was way too still for his comfort, like the world was holding its breath in anticipation of tragedy. He slunk around the northeast side of the rectory, his eyes playing over its walls and windows, the grounds, the trees and the tombstones in the cemetery beyond. Nothing caught his notice, although the shadows had a sinister cast.

He rounded the back of the rectory, walked alongside the church to the parking lot. An outdoor mausoleum four units high separated the cemetery grounds from the parking lot, which sat empty. Peller continued his rounds, seeing nothing. He could keep an eye on the parking lot easily enough. There was only one way in. But if Beecham had walked, he could come from any direction, slip by unnoticed.

Corina's right, he mused. *We're in for a long day.*

†

Stonewalling never gets old, Dumas grumbled to himself.

"It was an ecumenical event," Carlyle Navin lied.

Mary Tyler sat on the sofa beside him, her hands folded in her lap, her eyes downcast, her mouth shut. Navin had probably told her to keep it that way.

"And the graffiti? Was that ecumenical, too?"

Navin gave him a withering look.

"How about the dog parts?" Theresa Swan asked. She'd elected to stand by the wall, in the background, from whence she could ambush the couple as needed. It worked.

Tyler looked ill. "The dog was already—"

"Shut up," Navin snapped.

Dumas picked up the thread. "Already dead. We know. How did it die?"

"Splenic—"

Navin turned on her. "Shut *up*, Mary!"

"You're too young to have graduated from veterinary school. You're a vet tech, right? How did you harvest the parts you wanted without being caught?"

Tyler squeezed her eyes shut. She was on the verge of tears.

Navin grumbled, "Damn it, Mom was right. I'll never live this down." He fished in his pants pocket for his cell phone. "We aren't saying anything until Mr. Bedi is here."

Dumas shook his head in mock disappointment. "Why don't you put that away and talk to us."

"Because you want us in jail." He tapped a contact and put the device to his ear.

"Believe it or not, we want to protect you. You might be in physical danger. If we walk, you're without a shield."

Mary looked up in alarm. Navin didn't. "Good story," he grumbled. "Tell me another."

Dumas sighed.

Navin's call went to voice mail. "Hi Mom. The cops are here again. I guess you'd better get Mr. Bedi. Call me." He dropped the phone on the sofa next to him.

"Okay," Dumas said. "I'll tell you another. Don't say a word. Just listen. Real hard."

Navin rolled his eyes.

"Mary's father was killed six years ago, shot to death in Centennial Park. No weapon was found, no suspects emerged. The case went cold. Then vandalism started to appear at a pair of Catholic churches, one where Mary's uncle is a priest and the other where you, Carlyle, are a parishioner. Handwriting analysis shows you wrote the messages at St. Paul. It's a good bet Mary wrote those at St. Augustine. Incidentally, that first message was written while I was inside getting married. I really appreciate that."

Tyler leaned into Navin, who put a protective arm about her.

"The messages," Dumas continued, "were about sin and confession. We know your father was in trouble, Mary. Father Ed was reluctant to talk about it, but eventually he did. We also know Father Ed's housekeeper is in trouble. The connection is a man calling himself Warren Beecham. He's involved in espionage. It's likely Beecham was pressuring Mary's father to hand over government secrets, but he refused to play ball. That's why he died."

"He was a good man," Mary whispered.

Dumas nodded. "I'm sure he was. Beecham's house of cards is starting to fall. He was stabbed last night. This morning, he left the hospital without release. We're operating on the theory that he intends to eliminate anyone who might know about your father's death, including Father Ed, Father Walter, and possibly the pair of you. Isn't that a fine story?"

Tyler buried her face in Navin's shoulder. He wrapped her in his arms and kissed her hair but said nothing.

That kid was going to play stubborn all the way to his funeral. Dumas gave up. He stood. "Okay. Let us know when your attorney is ready to meet. I hope you live that long."

The detectives' shadows hadn't even reached the door before Mary cried, "Wait! Please!"

They turned back. Navin was all but wrestling Mary to keep her on the sofa while she pushed at him, half sitting, half standing. "Mary," he snapped. "Calm down. It's a trick."

"You saw the letter, Carlyle! He was after her. He wanted to kill her. He'll kill us, too!"

Not much would have surprised Dumas, but that did. He returned to his seat. Swan stood behind him now, her hand on the back of the chair.

"Don't get hysterical." Navin pulled Tyler close again.

She allowed it, but she'd had her fill of enforced silence. "Two months ago, I got an anonymous letter. The return address was Richmond, Virginia. It was an apology for killing Dad." She choked back a sob. "It was written by a woman. She was hired to…to trick Dad into giving up secrets, but he didn't. He confronted her. She got scared and shot him. She said she was sorry."

"No name on the letter or envelope?" Dumas asked.

Mary shook her head, twined her fingers, squeezed so hard they turned white. "Nothing."

"Did she say anything else?"

"She said she confessed but the priest wouldn't give her absolution."

"Which priest?"

"I don't know. She only said she went to 'his bother's church' to confess. His brother. My uncle. Father Ed."

"Did she confess to Father Ed? Or to Father Walter?"

Mary shrugged.

"Did she say when she did this?" Dumas asked.

Another shrug.

Navin put up a hand. "No more questions."

Dumas had plenty to ask, but he backed off. He turned to Swan. "Six years ago, Father Ed had a deacon assisting him, but no other priests. Father Walter moved in three years ago. If AJ confessed right after the killing, Father Ed would have heard her. But he's always claimed no knowledge of his brother's killer."

Swan finished the thought for him. "Maybe AJ only made confession much later, to Father Walter. Why wouldn't he have given her absolution?"

"If she wasn't truly penitent. Or if she wasn't Catholic. I'm not aware of any other valid reasons. Corina would know if there are, I'm sure."

"AJ said she was sorry when she wrote to Mary."

"But was she at the time? Change of heart, perhaps. She's spent six years living with her crime." Dumas turned back to Mary, who was clinging to Navin and weeping. Quietly, he asked, "What else was in that letter, Mary?"

Tyler wiped her eyes and sniffled. "She said she was scared of her boss. She was going to run. Maybe leave the country."

"I understand now. That was the reason for the graffiti. You wanted the priest who heard her confession to come forward and ID her. You wanted her caught before she could leave the U.S."

"Wouldn't you?"

"But Mary," Swan said. She sat beside Tyler. "You know priests can't reveal what they're told in confession."

"My father was murdered! Why should a priest protect a killer?"

Swan looked to Dumas for help, but he had no answer, only more questions. "I get why you targeted St. Augustine. But why St. Paul?"

Navin threw up his hands in exasperation. "What the hell. Mary's already pled guilty, hasn't she? St. Paul was my idea. Two churches, two different writers, same general message. The priest who took this woman's confession would get it, but the police would write it off as a grievance against the Church, not an individual."

"Smart," Dumas said. "It could have worked. Do you still have the letter, Mary?"

"In my dresser."

"Can I have it? For evidence?" He could get a warrant, but he didn't want to do that to her, not after what she'd been through. She wasn't a criminal, not really, just a grieving, messed up kid. And Navin was just trying to protect her from herself.

"No," Navin objected. "Don't give them anything, Mary. At least, not until Mr. Bedi says so."

"It's over. We lost." Tyler looked up at Dumas. "I'll give it to you. But promise me something."

"What's that?" Dumas asked.

"Find her. Make her pay. Make her suffer."

"She already has," Swan said. "She's been on Beecham's hit list for six years."

†

There was no shoulder alongside Highland Road south of Brighton Dam Road at the line of pines where Paniagua had surrendered himself, so Holly Ross pulled onto the grass about where his car had come to rest. His mad dash for unattainable freedom had ended here. This was the spot—the most likely spot, anyway—where he realized he had to ditch that envelope.

There was nothing in the grass. She didn't expect there would be, but she knew where to look. Paniagua had made a show of running for it. He hadn't gotten far before falling, and not because he twisted an ankle. Ross examined the bed of brown pine straw beneath the trees. A disturbed patch caught her eye. There, sheltered by the boughs, buried in a shallow grave, she found it. A white envelope, a bit the worse for wear but not disintegrated. She documented the location of the find with her cell phone camera, then pulled on gloves and collected the evidence. Returning to her car, she carefully opened the envelope and extracted the contents. As she expected, there were shreds of a photo, plus three others intact. Photos of a woman. Curiously, Paniagua wasn't in any of them, just the woman, pale, thin, dark circles beneath sunken eyes, worry lines marring her face. She might have spent the past decade hounded by demons.

Behind the photos, Ross found something else. A cashier's check. Ten thousand dollars.

"What the hell?" she muttered to no one.

The obvious made no sense. Beecham wanted the woman in the photo. He wanted Paniagua to—what? Find her? Kill her? Whatever the offer was, it infuriated Paniagua so much, he nearly gutted Beecham.

Ross began to speculate but checked herself. No flying to the moon. Dumas might offer up wild ideas, but he usually had something—at least instinct—to back them up. She had nothing but questions. Only one person could answer them, if she could convince him to cooperate. She pulled an evidence bag from her glove compartment and secured the envelope and its contents. Shortly, she was back in the interrogation room with Paniagua.

He looked ill as she spread the photos and payout in front of him. She didn't say a word, just gave him a questioning look and waited for an explanation.

Paniagua swallowed and looked away.

Ross gave him a few moments, to no avail. "Let's revisit why you're here," she said. "You stabbed a man in front of witnesses. You're not escaping that assault charge unless you cooperate."

The man's jaw might have rusted shut.

"You offered to cooperate, if we kept your name out of it. You don't want your family to find out."

A slight nod, but still no eye contact, still no voice.

"This envelope and its contents are now evidence. The prosecutor will use them at your trial. Moreover, when Beecham is caught—and he will be—your name and this envelope will come up at his trial. You see where we're going with this?"

He squeezed his eyes shut. He felt the metaphorical gun at his temple, but still he wouldn't speak.

Ross slapped the table. "For God's sake, Rodrigo, wake up! You're not stupid. You know the only safe exit is to talk!" She swept her hands over the evidence on display. "I'm trying to help you. What's this about?"

He buried his face in his hands. "Her name is Amelia. Beecham wants her dead."

"Amelia Jenkins?" Ross peered at the photos again. So this was AJ. No wonder she looked like a walking corpse.

Paniagua dropped his hands and stared at Ross, shocked.

"Yeah, we happened on her name. How do you know her?"

"Never mind that."

"Never mind any chance of a deal, then."

"Look—"

"Was she your lover?"

Paniagua pinched his lips.

"Of course she was. That's what Beecham was holding over you."

"I never betrayed my country. I never gave him anything. Not one thing."

Which meant AJ was indeed another Clare Fleming. "You knew what he was up to?"

"Of course I knew!"

"Why didn't you report him?"

"Because he threatened to tell my wife about... Look, Beecham was controlling Amelia. She didn't want... She wasn't like that, okay? But she didn't have a choice."

Interesting. He was defending the woman who had seduced him and tried to recruit him for espionage. Which meant... "You're in love with her."

He didn't admit it, but he didn't have to. He looked too miserable for it to be false.

"Okay," Ross said. "I get that. And I get that if you turn Beecham in, Amelia goes down, too, which you don't want. You want to protect her. But damn it, he's blackmailing you."

"Worse than that," Paniagua said. "The guy's a twisted psycho. He threatened to kill me. Said he's make it look like suicide. He even forged a note in my hand, whining about how tortured I was over the affair. It was a good forgery. Even I couldn't tell it wasn't my writing. And it wasn't a bluff. He would have done it."

Ross was starting to hate this Beecham guy. If she had him here now...

Keep a lid on it, she told herself. "What did he want from you?"

"Sometimes he needed to...to expand his staff."

"More women." Really, really hate him. Her trigger finger was twitching.

Paniagua nodded. "From time to time I found a likely candidate and introduced her to Beecham."

"Clare Fleming?"

He started. "How do you..."

"She got spooked. She's cooperating with the feds. I suppose she can ID you."

He squeezed his eyes shut.

"Where did you find her?

"At Christmas mass at St. Paul. She was filling in for their rectory housekeeper. She seemed…" Paniagua shook himself. "Damn it. If Beecham finds out, we're both dead."

"I expect the FBI is doing their best to make sure he doesn't. She's their star witness so far. And he won't get to you while you're our guest." Ross pushed the cashier's check toward Paniagua. "Tell me about this."

Having gotten this far, Paniagua's resistance evaporated. "Beecham tried to kill AJ before. Several times. But she always gave his assassins the slip. He decided to try something different. He figures I've maintained contact with her. He wanted me to convince her to meet me. He'd be waiting to grab her. I told him…well, you know what I told him."

"I'm sure he got the message. Have you maintained contact with her?"

"Not frequent, but yes. She doesn't have anyone but me anymore. She texts or calls from time to time. But she never tells me where she is. I only know she's moved around a lot since…since leaving Beecham's employ."

"Since she killed Mark Tyler in a panic."

Paniagua looked miserable. "She didn't mean to."

"Thus 'in a panic.' But she did it, and that wasn't on Beecham's agenda. That's why she's been on the run."

Paniagua nodded. "She's changed phone numbers several times, but she always lets me know her new number."

Risky, but it worked for six years. Except Beecham knew or suspected. "Can I get her number from your cell phone? To offer protection?"

"Do you need to ask? I'm sure you've already searched my contacts."

"We have everything of interest that was on your person and in your car, but no phone. Where is it?"

He gaped at her. "It was in my left pants pocket. I swear it was."

Panic gripped Ross. "Are you sure?"

"Of course, I'm sure. I don't go anywhere without it."

Damn it. Beecham could have lifted it in the confusion. If so, he'd find AJ's number and use it to get to her. Ross bolted for the door, calling over her shoulder, "Someone will escort you to your suite!"

Chapter 19

Too much information poured in from too many directions to piece together, so Peller asked Captain Morris to set up a conference call and bring the scattered team into it. The upshot proved simple, in a convoluted way. Beecham, whoever and wherever he was, was after Amelia Jenkins, wherever *she* was. Paniagua had AJ's phone number, but his cell phone was missing. It was a good bet Beecham pilfered it in the scuffle. It might have been among his effects at the hospital, but those had vanished along with the patient. That gave Beecham the capacity for a series of killings to eliminate potential witnesses: AJ, Fathers Tyler and Walter, and—if Beecham knew about her— Mary Tyler, who had AJ's letter. Paniagua, being locked up, would be safe, as would Clare Fleming, who the FBI had hidden away somewhere.

Standing on the rectory porch, Peller addressed the disembodied voices on the phone. "AJ said she might leave the country. Even if Beecham calls her, it's unlikely he'll find her. He probably doesn't know she sent Mary that letter, so Mary and Carlyle should be safe. That leaves the fathers, and Corina and I are here with them. We need patrols in the St. Augustine area. Beecham may be ambulatory, but he's injured. I can't see him running far or fast."

"Don't cross AJ off the list," Ross said. "If Beecham realizes the priests are protected, she'll be his next logical target."

"But how does he get to her?" Montufar asked. "He can't just call her and say, 'Hey babe, come see me.' She'll bolt."

"All he needs is bait to lure her back, and damned if he doesn't have some."

After a momentary silence, everyone including Captain Morris simultaneously said, "Paniagua."

"Bingo," Ross affirmed. "They're in love, and she doesn't know he's in custody."

Peller didn't doubt Beecham would try. AJ described him as a monster. Offering Paniagua money to lure his lover to her death was without doubt beyond cruel. "Unfortunately, without that cell phone, we have no way of reaching AJ. We need to find Beecham."

"I'll get patrols dispatched," Morris said. "We have an APB out, but he won't be cruising about in the open. My good friend Agent Pack is on her way over. I can't wait for that meeting. Meanwhile, send me status updates and any brilliant ideas. I'll keep everyone in the loop."

When the call ended, Peller drew a deep breath and scanned the church, the courtyard, the cemetery, the trees. Everything, even the breeze, was still. He didn't hear a single car pass by on the road at the bottom of the hill.

The silence left him edgy.

†

The cops were still there, wandering in and out, one always inside, the other—sometimes the man, sometimes the woman—strolling about as though taking in the architecture.

They were looking for him. Beecham knew because in the past hour, three police cars had passed by on the road below the cemetery. That complicated matters. If he took the detectives down, the patrols would close in. He was thirsty and hungry and feeling the sutures holding his guts in, and he was trapped. No way to get to the priest unseen, no way to reach his car unnoticed. Someone might even have reported the vehicle by now, although most people were unobservant fools. It could sit there a year before anyone wondered about it.

Beecham dug the cell phone from his pocket and examined it. Nice little gadget, one of the pricier ones. He'd watched Paniagua unlock the thing often enough, so he knew the PIN. He entered it and accessed the phonebook.

Ah, there she was. The stupid bitch who ruined everything. The only smart thing she'd ever done was hide the gun. Yeah, she told Paniagua all about it, and he regurgitated the details while pleading with Beecham for his little jezebel's life. Beecham could almost see the scene. Mark Tyler threatening to turn her in, demanding to know who she was working for, standing fists to hips like an idiot as she trained the weapon on him. Refusing to budge while she pleaded and pleaded and pleaded for mercy.

Pleaded for mercy with her gun aimed at his chest. She couldn't even get that right. If you're going to shoot somebody, damn it, *shoot* them.

What little brain she had only kicked in once Tyler was bleeding out at her feet. She ran, hid the gun, ran and ran and kept on running. Beecham never would have found her, but she couldn't leave her dear, sweet, adulterous Rodrigo. Not entirely. Paniagua's tongue slipped once over drinks. He admitted to hearing from her, pined for his lost love. Beecham knew what to do. A little alcohol here, a little there, and he gradually collected scraps of Jenkins' miserable new life, no one thing revelatory by itself, but enough to stitch together. Enough to locate her. Enough to have her put out of her misery. Three times over, in fact, but every damn time she wised up long enough to skip town.

Those photos were the closest Beecham had come to her. That was over a year back, when his private investigator caught up with AJ in Parkersburg, West Virginia. They were beautiful photos, telling the story of a haunted, hunted woman living a life of gloom. Beecham ate her despair for breakfast every day while dreaming of delivering her to the peace of oblivion. She deserved that sort of release. You can't know you're at peace when you don't exist.

Then he hit upon a plan, a truly beautiful plan to give both Jenkins and Paniagua their due. Beecham wouldn't deal the blow, nor would a hireling. Paniagua would do it. Her lover, her confidant, her friend would pull the trigger. Alas, that idea proved too delicious. A poison apple. He shouldn't have let it seduce him. The payoff was a knife in the gut.

But now…

Now he had another idea. A better idea.

Beecham placed a call.

†

Special Agent in Charge Miriam Pack was more dragon than ever, but at least she couldn't blame Captain Morris for this one. Beecham ran off while Pack's people were camped at the hospital to make sure he didn't. She wasn't volunteering details on the screw-up, and actually, Morris didn't blame her for it. Even simple operations could go awry with surprising ease. But at least Pack wasn't biting off any HCPD heads this afternoon. In fact, she was almost grateful for the quick action.

Almost. She stormed Morris' office, threw herself into a chair, and slapped the desktop for no apparent reason. "Go," she snarled.

Morris laid out the speculations, the deployment details, everything.

"The only potential target we don't have covered," Pack said, "is Amelia Jenkins, and we have no way of finding her. Is that right?"

Morris didn't know why she was saying "we," since the FBI wasn't covering anything yet, as far as she knew. But she ran with it, just to be civil. "We don't. Unless she's shown up on your radar."

Pack shook her head. "Once Peller supplied the name, we dug into her background, but nothing surfaced. She's like most people. Never in any serious trouble, not working in any capacity that would generate a background file or fingerprints." She thumped Morris' desk again before continuing. "The number stashed in Tyler's phone pointed us to an apartment where somebody else now lives and a restaurant where Jenkins worked for a couple of years. Her employer had her Social, which led to an expired credit card and a closed bank account. Then, puff of smoke, she vanished. Probably never went by Amelia Jenkins again. I don't know how the hell Beecham found her. We sure can't."

"Probably from Paniagua," Morris said. "He and AJ kept in touch. He might have dropped a few clues without realizing it. And now his phone's missing. We think Beecham lifted it during the struggle when Paniagua stabbed him."

Pack ground her teeth, then slammed her fist on the desk. Morris jumped. Her family photos fell face down.

"Are you always this high strung?" Morris snapped as she righted the pictures.

"When nothing goes right? Yes!"

"So how do we fix it?"

"How do you think? We find Beecham before he finds AJ."

"In her letter to Mary Tyler, AJ said she was preparing to leave the country. The postmark was Richmond, Virginia. That was two months ago."

"Just because she mailed it there doesn't mean she lived there."

"I realize that."

Pack shook her head. "Even if she did live there, Richmond's a big place."

That's not the point, Morris grumbled to herself. "The world's bigger. What can Beecham do with her phone number? Unless she's incredibly stupid, which she's not—"

"How do you know?"

Morris picked up her pen, started to click it, almost didn't. But this wasn't her team. Pack deserved it. She clicked away, several times. "Because she's evaded Beecham for six years. There won't be any publicly available links between her phone number and her address. She probably isn't even at the same address anymore, Richmond or not."

Pack pinched the bridge of her nose and squeezed her eyes shut as though trying to force thoughts from her brain. "We need patrols."

"I have patrols. And an APB."

"Not your patrols. Mine. Suits, not uniforms."

Morris had her suits on the scene, too, but she supposed extra eyes wouldn't hurt. "Do what you must. But I still don't see what Beecham can do with Paniagua's—"

Damn it. She did, too.

The same thing occurred to Pack. "Trick AJ into coming back," she said. She thumped the desk again.

†

"Rodrigo. I can't talk now." Her voice was the barest of winter breezes.

His was stronger, colder. "No matter, my precious slut. Rodrigo can't, either."

Her legs gave out. She collapsed and fell to the floor like a slab of plaster peeled from the water-stained ceiling, pulling her open suitcase from the bed. Its contents spilled about her, onto her. She might have been one of the garments herself, without bone or muscle, a piece of limp fabric tossed aside and forgotten.

"Are you there, honey? I need your attention. It's important."

He'd found her again. Any moment the door would explode in a rain of splinters, he'd stride in, shoot her or stab her over and over in every nonlethal spot he could find until she died as much from pain as blood loss. He'd threatened that once, years before, the last time they'd spoken. He tricked her then, too, tricked Rodrigo, stolen her phone number from him somehow, called and told her exactly what her punishment would be.

Which was unnecessary. She knew. She'd killed Mark Tyler not because she feared the FBI, but because she feared Beecham. The moment Tyler threatened to turn her in, her life was over. She couldn't let him do it, but she couldn't plead her way out of it. She was dead either way.

Amelia Jenkins pulled herself up, leaned her back against the bedbug-ridden mattress, tried to think. He had Rodrigo's phone. How had he gotten it? "I'm listening," she said, voice trembling in time with her body.

"Wonderful. I was afraid you had a seizure. That would be terrible." He laughed. "I so want to kill you, darling."

She wanted to defy him but didn't know how. Maybe once she could have, but no longer. "I know."

"Alas, I have a problem. Your true love has made a mess of things."

Oh God, Rodrigo, what have you done now? "I'm sorry," she said, but not for Beecham. For Rodrigo. For herself. For what could have been, if only they had met some other way.

"You should be. None of this would have happened if you hadn't been so pathetic. But you know what? I'll give you a chance to fix it. I'm generous like that."

He wasn't. It was a trick. A trap. Whatever it was. "How?"

"Be my sweet whore one last time. Come back to Rodrigo. Convince him to do the right thing, and I'll release you both from my service."

Release? Could she dare hope? But no, Beecham's release wouldn't be freedom. It would be death. "What's the right thing?"

"Do you know your Bible?" Beecham laughed. "Scripture is in the air these days."

She went to church as a child. Her parents were Methodists. But she remembered little of it aside from snatches of hymn, and after they were killed by a drunk driver, she drifted away from religion. It had given her no comfort, no security.

"You should study more," Beecham said. "John 5:13. 'Greater love has no one than this, that a person will lay down his life for his friends.' Do you love Rodrigo, Amelia?"

She did. Rodrigo wasn't like the others. He was kind and gentle, even though he knew from the start what she was after. He turned aside her efforts, but not her. In her entire adult life, he was the only one who truly cared for her.

"Would you die for him, Amelia? Would he die for you?"

She liked to think she would. She didn't want to die, but for Rodrigo, maybe she could. "I don't know."

"Come back to me and find out."

   The Wages of Sin

"You said you'd release us."

"Indeed, I did."

Her fear sublimated into anger. He was toying with her again. She was sick of it. "Tell me the truth for once!" she snapped. The hatred in her voice surprised her. It must have surprised Beecham, too, because he didn't respond, didn't laugh, didn't make a sound. "Just tell me, damn you!"

"Very well. Talk to him. Convince him to do the right thing. If he agrees, he can return to his old life. I will destroy all evidence I hold against him and forget he ever existed."

His old life. His family. His wife. Not his AJ. She almost refused. She wanted *him*, nothing more, nothing less. But what kind of life could they have together? None. They had none now, hadn't for six years. Beecham was right. If she loved him, she had no choice but to give him up so he, at least, could find happiness again.

Except...

"What's the right thing?"

"You already know."

She almost threw up.

"Come home, Amelia. Come home and save your love. Come home to die. I promise, he will make it quick."

"Where's Rodrigo now?"

Another pause. Beecham hadn't expected her to ask. He hadn't expected her to be that clever. Not that it was, really. It was a natural enough question. But for some reason, it caught him off-guard.

"Tell me!"

"In bed with his wife, I expect."

"You're lying again." Rodrigo wouldn't be at home now. He would be at work. Beecham probably said that to hurt her, except it didn't. Jenkins had never been jealous of Rodrigo's wife. More than the time of day, though, it was how Beecham said it. He wasn't so cocky. A hint of uncertainty had invaded his voice. "You don't know where he is," she said. "You can't get to him. You said he made a mess of things. What's he done, gotten himself arrested? Does the FBI have him?"

Beecham laughed, but it wasn't his usual laugh. It was forced. "The FBI doesn't have him."

"The police?"

"Come home, Amelia. Come back to church. Meet me in the churchyard, and I'll tell you how to save your love's life."

Save his life. Yes. If she could, she would save Rodrigo's life. A spark of hope flashed. Before it flickered out, she asked, "What time?"

Beecham said nothing, but she could see his predator smile as clearly as if he stood before her. Damn it, she told him! She hadn't asked for a date, only a time. She flat-out told him she was nearby!

But it didn't matter. She would never see Rodrigo again, never get to say goodbye, certainly never save him. She couldn't even save herself. She either vanished now or played into Beecham's hands, let him tear their souls to pieces and pin her killing on Rodrigo. Rodrigo would spend the rest of his life in prison, immersed in the hell of guilt and grief. *That's* what Beecham wanted. And he thought she was dumb enough to fall for it.

"Go to hell!" She cut the connection, ripped the back off the phone, yanked the battery from the case, and threw the pieces across the room. She rummaged under the bed where she had stashed bits and pieces of her life in cardboard boxes. She had a few tools there. She grabbed the hammer and smashed the life out of the phone. Then she curled into a ball on the floor and cried. She cried for half an hour. She'd never memorized Rodrigo's number. Never had to. He was always just a tap away. Now he was dead to her, and she to him. She had murdered them both, as Beecham wanted. At least, the effect was much the same. In the end, she'd done his bidding anyway.

Except...

Except...

She knew where he was.

And he thought she wouldn't show.

She sat, wiped away the tears, pondered the possibilities. She had a handgun, a nine millimeter Smith & Wesson M&P bought under the table, and she had learned how to use it. For protection. From Beecham. Ironic that he had driven her to acquire the means to take him down.

She wasn't so stupid as he thought, or as she herself once thought. She had only lacked purpose, and now she had it. Beecham gave her that, too. Purpose and resolve.

Yes. She would do it. She would give her life for Rodrigo. Willingly.

But not on Beecham's terms.

Chapter 20

Morning bled into afternoon. Patrols circulated the St. Augustine neighborhoods and cruised the Plum Tree Apartments parking lot and vicinity. The priests went about their business, Father Ed in his upstairs office and Father Walter in his room. Daily mass was at seven in the morning, so that was well over, and there were no further activities at the church that day. All was quiet, normal, as though no danger lurked in the shadows. Even the weather cooperated, with sunshine and a warm spring breeze.

But Peller grew increasingly uneasy as he made another circuit around the church property. Beecham wasn't a fool. He would notice the police activity, would monitor it and wait until it died down. That's what Peller himself would do were their places swapped. They couldn't let Beecham strike at a time of his choosing, when he had the upper hand. They needed to trick him out of hiding, and Peller saw only one way to do that. It was dangerous, but not so dangerous as yielding the whole battlefield to the enemy.

Returning to the rectory, Peller found Montufar on the sofa, lost in thought. Or maybe just bored to death. He sat in a chair facing her and leaned forward, but she ignored him, as though she didn't know he was there. She did, of course, but he took a back seat to whatever was on her mind.

"I have an idea," he said.

"A bad idea."

She'd arrived at the same conclusion. Of course she had.

"But I can't find a way around it," Montufar added. "And I'm not sure Captain Morris will approve."

"Well, then. Let's find out." He placed the call and put it on speaker. When Morris answered, he gave her the details, such as they were.

"You're nuts," the Captain said.

"We know," Peller replied.

"But you're both on board."

"We are."

"And Eric?"

"I haven't told him yet, but he'll agree."

"Cocky today, aren't you?" Morris clicked her pen a few times. The phone reproduced the sound faithfully. "Be damned careful, Rick. Beecham is no idiot."

"Neither am I. It's a calculated risk, yes, but we'll make it work. We have to."

"I sure hope so. Lives are at stake. And not that this is priority one, but Pack will have my head if we blow it."

"You want to tell her?"

"Hell, no. Her guys are invisible in their plainclothes and unmarked vehicles. They might get lucky."

Peller didn't know about that. Beecham might be skilled at spotting feds. But he didn't want to rock a boat that might capsize, not with his captain in it.

Next order of business was to fill in Dumas and Ross. Dumas took the call with curious calm and only said, "Understood."

"Keep your eyes open," Peller said, then wished he hadn't. Dumas wouldn't drop his guard.

"I will. Although honestly? I think you're on the front lines. Keep my wife safe, will you?"

"I will," Peller promised.

"And Sergeant, you keep the boss safe."

Montufar smiled. "You got it, Sergeant."

Peller allowed fifteen minutes for word to spread to the patrols, then he called the priests to the living room. Father Ed came down from his office, Father Walter from his room, cane in hand. When Peller related the plan, they took it in stride, as though he'd suggested calling out for pizza. Maybe they didn't believe the danger was real, or maybe they were ready to accept whatever fate befell them. Either way, the trap was set, although it wasn't clear for whom.

With a nod at Peller, Montufar retreated upstairs. Father Ed escorted Peller to the front door and stepped outside with him.

"You shouldn't be out here," Peller warned.

Father Ed shrugged. "Don't worry about us. Whatever God wills, it's for the best."

Peller didn't disagree with the sentiment, but often he didn't understand the Almighty's gameplan. Often, it was hard to swallow. Why had Sandra died? Why had Shania North suffered as she had? Why was this happening now? "Sergeant Dumas tells me the Muslims have a saying," he said. "'Trust God, but tie your camel.' I just hope I'm using the correct knot."

The priest smiled and extended his hand. Peller grasped it. "All will be well," Father Ed promised.

Peller sauntered toward the parking lot without searching his surroundings. No need to search. He was giving up for the day. Beecham had vanished, maybe never to be found. He tried to project that sentiment, in case the suspect was out there watching. Peller drove away at a sedate pace, making southwest on Old Washington Road. When he came to Hanover Road, he turned left and doubled back through the residential area, returning to Augustine Avenue. Just before reaching Old Washington and the church on the other side, he turned right and parked along the curb behind a VW Jetta, a rental with New York plates. The license made him think of Lockport, New York, where he grew up and joined the police force and met Sandra.

A poor time to get lost in that, but he couldn't help it. He replayed their meeting, the freak accident in which she'd run into his patrol car when a stray dog cut in front of him and he slammed on the breaks. The dog that later became theirs. Talisman, she'd named him. Curiously appropriate, given that he brought them together.

He wondered who the Jetta belonged to, where in New York they lived, who they were visiting.

Then he wondered if they were visiting anyone. Beecham had slipped from the hospital, where he had no transportation. If he was here intent on murder, there was but one option affording him a quick escape: a taxi from the hospital to a rental agency, then a rental car to church. Well. Unless auto theft was in his bag of tricks.

It was, anyway, worth a look. Peller called in the plate and asked for a check on the renter. Without a warrant or subpoena, the rental company wasn't obligated to provide the information, but maybe they would, given the circumstances. It would take some time for a response either way, so Peller went for a walk around the neighborhood. Later, he would return to the church, but not yet. Whatever Beecham was, he wasn't stupid. He'd wait, make sure the police presence really had dialed back, make sure Peller wasn't still around. The situation, for the moment, should be stable.

Peller walked past houses of modest size seated on modest lawns, shaded by trees of middle age. Not a fancy neighborhood but well-groomed. The land rose and fell, testing his stamina. He wasn't as young as he used to be and started to feel the exertion sooner than expected, but he maintained his pace. An hour later, winded and more than ready for a break, he returned to his truck just as a text arrived. The rental car company had supplied a name, address, and photo. William Ross, domiciled at a Bethesda address that wouldn't map, a discovery that prompted the company to hand over the info without complaint. In the photo, a bespectacled Warren Beecham smirked at the camera.

He was here, just as Dumas intuited.

Peller texted back the location of the car so the rental company could reclaim it, then he called Captain Morris and told her. That done, he made for the church, forcing himself to maintain a normal pace. It wasn't easy. In the adrenaline rush, his body was ready for a sprint.

†

The church lay quiet in the afternoon sun. Birds flitted through the leaves, chattering nonstop. Squirrels chased each other around the grounds and up tree trunks. The brooding gravestones testified in their silence to the common end of rich and poor, high and low.

Amelia Jenkins had circled the area in her car, inspected it as thoroughly as possible, seen nothing unusual. But then, those trees and hills could conceal much. Beecham might be anywhere on the grounds, even inside a building. She wouldn't put it past him to commit murder in a church.

She parked uphill from the school on a street lined with older ranch homes. She had a plan, of sorts. She would walk in alongside the school, where she could inspect the parking lot and catch sight of Beecham if he was there. Not that he would be. He would have done the same thing, parked somewhere else, walked in, probably kept to the shadows. Caution was in order. She had to study everything, make no move until she knew where he was.

A white fence separated the end of the school building from the road. Nobody was watching, so with some effort she hopped it and slipped along the back of the structure. She reached the convent, crept by, peered around the corner. The parking lot sat empty. Keeping to the wall, she stole to the front of the building and checked out that lot. Also deserted. So far, so good. She quickly crossed to the church. Although exposed to view as she went, she reached the front courtyard without incident. That, too, was empty. The rectory blocked her view of the cemetery, but there was no sign of anyone about, no sound but distant traffic.

The rectory. Windows on every side. A perfect place to keep watch, if the priest would allow it. He might not. Or rather, the rules might not allow it, and he was ruled by rules. Rules had prevented him from accepting her confession. They might refuse her need now. Then again, Jenkins had the gun, and this time the ends justified her means. The priest would have no choice. Beecham deserved death, and God had placed him in her hands.

Maybe that was the meaning of the past six years. Maybe all she had suffered had been leading to this moment. To justice.

Eyes flitting back and forth, she crept to the rectory's front door and rang the bell. The wait seemed interminable. If Beecham was out there, he would see her, but maybe he wouldn't recognize her. He wasn't expecting her, and time had ravaged her. She'd grown thin and pale, a ghost of her younger self. Her own skin might be her best disguise now.

The door unlocked and opened a crack. A single eye peered out, surveyed the visitor as though expecting a demon. "May I help you?"

The voice wasn't what she expected. She expected someone older, someone frail, the voice she remembered from her failed confession. But three years had passed, three years since she had been turned away, stripped of hope. Maybe the old priest had moved on or died.

"I need help," she said. That should have been enough. This was a church. That was their business wasn't it?

"This isn't a good time," the hidden man said.

"Good time?"

"We have...problems."

"So do I. Please, may I come in?"

The eye scanned her again. "One moment." And the door snicked shut.

He might as well have slammed it in her face. *Not even God will forgive me*, she had written. She had meant it, and the closing of the door made her feel it all over again.

But then it opened, and a black-clad priest was there, motioning her inside. He all but slammed the door behind her.

Some problems, he'd said, but no problems were in evidence. He looked worried, even grim in his black clothing. Yet she had stepped into a serene space, comfortable, well-kept. Another priest—the older one to whom she had tried to confess—was seated in a chair with a cup of coffee on the table before him and a cane at his right hand. He smiled a grandfatherly smile.

Jenkins almost tripped over her own feet. He hadn't spoken a word, but his voice came back to her as though only a moment had passed. "I can't. I'm sorry, but I simply can't. You aren't Catholic. All I can do is advise you."

"Then I'll be Catholic!" she had pleaded. "I'll convert right now! Please, I'll do anything!"

"It doesn't work that way. You must go through the process. It takes time."

"I don't have time!"

But her plea fell on deaf ears. He wouldn't budge, wouldn't bend the rules, not even a little.

She looked away, tried to banish the image.

The other, the priest who had opened the door, locked the deadbolt and motioned her to the sofa. He glanced back as though the door was nothing but mist, as though anything might pass through it. "How can I help?"

Jenkins sat. "Someone told me to meet him here. He wants to hurt me."

The old priest cocked his head. "They why did you come?"

"Let me watch for him here. In the rectory." She opened her purse and pulled out the Smith & Wesson. "When he shows, I'll kill him." She pointed the barrel at the ceiling. The priests gaped, then she tucked it away and turned to the older man. "He's probably after you, too."

"Why would he be after me?"

"Because you know what I did. You heard my confession. At least, you listened. You wouldn't absolve me. Just because I wasn't your religion, you wouldn't absolve me. I guess I'm going to hell, so it doesn't matter what else I do, does it? I may as well kill him. Believe me, he deserves it."

The younger priest, his face a palette of shock and fear, sank onto the sofa next to her. "Amelia Jenkins?"

How had he known her name?

"I'm Father Ed. This is Father Walter. Mark Tyler was...my brother."

Jenkins leaned away as though an invisible hand had reached from behind and grabbed her by throat. She almost couldn't find her breath.

"You say you aren't Catholic."

She couldn't answer, but Father Walter said it for her. "She's not. I wish…" He closed his eyes. "I wish I could have helped you, Amelia. I really do."

What did it matter anymore? She had only one hope left, that she could stop Beecham and free Rodrigo.

"For what it's worth," Father Ed said, "I forgive you. We can't offer absolution through the sacrament, but I forgive you. And God will, too, if you turn aside from this path."

As soon as he said it, he straightened as though an enormous weight had been lifted from his shoulders. He drew a long breath, rose, and marched to the foot of the stairs. Looking up, he said, "It's time to end this. I'm opening the door."

Jenkins gaped at him. Surely, he didn't think God lived in the attic? What was he doing?

She found out a moment later, when a woman hidden above replied. "Not yet. Let's give Lieutenant Peller time to get into position. Beecham is in the area. I just got word his rental car was found parked across the street. And Ms. Jenkins, please stay out of the way. Let us handle him."

Jenkins shook her head to clear it. Nothing was making sense. "Us? Who are you?"

"Detective Sergeant Corina Montufar, Howard County Police. You should come upstairs. You'll be safe here."

Why were the police here? How did they know about her? How did they know about Beecham?

It didn't matter. She had come to stop Beecham, and by God, she was going to do it. She sprang to her feet and made for the door. "I'm done taking orders. Beecham dies. Now."

Father Ed sprang after her, but before he could reach her, she unlocked the door and threw it wide. Drawing her gun from her purse, she stepped outside.

Chapter 21

Peller wanted Beecham to think the cops had pulled out of the area. An hour of inactivity ought to do it, or so he hoped. Patrols gone, Peller himself gone. Montufar was still there, but even if Beecham realized it, he might make a move, assuming in his hubris that a female cop was no match for him.

The terrain gave Peller an advantage. Although he didn't have the high ground, he could approach largely unseen, concealed by the trees and the school. The parking lots, the courtyard, and both rectory doors would all be in plain sight. Father Ed had given him a key to the side door. If Beecham was skulking about the cemetery, he wouldn't likely see Peller return.

His reentry plan worked like a charm, to a point.

Peller crossed Old Washington road. He checked the drive and what little he could see of the parking lot. Empty. He strolled up the sidewalk toward the church, turned up Augustine Avenue, saw no movement, nothing out of place. He walked the school's exit drive, passed by the red brick building, reached the convent. All was still. No cars, no people, nothing. He made for the herringbone pavers at the front of the church and palmed the rectory key.

He had just pulled it from his pocket when he saw Beecham pass through the front door.

†

Amelia Jenkins was ready to do what she'd come for. She just wasn't ready to blunder into Beecham on the porch. As she stepped through the door, his hands clamped onto her, his right on her shoulder, his left on her wrist. He twisted her arm to point her gun off to the side, then he yanked her body into his. His breath washed over her face. She yelped and tried to break away, but he was too strong, she too weak. He squeezed so hard, she feared he might pull her hand clean off.

"Be a good girl and drop it," he whispered.

"No!"

He squeezed harder and shook. Her fingers opened of their own accord and the weapon clattered on the deck. "Inside." He shoved her backwards. She almost fell through the open doorway. No sooner had she regained her footing than he shoved her again. She sprawled on the floor at Father Ed's feet.

The priest, who had followed in a vain attempt to prevent her leaving, bent down, gave her his hand, helped her up. He smiled. It was the gentlest smile she had ever seen. "Behind me," he whispered.

Jenkins skittered behind Father Ed and looked for her gun. It was on the porch in plain sight. If she could just get to it...but no, she couldn't, not with Beecham in the doorway, his own weapon in hand.

"I actually came for you," Beecham said. He waggled the gun at Father Ed. "I didn't expect my beloved Amelia to show up. Didn't you tell me to go to hell?"

"That's where you belong," Jenkins said.

"You and I both. Fortunately, there is no hell, only the common void of oblivion."

"You're sadly mistaken," Father Ed said. "Put the gun down and let's talk."

"No, Father. I'm here to simplify matters." He considered Father Walter for a moment, then said, "Three witnesses in one room. Two of you won't be leaving. The third..." He grinned at Jenkins. "We're going to find your love and conclude the deal I offered."

"Don't bet on it," she said. Her fear had sublimated, maybe in the glow of Father Ed's courage, maybe in the heat of her hatred for Beecham.

Beecham laughed. "Why not? I hold the aces." He raised his gun, trained it on Father Ed's heart.

Father Ed didn't flinch. He looked Beecham in the eye.

"But not the joker." Montufar descended the stairs, weapon trained on Beecham. "Howard County Police. Set it on the floor. Slowly."

Beecham squinted at the newcomer and muttered, "What the hell," but he didn't comply.

Montufar stopped two steps up, giving her sufficient high ground for a clear shot. "You're allegedly smart. You wouldn't be so stupid as to commit first degree murder in front of a cop, would you?"

Beecham shifted his aim to Montufar. "That depends."

"Don't play chicken with me. You'll regret it."

"In my experience, girls with guns aren't that formidable."

Another voice intruded from the porch. "That one is. And she's got backup."

Beecham whirled. "Damn it," he snarled. "I thought you'd left!"

He aimed for Peller's heart.

Amelia Jenkins pushed Father Ed aside and rushed Beecham, striking him like a diminutive defensive tackle taking down an opponent. Beecham, not expecting the impact, tumbled forward onto his own gun, which discharged beneath him. Peller and Montufar swooped in to keep him down as Jenkins rolled away. Peller pinned Beecham's arms behind him while Montufar cuffed him. They rolled him over and checked him for wounds. Nothing. Wherever the errant shot went, he got lucky. Or unlucky. He stared up in terror, maybe at the detectives, maybe at an unexpected vision of eternity, be it the one he believed in or the one he didn't.

Another explosion sounded. Blood splattered and poured from Beecham's chest. The terror seeped from his eyes, replaced by nothingness.

Amelia Jenkins dropped her Smith & Wesson and slowly sank to her knees beside the body. She cocked her head and gazed into Beecham's blank eyes. She didn't cry, didn't whimper, didn't make a sound. She might have been dead, too.

Father Ed and Father Walter gaped at her handiwork. Montufar closed her eyes and whispered words the others couldn't hear.

Peller shook his head. "Oh, Amelia."

Jenkins shivered, then lifted her eyes to Father Ed. "It was him, you see. He really killed your brother. I was just the gun in his hands. I'm sorry. Mark was a good man. But this one…" She nodded at the corpse. "This one's on me, and I do not repent."

She snatched up the gun. Peller lunged, but before he could stop her, she shoved the barrel in her mouth and took one last life.

Chapter 22

The interrogation rooms buzzed the following morning. After considerable argument, Special Agent in Charge Pack agreed to conduct the necessary interviews at Northern District Headquarters, so the place swarmed with HCPD detectives and FBI agents all clamoring for turns with, in no particular order, Clare Fleming, Rodrigo Paniagua, Mary Tyler, Carlyle Navin, Father Ed, and Father Walter.

The FBI's focus remained on Fleming and Paniagua, since they alone could offer insight into Warren Beecham's network and, maybe, his real identity. Fleming, though, proved useless in that capacity. She provided enough detail to convict Beecham, if only he had been destined for court, but he had never given her information on other operatives. As far as she knew, she might have been alone in servitude to him, although she suspected she wasn't. The interest Beecham expressed in Father Ed was the sole piece of connecting evidence she provided. Given she had voluntarily gone to the authorities despite Beecham's threats, Pack let her slide. Morris was shocked but pleased. Fleming had suffered enough, and maybe she'd finally found an incentive to reform.

Paniagua had names. He steered twenty-three women into Beecham's grasp over the course of seven years. After Ross confronted him with the photos and the payment Beecham offered in exchange for killing Amelia Jenkins, he had nowhere to hide. He spilled the works, or as much as he knew, in exchange for a slap on the wrist. But it was a hard slap. He lost his security clearance, lost his job, lost everything but his family. Ross kept tabs on him in the coming months, largely through Carlotta Becerra, who was no longer a menace to poorly parked vehicles. But she made up for it by playing drill sergeant to her son-in-law. She was determined to keep him in line. And his wife? Somehow, she swept the whole incident under the rug. Rodrigo wasn't bad in her eyes. He'd just been under a lot of pressure.

Mary Tyler and Carlyle Navin, whose activities inadvertently exposed Beecham's betrayal, walked. Father Ed prevailed upon Captain Morris to give them a break. The actual damage done by the vandals had been minimal, and his niece, he argued, had been through hell enough. And Navin? He had tried to dissuade her. He only went along with her plan in a vain effort to protect her. "I think they have a future together," the priest told Morris.

"A strange future," she countered.

Father Ed laughed. "Sometimes the most enduring romances are forged that way."

Morris didn't know about that. "It's not my decision, but I'll recommend the DA drop charges. They might want to talk to Father Dan about that, though, since his church was involved."

"I'll get to him first." Father Ed winked.

In the end, he got his way.

Which left Morris with her own flock to tend. Her detectives were no strangers to violence, but in Howard County it seldom struck so close and with such ferocity. Peller and Montufar had kept quiet most of the day. Hell of a way for Montufar to start her marriage, but at least she had Dumas to lean on. Morris called them in together and gave them the Employee Assistance Program spiel. They thanked her and promised all would be well.

And Peller? He was Peller. Always was, always would be. "I'm fine," he insisted once the Captain's door was closed. He didn't even wait for her to broach the subject.

"It would be natural for you to feel guilty," Morris said. "You had Beecham in custody. Jenkins—"

"Jenkins saw her opportunity and took it. Maybe we should have seen it coming, but everything happened so fast. And then she dropped the gun. Yes, we should have removed it, but…" He shook his head. "It was a blur. I'm just glad Corina didn't take a bullet."

"Or you."

"Well, sure. But better me than her."

"What about AJ?"

Peller looked out the window. It wasn't a bad day, a bit cloudier than before but with streaks of sunlight pouring down. Morris wondered what he was seeing. "I think God will forgive her. I hope so, anyway."

Morris didn't often hear him talk religion. Was that a sign of distress? Sadness? Regret? "You don't have to get through it alone, Rick."

He gave her a tight smile. "I've had the EAP number for years. I don't need it."

"I didn't mean that."

It took him a moment to realize what she did mean. "Not you, too."

"I'm not telling you what to do. I'm just saying, she's there for you. At least consider it."

His gaze returned to the window. "It might shock you that I already have."

Hardly. He wasn't a Vulcan. Not really.

†

Peller didn't drive home that evening. He climbed into his truck feeling a thousand years old, sat for ten minutes before starting the engine, then cranked it and headed for Joan Churchill's apartment. He gave her no warning, just showed up five minutes after she got home from work herself. When she opened the door in a bright blue dress, white heels dangling from her left hand, she looked so happy, she might have won the lottery. Then she saw his haggard expression and morphed from joy to alarm. She tossed the shoes aside, took his arm, and led him in.

"What's wrong?"

"Long couple of days. Long story."

She took him to the sofa and maneuvered him onto it, then sat beside him, a hand on his shoulder. "Tell me."

"You may not want to know."

"Someone's dead," she guessed.

Peller nodded.

"Police, criminal, or bystander?"

"Criminal."

"Did you shoot them?"

He shook his head. Now that it came to it, he wasn't sure he *could* tell her. He wasn't sure he wanted to think about it himself.

She put her arms around him and pulled him close. He nearly squeezed the life out of her, but she didn't complain, didn't make a sound, until he released her. Then she said, "Start at the beginning."

The beginning. He supposed he could do that. He related the events of that day—key events, at least—feeling like someone had pushed his fast forward button. The narrative couldn't possibly be comprehensible. Churchill didn't interrupt, asked for no clarifications, no explanations. Even when he got to the end, she maintained silence. The only signal she gave was the concern in her eyes. Concern for him.

"Then AJ shot herself," Peller finished. "I couldn't stop her. It was so fast. She put the gun in her mouth and..." He shrugged. "It was over."

Churchill touched his cheek. "You should've come last night."

"I needed time alone." That's what he told himself, anyway. That's what he always told himself.

"You needed Sandra."

He flinched. It was true, but hearing Churchill say it...why would she say that?

"I'm sorry she can't be there for you anymore. But I am. You know that, don't you?"

He certainly should have. "Old habits," he said, as though that excuse had any value.

She kissed him lightly on the lips. "I'm going to make us dinner, then you and I are going to do something frivolous, and you are staying here tonight." She tapped the tip of his nose. "Don't you dare argue."

He smiled, weakly. "Yes, ma'am."

And that's how it went. Broiled hamburgers with the works. Potato salad. A few episodes of *My Name is Earl*. Churchill goaded Peller into discussing ideas for turning Jason's old room into an office. And so forth and so on, until it got late and Peller could barely keep his eyes open. If that was her ploy to keep him overnight, it worked once again. In his semi-somnambulistic state, he found that amusing.

But there was one small twist.

That night, he didn't sleep on the couch.

Thank you for reading! Please leave a short, honest review wherever you purchased this book. I greatly appreciate it, and it will help others discover my books.

Acknowledgements

A few words of thanks are in order. Members of the North Baltimore Chapter of the Maryland Writers' Association offered feedback to strengthen the opening scenes of this book, particularly Jeff Elkins and Flo McCahon (who writes as Millie Mack). I'm sure there were other contributors, too. My memory for names can be woefully inadequate, but you know who you are.

Also, my gratitude to my daughter and editor Andrea Bullock, who has kept me out of trouble, at least in the literary sense, since her mother's passing. And of course, to the rest of my children and sons-in-law and grandchildren for making life a joy and supporting me in my writing mania.

Finally, my continuing love and gratitude to my late wife Kathleen, who spent decades whipping my writing into shape. I couldn't have done it without you. That particularly applies to this novel. Some months before her passing, I told her I thought *A Day for Bones* might be my last Howard County Mystery. She agreed, but shortly thereafter suggested vandalism at a Catholic church as a springboard for a subsequent novel. A Catholic herself, she was alarmed at the spate of vandalism committed against Catholic churches in the late 2010's and early 2020's.

I'm not sure this novel is quite what she had in mind, but as it's set more than ten years earlier, I had to fiddle it. I do hope she would have liked it, just the same.

Further Reading

Rick Peller, Corina Montufar, and Eric Dumas return in more Howard County Mystery novels, available in print and ebook through your favorite bookseller:

The Fibonacci Murder (HCM #1)

"I start with zero. Nobody dies today." The strange note delivered to Rick Peller proves to be a warning shot. He, Corina Montufar, and Eric Dumas are soon pursuing a cunning killer basing murders on the Fibonacci series, a mathematical sequence in which each number is the sum of the preceding two. And the only thing Peller knows for sure is that the series never ends.

True Death (HCM #2)

Four years ago, Rick Peller's wife Sandra died on a country road. The driver who rammed her car vanished without a trace, leaving police stunned and baffled. Now, a bungled robbery raises new questions. As Corina Montufar and Eric Dumas investigate, Peller's memories awaken, triggering a series of insights that shine new light on Sandra's death.

Ice on the Bay (HCM #3)

A veterinary technician vanishes without a trace. A arson in an exclusive area bears the marks of an arsonist currently serving a prison term. A murder victim leaves behind an address book full of suspects. While temperatures plummet, cold cases collide with new crimes, and somewhere a killer with blood as icy as the waters of the Chesapeake watches and waits.

A Day for Bones (HCM #4)

A catastrophic flood scatters a human skeleton along Main street in Ellicott City, Maryland. As Detective Lieutenant Rick Peller investigates, the dark secrets of a successful family emerge, until someone lurking in the shadows resorts to murder to keep them hidden.

About the Author

Dale E. Lehman is an award-winning writer, veteran software developer, amateur astronomer, and bonsai artist in training. He principally writes mysteries, science fiction, and humor. In addition to his novels, his writing has appeared in *Sky & Telescope* and on Medium.com. He owns and operates the imprint Red Tales. He and his late wife Kathleen have five children, six grandchildren, and two feisty cats. At any given time, Dale is at work on several novels and short stories.

Visit https://www.DaleELehman.com to find out more about Dale's books.